THE MAGIC MAKER

MICKEY DUBROW

OTHER BOOKS BY MICKEY DUBROW

Bulletproof
American Judas
Always Agnes
Love and Lies at Martha's Hair Done Right

Library of Congress Control Number: 2024942174

Cover Design by: Alexios Saskalidis
www.facebook.com/187designz

For information please contact:
Brother Mockingbird, LLC
www.brothermockingbird.net
ISBN: 978-1-960226-16-7 Paperback
ISBN: 978-1-960226-22-8 EBook

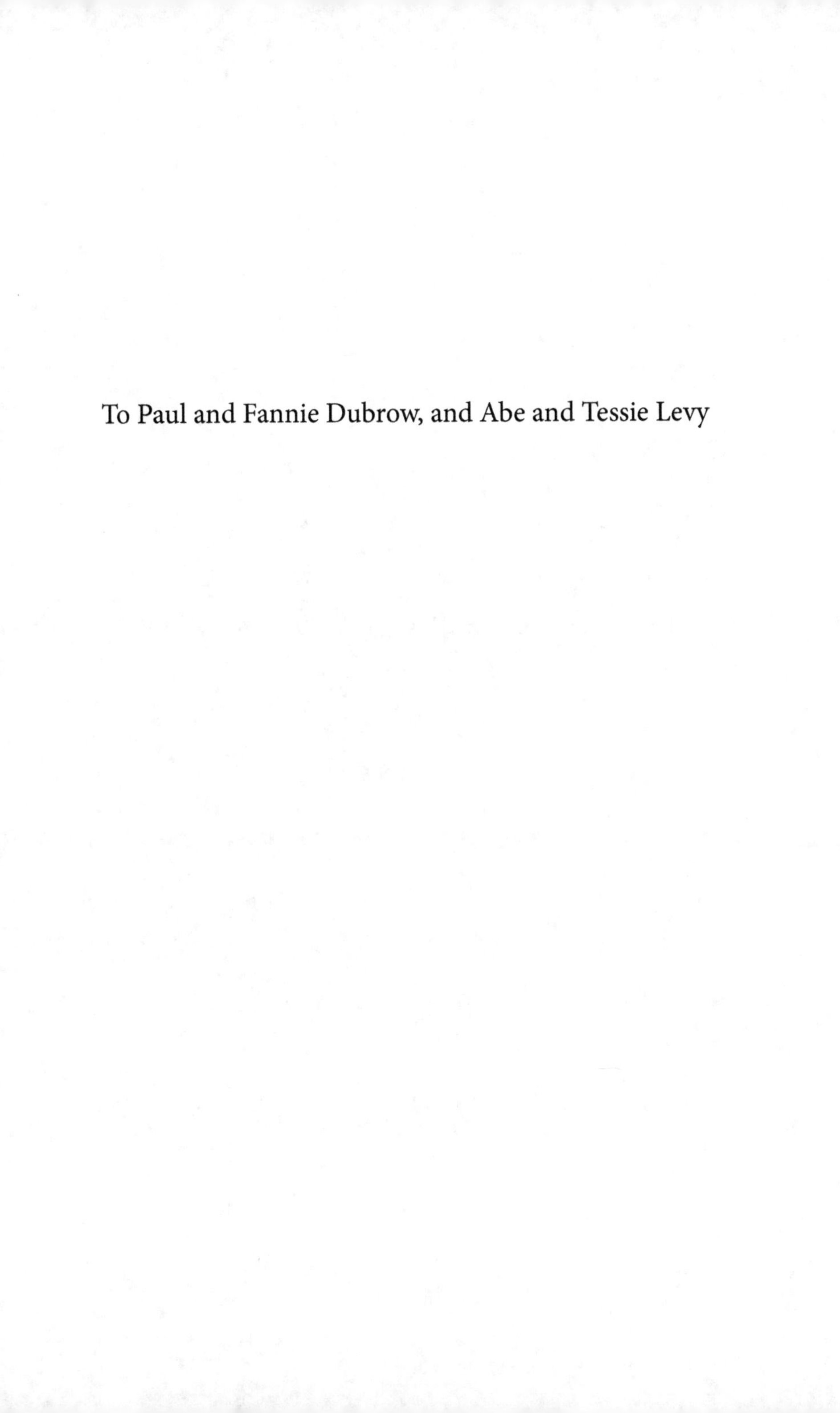

To Paul and Fannie Dubrow, and Abe and Tessie Levy

"If Jews were magicians, their every act a charm, then their magic

devices could aid as well as harm."

Joshua Trachtenberg, *Jewish Magic and Superstition. A Study in*

Folk Religion

CHAPTER ONE

2017

Walking on a New York City sidewalk on a frigid January morning, Esther Luna felt like a salmon swimming upstream through a river of humanity. She looked forward to the comfy warmth of the employee break room where the overhead fluorescent lights hummed like hungry mosquitos and the smell of stale cookies had taken permanent residence in the cupboards. She even looked forward to a cup of Stan's terrible coffee to thaw her out before her workday began as a Tenement Museum educator.

The museum was a former tenement building located at 97 Orchard Street. After being shuttered for over fifty years, the brownstone was reopened and some of the apartments were restored to show how immigrants from Poland, Germany, Ireland, and Italy had lived at the turn of the twentieth century.

As Esther walked past the museum on her way to the staff offices in the building next door, she thought she saw someone looking out of a fourth-floor window. Either that or she had been tricked by the sun glinting off a windowpane. She stopped to investigate.

There was definitely someone at the window. A girl, a third or fourth grader, with a yellow bow in her hair. She waved at Esther. Without thinking, Esther waved back.

She checked the museum's front entrance. The door was locked. Peering inside, she could see the red light for the alarm was on. Esther went back to the sidewalk and stared at the girl. She wasn't supposed to be up there.

Esther went to the main office and used her passcode to get inside, barely noticing the blast of heat that greeted her. As she hurried through the winding hallways, her footsteps echoed off the tile floor. She spotted Stan Jolly alone in the break room. He was reading a book about the Great Famine in Ireland. He pulled himself away long enough to acknowledge Esther's arrival before diving back in.

"There's somebody on the fourth floor of 97," Esther said.

Stan put down the book. "But we haven't started tours yet."

"It's a little girl. Nine or ten. Yellow bow in her hair."

Stan scratched his head. "You saw all that from the sidewalk?"

"Yes, Stan. I did. She waved at me. Can you believe it?"

"Was she with somebody?"

"I only saw her. I think she's alone."

"That's not good. Kids shouldn't be in the building without an adult."

"Nobody should be in there before we open. I'm going to find out what the hell is going on."

Esther stood by the table. Stan glanced at his book and then at Esther.

"You want me to go with you?" Stan asked.

"Duh."

They went to the main office and Esther got the keys to the museum's front door and to the fourth-floor right side front apartment. Outside, Esther led the way to the tenement building and pointed at the window.

"That's where I saw her," Esther said.

Stan hadn't brought his coat and rubbed his arms for warmth. "I don't see anybody."

"She could be anywhere in the building."

Esther unlocked the front door and turned off the alarm. She flipped on the hallway lights revealing the decorative tin ceiling and burlap wall coverings. The lemony scent of wood polish hung in the air. Esther and Stan climbed the creaky wooden stairs that generations of immigrants had climbed.

Going up the stairs always made Esther feel like she was entering a time machine to the past when immigrants had lived here. That feeling was part of why she loved her job and why she wanted to protect the museum.

"Who could be in the apartment?" Esther asked.

"Can't be squatters or graffiti artists," Stan said. "They'd never get past the security system."

"Which begs the question, how did the girl get inside?"

"You said she had a bow in her hair?"

"Yeah. A yellow one. Big enough that I could see it from the street."

"Do you think maybe she's one of the actors?"

Recently, the museum had hired actors known as living history reenactors, costumed interpreters playing actual residents of the building who told visitors the residents' life stories.

"They don't use child actors," Esther said.

"Could be a new thing," Stan said. "And this is rehearsal."

"Without first checking with us? If that's the case, then they're in big trouble."

When they reached the fourth floor, Esther led Stan to the apartment where she'd seen the girl.

"Wait a minute," Stan said.

"I don't think she's dangerous."

"It's not that. These apartments were closed for decades. Restoring them to be historically accurate takes a lot of time and money. Rather than do all of them at once, the museum has been restoring them in small groups."

"I know, Stan. I work here too. What's your point?"

"This one hasn't been scheduled for restoration yet. In fact, it hasn't even been opened. Nobody has been inside for over seventy years."

"Until today. Somebody broke in."

Esther slid the key into the ancient keyhole, but it wouldn't turn.

"The lock is rusted shut," Stan said. "We'll need a locksmith to get it open."

"Somebody already got inside. Either the lock's broken or the door's not locked."

Esther turned the doorknob. The latch clicked, and she pushed the door open. It was like opening a tomb. They covered their noses, which did little to keep out the stench of decay and mildew.

They stood in the doorway and peered inside. "Anybody in there?" Esther called. "You're in big trouble if you don't come out right now."

Nobody answered.

She was about to enter when Stan grabbed her arm. Esther jumped.

"Don't do that!" she said.

Stan aimed his phone's flashlight at the floor.

"Look at the dust on the floor."

"It's only dust," Esther said. "It won't kill us."

"That's not the point. If anybody had been in here recently, they would have left footprints."

Esther took her phone out of her purse and turned on the flashlight. Her beam of light traveled over the peeling paint on the walls and ceilings. Chunks of plaster had succumbed to gravity, exposing the wood lath underneath. Peeling wallpaper revealed older layers of wallpaper each with its own design, creating a collage of wallpaper history. The linoleum curled at the edges uncovering the rotting wood floor.

The apartment didn't just smell like a tomb, it was also as cold as one. Her breath steamed in the frigid air.

"Footprints or no footprints," Esther said. "I'm going in."

She entered the apartment with Stan close behind her. They searched all three rooms. Except for a broken table and a mummified rat, they were empty.

Esther went to the living room window and stood where the girl had stood. Only a few weak rays of sunshine managed to make their way through windowpanes coated with decades of collected grime. Esther could barely see the street below which meant no one on the street could see her.

"Are you sure the girl was in this apartment?" Stan asked.

"Absolutely,"

Stan swung his light around the room.

"There's nobody here, Esther."

"You believe me, don't you Stan?"

"I believe that you think you saw somebody."

Esther trained her light on the windowsill. The dust covering the sill was undisturbed.

"She was standing right here," Esther said. "Where did she go?"

Stan shone his light under his chin, giving him a spooky face. "We've all heard the ghost stories about this place."

"She wasn't a ghost."

"Then what was she?"

Esther's scalp tingled as a sense of dread enveloped her. It happened so quickly that it took her breath away.

"There's something wrong with this room. We shouldn't be in here. We need to leave."

Esther didn't wait for Stan. She rushed out of the room, fled down the stairs, and out of the building. As she crossed the street, a car had to slam on its brakes to keep from hitting her. The driver honked and cussed her, but she didn't notice.

She spun around, looked up at the window, and screamed. The girl was looking down at her. They watched each other as Esther's heart pounded in her ears. As if she sensed Esther's fear, the girl put her hand on her chest and shook her head. Then, she disappeared from the bottom to the top so that only her bow was visible before she was gone completely.

Esther's head swam, and she hugged a light pole to keep from falling. People glanced at her as they walked by, but no one stopped to ask if she was all right.

Stan came out of the building and hurried over to her. He put his arm around her shoulder and led her to a stoop. As they sat, he nodded at a cluster of people huddled outside of the museum's gift shop.

"I don't know why they get here so early," Stan said.

Esther hugged herself and rocked back and forth. She shivered from a cold more inside her than outside.

"Aren't you scheduled to lead the first tour today?" Stan asked.

Esther nodded.

"Go home," Stan said. "I'll cover your tours today."

"I saw her."

"The apartment was empty. We didn't see anything."

"I saw her! Just now. Right there."

She pointed at the window as tears streamed down her face.

"You're in no shape to get home on your own," Stan said. "Let me get you a cab."

"I don't want a cab."

"Are you sure?"

"I don't want to be here one second longer than I have to."

Esther struggled to her feet, swayed slightly, and left Stan on the stoop. She made sure not to look at the building as she walked away. When she entered the subway station, she realized she'd been holding her breath. She stared down at her hands during the entire forty-five-minute ride to East Harlem. She didn't dare look at the other passengers. The girl might be among them.

She entered her apartment and locked the door. Her caramel-colored cat, Flan, came out of the kitchen and peered at her. Esther shrugged off her coat and left it on the floor before tossing her purse on the couch. She picked up Flan. The overfed cat's solidness and soft fur comforted her. She thought about calling Gus, but he would insist on coming home and she wasn't ready to talk about what happened.

She went to the bedroom and placed the cat on the bed before closing the curtains to shut out the morning sun. She kicked off her shoes but didn't bother to undress further before crawling under the covers. Flan curled up next to her. Esther said her rosary and asked God to keep away dreams about the girl in the window. Her prayers were not answered.

CHAPTER TWO

Rabbi Meir Poppers had been a guest in Rabbi Sidney Burd's home on many occasions, but this was the first time he'd been here to celebrate Pesach. Outside, the air was thick with green pollen that covered cars like snow. Inside, the house smelled of overcooked brisket and simmering matzo ball soup. Meir removed his black Trilby hat and put it in the hall closet before handing a bottle of wine to Sidney's delightfully zaftig wife, Yetta Burd.

"Here is my contribution to this evening's seder," Meir said.

"Thank you, Meir," Yetta said. "I was worried we wouldn't have enough."

She led Meir to the living room where family and friends had gathered. Yetta and Sidney had four young sons. Meir was used to seeing their living room covered with toys, books, and sippy cups. But now it was tidy, and adults outnumbered the children.

Yetta steered Meir to the couch where an attractive woman was seated. She had auburn hair, intelligent brown eyes, and a smattering of freckles on her cheeks.

"Meir," Yetta said, "I don't believe you've met Nona."

"I can't say that I have," Meir said.

"Nona Sayers. Rabbi Meir Poppers."

Nona offered Meir her hand. She had slender fingers and wore a turquoise bracelet.

"Nona is new to Atlanta and doesn't know anybody. Why don't

you keep her company?" Yetta said. She scurried away before Meir could respond.

Meir sat stiffly next to Nona, who was not a shy person. He quickly learned that she was originally from Dallas, Texas, was an executive at a data processing company, absolutely adored her two corgis, and was an excellent cook. She was also, like Meir, Jewish and single.

Meir knew a set-up when he saw one. He wasn't opposed to the idea but preferred some warning beforehand. Meir was thirty-five and eager to get married, and though he possessed many amazing talents, finding a nice Jewish girl was not one of them. He often blamed his failure with women on the fact that he was at that awkward age between birth and death.

"I thought Yetta was exaggerating," Nona said, "but you really do look like that actor."

"Which actor?" Meir asked.

Nona twirled her finger. "You know. The one who was in that movie. Tall with a long face. Curly black hair with blue eyes. He even had a beard like yours. Well-trimmed. Not bushy like a hipster lumberjack. He's also been known to wear a Frank Sinatra hat. I swear you could be his twin."

"This actor. Is he handsome?"

Nona grinned. "Yes. He's very handsome."

Meir felt a nervous flutter in his stomach. He wasn't accustomed to getting compliments from a woman he wasn't related to.

"I need to see this movie," he said.

Nona wrinkled her nose. "Don't bother. It's a terrible movie. He was the only good thing about it."

"Thank you for saving me the trouble."

"Yetta said you weren't Orthodox."

"I'm not."

Nona nodded at Meir's head. "Then why the kippah?"

Meir touched the black with gold trim yarmulke clipped to his hair. "My sect is not Orthodox, but we cover our heads to honor God the same as Orthodox Jews."

Nona patted her hair. "Yetta tells me that besides being a rabbi, you're a ketchup maker. What exactly is that? Do you make some kind of special kosher ketchup?"

Meir shook his head. "Not ketchup maker. I'm a *kishef macher.* A magic maker."

"Oh, I see. You're a magician. Do you do bar mitzvahs? My nephew is having his soon. Maybe my sister could hire you for his party."

"I'm not that kind of magician. With God's help, I create traditional Jewish magic."

"Does that mean you pull a rabbi out of your hat instead of a rabbit?"

Nona laughed. Meir didn't. He'd heard the joke before and never found it funny.

"I don't do tricks. My magic comes from the Talmud."

Nona narrowed her eyes at Meir. "You're going to have to do better than that."

The nervous flutter in Meir's stomach turned into a belly ache. He was asked to explain what he was frequently enough that he should have had a good answer by now. Glancing around, Meir had a sudden inspiration. He gestured toward the dining room. Two tables were ready for the Passover service with bottles of wine, a seder plate with the six essential items (shank bone, hard-boiled egg, haroset, parsley, celery, and horseradish), bowls of salt water, Elijah's cup, matzo, and Haggadas. Pillows rested on every chair.

"The Passover story is the story of the Jews escaping bondage in Egypt," Meir said. "They were led by Moses, the greatest kishef macher of all time. Exodus is full of Moses performing Jewish magic with God's assistance. Moses turns his staff into a snake-eating snake, parts the Red Sea, and makes bread fall from the sky."

"Are you telling me that you're like Moses?" Nona asked.

"I've never done anything as big as parting a body of water, but yes. I'm a kishef macher like Moses."

Nona adjusted her bracelet. "I should see if Yetta needs any help." She darted into the kitchen.

A woman with many rings on her bony fingers sat in the space vacated by Nona. She tapped Meir's arm.

"You really screwed the pooch with that one."

"Excuse me?" Meir asked.

"Hi, I'm Sylvia. I know you're Rabbi Poppers because I was eavesdropping. Bad habit, I know, but you hear such interesting things."

Meir was about to move away but his curiosity got the best of him.

"What did you mean when you said I screwed the pooch?"

Sylvia looked to be in her seventies and was very thin, which made her mouth seem larger than it already was. Her white hair was stylishly short and spikey. The seafoam green frame of her oversized glasses couldn't hide the twinkle in her eyes.

"The young lady is not coming back," she said. "Then again, you never had a chance with her."

That couldn't be true. Nona had said Meir looked like that actor. It didn't matter which actor as long as she thought he was handsome. Meir thought Nona was attractive too. He liked her freckles and she smelled nice. Despite a few bumps, he felt they had made a connection.

Meir crossed his arms. "I don't see where it's any of your business."

"Actually, it is my business." Sylvia fished a business card out of her gold purse and handed it to Meir.

"Sylvia Solomon," Meir said, reading the card. "You're a *shadchanit*."

She tapped Meir's arm again. "I'm impressed. You used the correct term for a female matchmaker. I don't mind being called a shadchan, but I can't stand it when somebody calls me a *yenta*. Remember her from *Fiddler on the Roof*? Yenta was her name. Finding matches and catching catches was her occupation."

Meir thrust the card toward Sylvia. "I don't need a matchmaker."

Sylvia gently pushed Meir's hand away. "You told that nice girl that your job is performing miracles and you're not a doctor. Plus, you're a rabbi which is almost as good as being a doctor and you still bombed. Boy, do you ever need a matchmaker."

Meir's cheeks flushed. "I can't just call on God to create Jewish magic as if I were an entertainer at a bar mitzvah. I have to have a good reason for doing it."

"Don't tell me. Tell the nice girl."

Meir pounded his fist on his leg. "I will. During the seder."

Rabbi Sidney announced that it was time to begin. Meir stuck Sylvia's business card in his pocket and moved to the dining room. He saved the chair next to him for Nona. Women poured out of the kitchen. Nona walked past Meir and took a seat at the other table, as far away from Meir as a person could possibly get and still be part of the seder. The shadchanit took the chair Meir had saved for Nona.

Yetta lit the Yom Tov candles and said the blessing. Rabbi Sidney lifted his wine glass to begin the Passover service. Adults and children each got a chance to recite part of the service. Sidney and Yetta's son Ira was the youngest person at the service, so he got to sing the four questions. Meir kept stealing glances at Nona. She ignored him until the reciting of the ten plagues. As she dipped her index finger in her wine and touched her plate, she turned toward Meir and gave him the stink eye. Apparently, whatever connection Meir thought they had only existed in his imagination.

Though he had known Nona Sayers for less than an hour, Meir was devastated. He should have been used to it, but he wasn't. Maybe this time it stung more than usual because she had started out flirting with him. He liked her. She seemed to like him until she found out what he was. His teachers at Falk Yeshiva had warned Meir that life as a kishef macher would be difficult, but they never said a word about how lonely it would be.

The Seder progressed to the Hillel sandwich which combined maror, bitter herbs, with charoset, sweet apples and nuts, on pieces of matzo. Meir spooned charoset on a piece of matzo and passed the bowl to Sylvia. She passed him the bowl of maror. Meir bit into his Hillel sandwich. Bits of matzo and apple fell to his plate. He noticed

Sidney heading toward the living room. Sylvia noticed Sidney's exit as well.

"He's hiding the *afikomen*," Sylvia said. "My late husband Harold was a master at hiding the afikomen. It would take our children forever to find it."

"Did you know that during medieval times, people used the afikomen as an amulet against the evil eye?" Meir said. "They would carry pieces of it in their clothes."

"Should I slip a piece of matzo in my purse for good luck?"

"Only if you want crumbs in your purse."

Meir and Sylvia weren't the only ones who'd observed Sidney's exit from the dining room. Even though there wasn't a separate kids' table, the children had self-segregated from the adults by occupying the chairs at the far end. They grinned and stole glances toward the living room. Meir imagined that they were discussing how each would spend the five-dollar reward for finding the afikomen. He remembered similar conversations with his brother Morris when they were kids.

After the Hillel sandwich came gefilte fish and hard-boiled eggs.

"I have two daughters," Sylvia said. "They both found wonderful husbands with no help from their mother and have blessed me with three beautiful grandchildren. Joyce lives in Seattle and Mable lives in Houston. They both invited me to spend Passover with them."

"Why didn't you go?"

"Passover is the hardest holiday for Jewish singles. Forget Hanukkah, Rosh Hashanah, and Purim. Forget Thanksgiving. Passover is the ultimate Jewish family holiday."

"When Yetta invited me to their seder, she referred to me as an orphan because I'm here alone instead of with a family."

Sylvia sighed. "First thing tomorrow, the orphans will be calling me. They'll be in such a hurry that they'll want to be married and have a family in time for the second seder."

Women came out of the kitchen bearing steaming bowls of matzo ball soup. Meir blew the oily surface before tasting the broth. He chopped the matzo balls into chunks with his spoon. How Yetta got them to be so fluffy and mouth-wateringly delicious was a type of Jewish magic.

"I have a potential client flying in from New York tomorrow," Meir said. "Otherwise, I would be at my parents' house."

"Where do they live?"

"Minneapolis. I grew up in the Twin Cities."

"This client you're meeting tomorrow. Man or woman?"

"Woman."

"Does she want you to make her a love potion? Maybe we can go into business together."

"She claims she saw a ghost that isn't a ghost."

"And I thought I had difficult clients."

After the matzo ball soup, dinner was served. Yetta had done the lion's share of the cooking. Sidney's parents had brought a brisket. Next-door neighbors Lenny and Elaine provided a kugel. Yetta's sister and brother-in-law brought macaroons, fruit salad, and chocolate-covered matzo. Everything was excellent.

Once the dishes had been cleared it was time for the children to find the afikomen.

"We can't finish the service until you find it," Sidney announced. "You don't want us to be stuck here all night, do you?"

The children made a mad dash into the living room and kitchen in search of the hidden matzo. Sidney and Yetta beamed as their boys opened cabinet drawers and looked under seat cushions. A cousin found the afikomen in the bookcase between a history of Israel and a collection of Jewish humor. She held it up triumphantly. Sidney gave her a five dollar bill for the afikomen.

Meir turned to Sylvia.

"You said I never had a chance with Nona," he said. "How do you know?"

"I've been doing this for over thirty years. I can tell just by looking at their shoes that two people aren't right for each other."

Meir looked down at his black Adidas. "I have flat feet. Running shoes have good arch support."

"Nona is wearing suede pumps. She's looking for a man who wears fancy shoes even to a weeknight family seder."

Meir watched Nona talking to another single man who'd come to the seder. He couldn't see the man's shoes, but they probably weren't running shoes.

"Okay, Sylvia," Meir said. "You're hired. Find me a match."

Sylvia put her hand on Meir's arm. "I've got my first orphan and the seder is not even over."

CHAPTER THREE

1917

Sadie Rosenfeld was almost done setting the table for the seder. The utensils, plates, and wine glasses were in place. A pillow was on every chair. The only things left were the Haggadas. Pages were stained and brittle from drips and splatters during previous years' seder meals.

As Sadie placed them on the table, she imagined who would get each one. Papa would sit at the head of the table and lead the service. Nathan, the oldest, would sit to Papa's right. Mama would sit to Papa's left in the chair closest to the kitchen. Sadie would sit next to Mama so that she could help her serve the seder meal, and Jacob would sit between Sadie and Nathan.

A wooden mannequin wearing an almost completed dress would watch over the service from a corner of the room. The Rosenfelds made excellent dresses, well stitched and in the latest styles, but Papa didn't want to make dresses forever in the family's fourth floor apartment in the tenement building at 97 Orchard Street. He dreamed of owning a clothing store someday called Rosenfeld and Son. Nathan was the Son who would work beside his father and one day take over the business when Papa was ready to retire.

Papa didn't know that Nathan had his own dream. Nathan was in love with Edna Oxenhandler. She lived with her family on the second floor of the tenement. Once Nathan saved enough money of his own, he planned to marry Edna and move into his own apartment.

He had a friend who assured Nathan that he could get him a job at his uncle's bakery.

Nobody was supposed to know about Nathan's plans, but secrets were hard to keep in a tenement building. The only person who didn't know was Papa. Sadie thought Nathan's plans were brave and romantic. Mama understood Nathan's desire to strike out on his own, but she thought he could do better than Edna Oxenhandler. Sadie overheard Mama tell Mrs. Matzkin that what little brains and common-sense Edna possessed were buried deep inside her ample bosom and that a man needed a wife with a strong heart and a sharp brain to survive in this world.

Sadie looked at Mama in the kitchen. She was such a wife to Papa. Mama often reminded Papa that Nathan, Jacob, and Sadie were not just his employees. They were his children. Sadie once asked Mama who was her favorite child, thinking that she would say Sadie since she was her only daughter. Mama said all her children caused her back to ache equally. And then she laughed. Sadie laughed too even though she wasn't sure why.

If Sadie were asked which of her two brothers was her favorite, she would say Jacob even though he sometimes pinched her when no one was looking. She liked Jacob more because they were closer in age and Nathan, the oldest, sometimes acted like he was a third parent.

Jacob was only thirteen and already girls were noticing his curly hair and blue eyes. He noticed the girls, but he feared them. When they greeted him, his cheeks turned apple red. At least he didn't pinch them.

Sadie turned to Jacob. He was sitting by the window and fidgeting like a squirrel.

"Do you see them?" Sadie asked.

"Mama asked me to watch, not you," Jacob said.

He had wanted to go outside but Mama wouldn't let him because his clothes were clean and pressed. To give him something to do, Mama had him keep watch for Papa and Nathan.

Jacob left the window and hurried into the kitchen. Sadie followed him.

"Papa and Nathan are coming up the stairs," Jacob said.

Mama was bent over a steaming pot. She tasted the broth and nodded her approval. "Good. Dusk will be here before you know it."

"There's a man with them," Jacob said.

Mama put the lid on the pot and wiped her hands on her apron. "A man? Who is this man?"

"I don't know. I've never seen him before."

"Isn't that wonderful? Just like Baruch to bring someone home at the last minute. Sadie, set another place at the table."

Sadie quickly moved the chairs around to make room for a sixth. She had just gotten a place setting and a Haggada on the table and a pillow on the chair when Papa opened the front door. He and Nathan entered the apartment followed by a smiling beggar who strutted into the apartment as if he were a king.

He appeared to be the same age as Papa, but that was where their similarities ended. His red hair and beard seemed to shimmer like Moses's burning bush. He wore layers of tattered clothes, and a thin blanket draped over his shoulders like a *tallis*. Sadie's eyes teared from his rank body odor. She wasn't sure if it was because he wasn't anchored to a home or if it was because he looked like a vulture ready to pounce, but he scared her so badly that she had to hold herself to keep from shivering.

Mama came out of the kitchen to greet the stranger.

"Rebekah," Papa said. "This is Eli. I invited him to join us for the seder tonight."

"*Gut yontiff*," Mama said.

Eli grinned at Mama as if it were her good fortune to meet him.

"*Chag Sameach*," Eli said. "*Nu?* How many children do you have?"

"The three you see here. Two boys and Sadie. She's the youngest."

Eli held up a dirty forefinger. "The Torah commands Jews to be fruitful and multiply. You've done well, Rebekah Rosenfeld."

Mama gave Papa a sidelong glance.

"I'm glad you approve," she said.

Papa snorted, and then offered Eli the only stuffed chair in the front room, which was also the dining room. At night, it was the boys' bedroom. Eli accepted the offer and settled in. Papa stood next to the mantle and Mama went back to the kitchen. Nathan and Jacob took chairs from the dining table and sat facing the beggar. Sadie went to close the front door.

Before she shut it, she peered out. The gas lights gave the narrow hallway an orange glow. The sound of babies crying, children laughing, and mothers shouting orders echoed off the walls. She'd spent the day helping Mama prepare for tonight and hadn't been able to go out and play for even a minute. But there would be plenty of time tomorrow. Sadie closed the door. She held her breath to avoid smelling Eli as she went past him on her way to sit on the windowsill.

The family stared at the beggar. He continued to smile. Considering he was a beggar, he seemed very pleased with himself.

"Tell me, Baruch Rosenfeld," Eli said. "Are you certain you want a stranger in your home? I could leave now if you like."

He started to rise from the stuffed chair. Papa held up his hand to stop him.

"You're a Jew," Papa said. "I'm a Jew. We're not strangers."

Eli settled back into the chair. "We may both be Jews, but you still don't know me."

"All Jews are *mishpocha*. What else do I need to know?"

Eli chuckled. "Nothing. Nothing at all." He turned Nathan and Jacob. "Tell me boys, which *cheder* do you attend?"

Nathan and Jacob glanced at Papa.

"They go to a public school because the law says they have to," Papa said. "They work when they get home. We're a family business. Everybody works, even my youngest."

Eli's smile melted away. "But studying Torah is important."

"So is eating," Papa said. "We can't afford for them to go to public school and cheder."

Eli pointed at Nathan. "You're the oldest?"

"I am," Nathan said.

"Yesterday was the Fast of the First Born. Did you at least fast yesterday?"

"Yes, I did."

"That's not the same as attending cheder, but it's something."

Papa took his pocket watch out of his vest and compared the time with that of the clock on the mantle. He wiped soot off a windowpane and peered outside. "Sunset will be here soon. Eli, if you'd like to use the water closet, it's just down the hall."

Eli shook his head. "I'm fine."

"Would you like something to drink?" Papa asked.

"A glass of water."

"Sadie. Get our guest a glass of water."

Sadie hurried out of the room. Mama had been watching from the kitchen. She took a glass off the shelf, filled it with water, and handed the glass to Sadie. When Sadie returned, Eli was examining the nearly completed dress on the mannequin. He pinched the silk hem with his grimy fingers.

"Nu?" Eli said. "You make dresses for *goyim?*"

"I make dresses for women," Papa said.

"And these dresses are why your boys aren't learning to be Jews?"

Papa glared at Eli.

"These dresses are why we can afford to celebrate Passover this evening."

Sadie handed the glass of water to Eli. Papa's annoyance with the beggar made her less afraid of him.

"Are you a fisherman?" Sadie asked.

"What makes you think I'm a fisherman?" Eli said.

"You're wearing a fisherman's hat, and you smell like dead fish."

"Sadie!" Papa said.

Eli threw back his head and laughed showing his yellow teeth. He lunged forward and squeezed Sadie's arm. Pain shot through her as his fingers dug into her flesh. Her fear of him returned.

"She's just being honest," Eli said. "Listen to me, young lady. You should always be honest."

Eli let go and Sadie ran to Papa. He hugged her and rubbed her sore arm. As Eli sipped his water, his eyes grew wide, and he pointed a shaky finger at the table. Nathan and Jacob looked at each other thinking that he was pointing at one of them.

"What is that?" Eli demanded.

"What is what?" Papa asked.

Eli placed the water glass beside the stuffed chair, went to the table, and slapped a box of Manischewitz's matzos to the floor.

"Machine matzo!" Eli said. "It's *chometz*! It's not kosher. But wait. I can fix it." He reached inside his clothes and took out a soiled white cloth. He carefully unwrapped the fabric to reveal a flat oval of unleavened bread. It was brown with chipped edges.

Nathan stared at the matzo. "He was carrying that inside his clothes. Makes you wonder what else he has hidden in there."

Eli placed his handmade matzo on the table where the box of machine-made matzo had been. "Here! Use mine. It's *Shmurah* matzo."

Jacob grimaced. "I'm not eating that! It's been next to his sweaty skin."

Papa retrieved the box from the floor and held it close to Eli.

"This matzo is perfectly fine." Papa pointed at writing on the box. "Look here. It says, *guaranteed to be strictly kosher for Passover*."

"I should believe a box?" Eli asked.

Papa put the Manischewitz's Matzos on the table and handed Eli's matzo back to him.

"I'm sorry my home isn't good enough for you," Papa said. "You're welcome to leave at any time."

Eli wrapped his matzo and tucked it inside his coat. "My apologies, Mr. Rosenfeld. I know I'm just a lowly beggar, but I'm also a Jew who is very worried about our people. All these modern changes, they lead to assimilation. If we don't hold onto to our traditions, then surely Judaism will perish."

"This is America," Papa said, gesturing at the window. "It's not perfect, but it's much better than where we were before. We haven't stopped being Jews, but now we're American Jews who eat kosher matzo that comes in a box."

Eli gazed out the window. The sun was beginning to dip behind the buildings. "You are right. We are in America."

Eli sat in the stuffed chair and sighed as if he had just received terrible news.

Papa compared the time on his watch with the time on the mantle clock again. "I should see how Rebekah is doing."

He left the small front room for the equally small kitchen. Sadie went with him because she didn't want to be around the beggar without Papa. The smell of Mama's cooking made her stomach grumble. Mama had Sadie sit on a stool next to the stove. She rolled up Sadie's sleeve and pointed at Sadie's arm.

"Look what he did," Mama said.

Papa examined Sadie's arm. Eli's grip had left five red spots that were quickly turning purple. Sadie saw them as proof that the beggar was dangerous. Certainly, Papa would order him out of the house.

"She'll be fine," Papa said. "How's dinner coming?"

Mama rolled down Sadie's sleeve and buttoned the cuff.

"Everything is ready."

Papa glanced into the living room and then leaned against the sink.

"What could I do? I couldn't leave a Jew on the street during Pesach."

"I know," Mama said. "But couldn't you have found a more agreeable beggar?"

Papa shrugged. "He was the only one available on such short notice."

"I'm serious, Baruch," Mama said. "Out of all the Jewish beggars in New York City, you managed to find the most Orthodox *schnorrer*."

Papa wrapped his arms around Mama's waist. "It's just for tonight's seder. It's not like he's moving in."

"How did it go at Macy's?" Mama asked.

What with bringing Eli to the apartment, Papa hadn't had a chance to tell Mama about his business meeting. He fished a bag of coins from his pocket. They clinked as he poured them onto the kitchen's narrow countertop.

"I know I shouldn't have conducted business on *yontiv*, but Macy's insisted I meet with them today," Papa said.

"We've already gone over that," Mama said. "What did they say?"

Papa grinned. "They loved the dresses. They said that they'll take whatever we make."

Mama kissed Papa's cheek.

"That's three stores," Mama said. "Are you sure that's not too many? I don't want you overworking the boys."

"We'll hire some workers," Papa said. "Our business is growing. Soon, we'll have enough to move to a better place."

Mama took a metal tin off the kitchen shelf and started adding the coins to the money inside. They clinked as they landed.

"Wait," Papa said. He selected a Buffalo nickel from the pile and slipped it into his pocket. "To pay for the afikomen."

Mama put the rest of the coins in the tin and placed it on the shelf.

"You haven't forgotten what you promised the children, have you?"

Papa winked at Mama before studying the calendar hanging on the wall over the sink. The illustration for April was of a woman working in her garden.

"I don't remember promising them anything," he said as he looked over his shoulder at Sadie.

Sadie couldn't believe Papa had forgotten. She dragged the stool over to the sink, climbed onto it, and jabbed April 15 on the calendar.

"You said you'd take us to Coney Island the Sunday after Passover."

She plucked a postcard from the shelf and held it up so there wouldn't be any doubt of the location. The postcard was of the grand entrance to Coney Island's Luna Park. Papa took the postcard.

"Where did this come from?" he asked. He looked at both sides. "I don't remember receiving this in the mail. The writing on the back is smeared. I can't read a thing."

Sadie wished Papa would stop teasing her about the postcard. She had found it on the street and had cleaned the schmutz off with the hem of her dress. The back had gotten wet. A few letters in Yiddish were still clear but no words. Who the card was for and what message was sent had been lost.

Mama saw no reason why Sadie couldn't keep the card. When Papa saw how much Sadie was entranced by the card's image, he announced he would take the family there after Passover. Sadie couldn't believe they were really going to go to a real-life fantasy land.

"Papa," Sadie said. "You promised."

"Did I?" he asked. "That doesn't sound like something I would promise."

Sadie pouted and put her hands on her hips. There were some things too important to make fun of, like Coney Island.

"Yes, you did, Papa," Sadie said.

Baruch laughed and gave the postcard back to Sadie.

"Don't worry. I didn't forget." He checked his pocket watch. "Come on. It's time to begin."

The Passover Seder started at sundown without further comment from Eli. He sat slouched in his chair between Nathan and Jacob. Though he seemed more sad than angry, he still made Sadie nervous. Unlike the Rosenfelds, Eli did the service the Orthodox way. When it came time to drink the first cup of wine, he leaned so far to his right that Sadie thought he'd fall to the floor. While everyone else only took a sip, Eli drained his glass.

The seder progressed smoothly until they reached the four questions. Sadie didn't need her Haggada. She had memorized the words.

"*Mah nishtanah, ha-laylah ha-zeh, mi-kol ha-leylot. Mikol ha-leylot. Ha-laylah ha-zeh, ha-laylah ha-zeh, mikol ha-leylot.*"

"Enough!" Eli shouted, rising to his feet. "Matzo in a box. Boys who don't attend yeshiva. And now, a girl reciting the four questions. How can you claim to be Jews when you allow this?"

Papa slammed his fist on the table, causing his wine glass to tip over. Mama picked up the glass and mopped up the wine with a rag but couldn't remove the red stain that had already formed on the white tablecloth.

"Enough, you say?" Papa said. "I say enough. The four questions are recited by the youngest child."

"You dare tell me how to conduct a seder!" Eli said, his face as red as his beard. "Do you know who I am?"

"Are you not the beggar who I invited into my home and has done nothing but complain?"

"It just so happens that I am … just a beggar."

"The youngest child recites the four questions." Papa said, pointing at Sadie. "Sadie is the youngest."

"The youngest Jewish male recites the four questions. So, unless she's hiding a *schmekel* under her dress, she is forbidden."

"That's the way it was done in Europe. But we're in America. Here it's the youngest child, whoever they may be."

Eli crossed his arms. Sadie put her hand on her chest. Her heart was beating so quickly she was afraid it would burst.

"Earlier, you said I was welcome to leave at any time," Eli said. "Maybe that time is now."

Papa glowered at Eli. "Yes. Maybe it is."

"No," Mama said. "He should stay." Everyone at the table turned their attention to Mama. "The purpose of the Passover Seder is to remind us that God delivered us from slavery in Egypt. Does it matter how we tell the story as long as we don't change the story's meaning?"

Eli glanced at Papa before addressing Mama.

"Tradition matters. It's part of our covenant with God."

"Then you must be furious that we forgot the goat," Mama said.

Papa snorted. Sadie grinned. She didn't understand what Mama meant but she liked how Mama's words made Eli look unhappy.

"Only high priests can sacrifice sheep and goats," Eli said. "There will be no Passover sacrifices until the Temple is restored in Jerusalem."

"But it was the tradition until circumstances brought us new traditions," Mama said. "That's what America has done. Brought us new traditions."

"Like the youngest daughter reading the four questions," Papa added.

Eli stared at Sadie. Sadie glanced at Mama. Mama gave her a reassuring smile. Sadie returned Eli's stare.

"Very well," Eli said. "I will stay a little longer, if only to find out what is creating that delicious smell in your kitchen."

"How generous of you," Papa said. "Sadie, please continue."

Sadie picked up with the second question. While she sang, Eli left the table and didn't return until right before the end of the *Maggid* and once again leaned almost to the point of falling while drinking the second cup of wine.

During the Passover meal, Eli slurped the matzo ball soup, sucked on the bones of the roast chicken, and other than using a spoon to eat his soup, ignored his knife and fork in favor of his fingers. The only food on the table that he didn't touch was the matzo. When it was offered to him, he shook his head.

While everyone else was enjoying Mama's cooking, Papa slipped into the kitchen with the afikomen wrapped in a linen napkin. Sadie pretended not to notice. From where she was sitting, Sadie could see Papa hide the matzo in a cast iron pot on the same shelf as the tin of money and her Coney Island postcard. She suppressed a grin so that Nathan and Jacob wouldn't suspect she knew the afikomen's hiding place.

The meal ended. Papa talked to the family about how he planned to handle the extra dress orders coming in from Macy's. Eli got up, scraping his chair loudly on the wooden floor, stood by the window, and muttered. He also jabbed his finger in the air, giving Sadie the impression he was arguing with himself.

He stopped muttering, nodded once firmly as if he had made a decision, and left the apartment. Sadie hoped that either he was going to the water closet to wash off some of his stink or leaving the apartment for good.

Papa finished sharing his ideas for how they would expand the family business. Jacob and Sadie helped Mama clear the table. While they removed the dishes, Sadie was disappointed to see Eli return. He stood by the table and Sadie had to work around him. She was close enough to tell that he was no less dirty and smelly than before. In fact, he had somehow gotten new stains. Sadie wrinkled her nose at the fresh splotches of red on his coat and cap.

As the last of the dishes were carried into the kitchen, Eli started chanting softly. Nathan and Jacob exchanged glances but said nothing. Mama and Papa ignored him. Sadie strained to listen, but he was speaking too softly for her to make out what he was saying or in what language he was speaking. Still chanting, Eli moved to the table and scowled at the box of Manischewitz's matzos. He put his hand on the box and deliberately turned it so that the front of the box wasn't facing him.

Nathan stared at the ceiling. "Did you feel that?"

"Feel what?" Papa asked.

"I don't know. I felt something. Like when you're walking by the shore and the wind shifts. You feel like the sea is calling you."

"God help me, my son is becoming a poet," Papa said.

With the table cleared, and the dishes stacked in the kitchen sink, Papa declared it was time to find the afikomen. Nathan felt he was too old for this game and stayed at the table. Sadie went straight to the cast iron pot and lifted the lid. The pot was empty. She wrinkled her nose. Papa must have caught her looking and changed the location. Perhaps this was his way of reminding Sadie that he was smarter than her.

She joined Jacob in searching the three rooms of the apartment. They opened drawers and lifted the mattress. They peered into the pots and under furniture. After what seemed like an hour, they collapsed in their chairs.

"We can't find it, Papa," Jacob said.

"We give up," Sadie said.

"Are you sure you looked everywhere?" Papa asked.

"Everywhere, Papa," Jacob said.

"Maybe you should give them a hint," Mama said.

Papa leaned back in his chair.

"Okay. It's in the kitchen and it's inside something your mother uses to cook in."

"We looked in all the pots, Papa," Sadie said. "It wasn't in any of them."

"Are you sure?"

"Yes, Papa."

"It's getting late, Baruch," Mama said. "Maybe you should show them."

Papa nodded. He, more than anyone, knew they had a lot of

work to do tomorrow. He went to the kitchen and took the lid off the iron pot.

"I don't understand. It's not here."

"Papa!" Nathan shouted.

Papa returned to the living room. Nathan stood by the mantle. His face was pale.

"What is it, Nathan?"

"The clock stopped ticking."

Papa checked the mantle clock. It had stopped at 10:45. He checked his pocket watch. He held it up so that the family could see. It had also stopped at 10:45. Papa tried winding the pocket watch, but nothing happened. His watch was frozen.

"Where's Eli?" Sadie asked.

The beggar was gone.

"Did anyone see him leave?" Papa asked.

No one had noticed his departure.

"It was rude of him to leave without saying goodbye," Mama said.

"What did he do that wasn't rude?" Jacob asked.

Nathan picked up the mantle clock and held it to his ear as if expecting a faint heartbeat.

"Something has changed. Can't you feel it?"

Sadie shuddered. "I do."

"Don't talk nonsense," Papa said. "Nothing has changed."

Jacob pointed at the window. "Look!"

Gray clouds blotted out the world outside. Jacob rushed to the front door and threw it open. He gasped and took a step back. The family gathered around him. The hallway was completely obscured by more dense gray clouds.

"It's just fog," Papa said.

"Have you ever seen fog this thick?" Nathan asked.

"No, but that's all it is. It must have rolled in from the East River."

"But what about the clocks? The fog didn't make them stop."

"I don't know why the clocks stopped, but I know fog when I see it. Wait here."

Papa lit a gas lantern and held it in front of him as he walked into the hallway. The family crowded around the door. The gray clouds swallowed Papa and his light.

"Where is he?" Sadie said. She cupped her hand next to her mouth and shouted. "Papa! Papa!"

"I'm here, Sadie," Papa said.

The family spun around. Sadie gasped. Papa stood behind them in the center of the living room. He held the lantern by his side. His face was pale.

"How did you get back in without us seeing you?" Mama asked.

"As soon I stepped outside the door, I found myself standing here. Nathan is right. Something changed."

"We have to get out of here!" Nathan shouted. He dashed out the door and immediately appeared next to his father.

They tried the windows, but they wouldn't open. They tried smashing them, but the glass wouldn't break. They tried hammering the walls, stomping on the floors, and crying for help. Nothing worked. Nobody answered. They were trapped.

"It's so quiet," Sadie said. "Where did all the people go?"

"I don't think they went anywhere," Nathan said. "I think we did."

CHAPTER FOUR

2017

Meir met with Esther Luna and her husband Gustavo, " Gus,"Ramos in the living room of his two-story condo. Esther and Gus had flown to Atlanta from New York City that morning. Though Meir had offered to pick them up at the airport, they had insisted on taking an Uber.

Esther had a round moon face befitting her last name and wore her straight black hair down to her shoulders. Her girl-next-door beauty made Meir jealous of Gus, a human barrel with muscular arms and a thin mustache that didn't flatter his pudgy face. Esther did all the talking while Gus did all the glaring.

"Thank you for meeting with me, Rabbi Poppers," Esther said. "I know this conversation could have been a text or an email, but I wanted to meet you in person."

"I'm glad you came," Meir said. "I prefer meeting face to face whenever possible."

Meir's gray cat, Alice, sauntered into the living room with her tail in the air. She hopped into Meir's lap. As he scratched her head, she closed her green eyes and purred. Esther touched Gus's arm and smiled at Alice. He ignored the cat and gazed out of the living room window at the bucolic neighborhood that surrounded Meir's condominium.

It was a breezy spring day, the kind of day with perfect weather that fooled visitors into believing that Atlanta was a great place to live, never suspecting that the merciless heat and humidity of summer was just around the corner.

"I didn't know who else to turn to," Esther said. "I didn't want a ghost hunter or an exorcist. Then I found your website. Rabbi Meir Poppers. Kishef Macher for Hire."

"Do you understand what a kishef macher is?" Meir asked.

"I have an advanced degree in Jewish history. I can read Yiddish and Hebrew. I know what you're thinking. Why would a Catholic girl from a Puerto Rican family study Jewish history? Scholars choose religions and cultures other than their own all the time."

"I suppose they do."

"I know what a kishef macher is, but I thought they only existed in Jewish folk tales."

Meir frowned. "Kishef machers used to be better known, but over the centuries, magic has fallen out of favor. As a result, our numbers dwindled, and we have retreated to the shadows. But the world beyond what people consider reality still exists. When someone like yourself encounters that world, it can be very unsettling. Even dangerous. Which is why they need someone like me who understands that world."

Esther looked at Gus. He crossed his arms. She turned back to Meir.

"This is not a ghost story," Esther said. "The girl I saw was not a ghost."

"What makes you so sure?" Meir asked.

Esther looked down at her hands resting on her lap. "I can't explain it. She was too far away for me to tell much about her, but somehow I know she wasn't a ghost. This is something worse. I can feel it in my bones."

"What happened exactly?" Meir asked. "Take your time. There's no hurry."

"I was on my way to work as an educator at the Tenement Museum. Are you familiar with the museum?"

"I am," Meir said. "The yeshiva I attended is upstate. Our teachers occasionally took us on day trips into the city. One time, they took us to the Tenement Museum."

Meir was seventeen when he and his classmates visited the museum. Their teacher, Rabbi Zelig Fruman, stated that the purpose of the visit was for the students to learn more about their ancestors who came to America so that they could have a better life. What Meir remembered most about that day was not the museum, but rather lunch at Katz's delicatessen. He had one of their huge pastrami sandwiches and the best cheesecake he'd ever tasted before or since.

"When you were at the museum," Esther asked, "you didn't see or feel anything unusual?"

Meir shook his head. "No. Nothing."

"Well, like I said, I was on my way to work when I looked up and saw a girl with a yellow bow in her hair looking out the window of one of the fourth-floor apartments. Nobody was supposed to be there, so I went upstairs to tell her to leave."

"What did the girl say when you confronted her?"

"She wasn't there. What's more, the apartment had been closed up for over seventy years. As I stood by the window where I'd seen the girl, I felt something was wrong. I was so scared I ran out of the apartment, out of the building. When I got outside, I saw her at the window again. And then she disappeared."

Esther threw up her hands. Gus looked at the ceiling.

"All at once or a little bit at a time?" Meir asked.

"Kind of like a wall going up in front of her. I freaked out. I skipped work and ran home. I went back to work the next day, but it wasn't the same. I kept imagining the girl moving around over my head. I started getting sick to my stomach. I was jumpy. I had trouble sleeping. After a month, I couldn't take it anymore, and I quit." Esther sighed. "I was there for five years. I loved my job."

"When did this happen?"

"Six months ago. I'm teaching at NYU now. I thought when I left the museum that was the end of the story. A spooky anecdote I would tell friends at a party. But I couldn't stop thinking about the girl with the yellow bow. I was sure she was real, but I had to prove it. This is what I found."

Esther opened a briefcase, took out a sheet of paper, and held it out for Meir. It was a photocopy of a page from the Yiddish language newspaper *Foverts*. The date at the top of the page was Monday, April 16, 1917. A news item had been circled with a yellow highlighter. He placed Alice on the floor before taking it.

"Can you read Yiddish?" Esther asked.

"Yes, I can," Meir said.

The highlighted story was about the mysterious disappearance of the Rosenfeld family. Neighbors noticed that days had passed since anyone had seen them. The landlord entered the apartment and found that it was completely empty. There wasn't a stick of furniture left.

The story claimed everyone liked the Rosenfelds. They had no disputes with the other tenants beyond a few minor quarrels. The head of the family, Baruch Rosenfeld, was known for his kindness and generosity. Friends were shocked that they had left without saying goodbye. A few neighbors speculated that Baruch couldn't afford the rent and the family fled in the dead of night. Other residents disagreed. Too many people inhabited 97 Orchard Street. It wasn't possible for the Rosenfelds to move their belongings down the narrow staircase and out of the building at any hour of the day or night without someone seeing or hearing them.

"How did you find this particular story?" Meir asked. "*Foverts* has been around for over a hundred years. That's thousands and thousands of daily newspapers."

Esther straightened her spine and spoke with obvious pride. "I used the research skills I learned in grad school. I went through the rental records of the tenement apartment and made a list of the families who had lived there. Then I searched census records to see if any of those families had a daughter die between the ages of six and twelve. I didn't want to completely rule out that the girl was a ghost. Two families fit the profile, but the girls were infants when they died. I went back through the rental records and noticed that in 1917, the landlord had written a question mark next to a family who lived in that apartment. The Rosenfeld family."

"Despite what the neighbors said, they could have moved out."

"That's the most logical explanation, but I kept asking myself, why the question mark? I knew there was a chance that I was going on a wild goose chase, but it was still a lead. I had to follow it. One of the places I looked for clues was the 1917 editions of *Foverts* and that's how I found the story about the family's disappearance."

Meir read the story again. There was something Esther was leaving out, but he wasn't sure what it was, but then it hit him.

"The Tenement Museum must have the rental records. How did you get access to them if you left your job?"

"One of my former co-workers at the museum let me into their offices after everyone had gone home," Esther said.

"That was nice of them."

"His name is Stan Jolly. He was with me the day I saw Sadie. He didn't see her, but he figured I wouldn't go through all this trouble unless I really saw something."

"Sadie?" Meir asked.

"I got her name from the census records. And the names of the entire Rosenfeld family: Baruch, Rebekah, Nathan, Jacob, and Sadie."

Meir handed the photocopy back to Esther.

"If the Rosenfelds had slipped out in the middle of the night, they could have changed their names and moved to another city," he said. "Another state."

"Oh, I know," Esther said. "Back then, it wasn't unusual for fathers to run off and change their names. Or for families so desperately poor, they sell their children. But an entire family running away and changing their names? I doubt it. I spent hours searching national archives for any of them. After April, 1917, the Rosenfelds flat out disappeared."

Meir scratched his beard. "How interesting."

"Another thing about the rental records. Once the Rosenfelds disappeared, the landlord had trouble keeping their apartment rented. Nobody stayed a full year, and it was empty for months at a time.

I think the tenants who lived there experienced the same thing I did. Something didn't feel right and that feeling drove them out."

Meir nodded toward Esther's briefcase.

"What else did you find?" he asked.

Esther took out another photocopy and passed it to Meir. It was a page from *Foverts* from Thursday, September 15, 1938. Esther had highlighted an interview with Bertha Lottie Rose, the author of *The Orchard Street Mystery*.

In the interview, Bertha told how she was living with her family on the second floor of 97 Orchard Street when the Rosenfelds disappeared. Bertha and Sadie were best friends. Bertha refused to believe that Sadie would leave without telling her goodbye. Or that her family would leave on Passover eve.

Meir stopped reading and looked at Esther.

"They disappeared on erev Pesach?"

"Is it important?" Esther asked.

"I'm not sure, though I wonder if they had a seder that night."

Meir continued reading the article.

Bertha was convinced that a terrible misfortune had befallen the Rosenfelds. Years later after she had moved away, married, and had children, she wrote a novel about what might have happened to the missing family.

"Why do I get the feeling you have a copy of Bertha's book in your briefcase?" Meir asked.

Esther grinned. "I couldn't find it online, but then I found a copy in a dusty corner of the Strand."

She took a small hardbound book out of her briefcase. It was inside a clear plastic quart-size Ziploc bag. She hesitated before passing it to Meir, but he handled it carefully. The book was in Yiddish. On the cover was an illustration of a girl with a bow in her hair.

"Bertha was a terrible writer with a great imagination," Esther said. "Her book is packed with ghosts, pirates, and parallel universes. The story doesn't make a lick of sense, but luckily, she was an excellent artist. She did this drawing of Sadie from memory." Esther pointed at the illustration. "This is the girl I saw standing at the window."

Meir studied the drawing. "She's a pretty girl," he said.

"Do you think I'm crazy?" Esther asked.

"I'm not qualified to pass judgment on your mental health. But I believe you did see Sadie Rosenfeld."

Esther's face brightened. "You do? That's wonderful! What convinced you?"

"Nothing specific, but so many odd things together. The question mark, the census records, the *Foverts* story, Bertha's book, and the fact that you and the tenants felt something was wrong in the apartment. But most important, what Jewish family disappears during a seder?"

"So, you'll help me?"

"I'll do my best. I'll warn you. We may discover that Sadie's father paid a kishef macher to help him skip out on the rent without being seen and then he moved the family to Buffalo."

The excitement in Esther's face drained away. "Then why did I see Sadie?"

"Who knows? Magic doesn't always work the way the kishef macher intended it to work. I won't know until I see the apartment for myself."

"Fair enough." Esther took a checkbook out of her briefcase.

Gus cleared his throat. Esther rolled her eyes. "Your website said that before you can begin, I have to pay you an honorarium."

"By accepting payment, I am making a promise to you to use all the resources at my disposal to solve your dilemma," Meir said.

Esther ran her thumb over the faux leather cover of her checkbook. "But your website doesn't list your rates. How much does something like this cost?"

"You can give me any amount you want. Give me a dollar and I'll work just as diligently for you as I would for someone who gave me a million dollars."

"That doesn't narrow it down much."

"What are you comfortable giving me?"

Esther glanced at Gus. He stared at the floor. Obviously, this was her decision.

"Fifty dollars?"

Meir shrugged. "Sure."

Esther filled out a check for fifty dollars, tore it out of the checkbook, and handed it to Meir.

"I can print a receipt or email it to you," Meir said.

"Email is fine." Esther sighed. "This is great. I feel like I'm finally going to get to the bottom of this mystery. I've been so wound up; I haven't been able to eat. I'm actually hungry right now. That's how relieved I am." She turned to Gus. He raised an eyebrow. She turned back to Meir. "Do you have something I could snack on?"

"Certainly."

Meir went into the kitchen, and Alice hopped into Gus's lap. His sausage fingers caressed the gray cat. Meir returned with a bowl of popcorn, a stack of napkins, and a glass of water. He put them on the coffee table. Esther peered into the bowl.

"Why is the popcorn pink?"

"It's a new flavor," Meir said. "It's not on the market yet."

"How is it that you have popcorn that isn't for sale?"

"It's my family's business. Mail-order, flavored popcorn. Maybe you've heard of Poppers Popcorn?"

"Meir Poppers. Poppers Popcorn. Why didn't I make the connection? Every Christmas we order a big can of Poppers jalapeño cheddar popcorn. I'm addicted to that stuff."

Esther grabbed a handful of the popcorn and put it into her mouth. Her eyes grew wide, and her cheeks puffed out like a chipmunk.

"Here," Meir said. He handed her a napkin. "You can use this."

Esther snatched the napkin, spit the popcorn into it, and folded the napkin.

"What the hell was that?" she asked.

"Clove bubblegum."

Esther grabbed the glass of water and drained half of it.

"That's the worst thing I've ever tasted!"

Meir carried the bowl back to the kitchen. He came back with a small trash can and held it out so that Esther could throw away the napkin.

"My father runs the company. He's always experimenting with new flavors," Meir said. "It's how he expresses himself creatively. Whenever he comes up with something new, he mails a sample to me. I'm his unofficial taste tester. I told him clove bubblegum was a bad idea."

Esther scowled. "If you knew it was bad then why did you let me eat it?"

"I wasn't sure. When Dad came up with watermelon coffee, I told him it was the most disgusting thing I'd ever tasted. He put it on the market anyway and it sells like hotcakes-flavored popcorn."

"You could have warned me."

Meir nodded. "You're right. I'm sorry."

Esther took a napkin from the stack and wiped her tongue. "Where's your bathroom? I want to rinse my mouth out."

"Down the hall, last door on the left."

Esther hurried out of the living room, leaving Meir alone with Gus. Meir smiled at Gus. Gus didn't smile back. Meir checked his watch. When Esther returned from the bathroom, he would offer to take them out to lunch.

"This is all bullshit," Gus said.

Meir was shocked to hear Gus's baritone after he'd been silent for so long.

"You don't believe Esther saw Sadie Rosenfeld?" Meir asked.

"She *thinks* she saw somebody," Gus said.

"What about the drawing of Sadie? It matched the girl Esther saw in the window."

"That doesn't prove anything. She saw the drawing and convinced herself that it was this mystery girl. The truth is she didn't see anybody. Esther imagined the whole thing as a way to deal with her grief. She doesn't even know she's doing it."

Alice was still in Gus's lap. Whenever he stopped petting her, she rubbed her furry head against his hand, and he resumed caressing her. Gus looked down the hallway to make sure Esther wasn't on her way back.

"Esther had a late miscarriage. It was a girl. We named her Sofia. You can see what's going on here. She wants this Sadie girl to be real because of Sofia."

Meir had assumed that Gus had come to Atlanta with Esther to make sure Meir wasn't a con artist who would take advantage of his wife. That was part of the reason, but not the main one. Gus was trying to protect Esther from further heartache. Meir was even more jealous of Gus than he was before. He wanted to love a woman as fiercely as Gus loved Esther.

"How long ago did this happen?" Meir asked.

Meir heard Esther's footsteps on the hardwood floor. Gus heard them too.

"Not long enough," Gus said. "Don't tell her I told you. You do, and I'll kick your ass."

Esther entered the living room and made a sour face. "I can still taste clove bubblegum."

CHAPTER FIVE

1917

Sadie Rosenfeld sat on the windowsill and watched Jacob slam the pointed end of Mama's iron into the windowpane again and again. The glass didn't break. His efforts didn't even chip the surface.

Jacob had taken over for Nathan who had banged on the window until he thought his arm was going to fall off. The window was just the most obvious way the family had tried to escape the three-room apartment after learning that they couldn't get out through the front door. They had tried digging through the walls, the floors, and the ceilings. In an act of desperation, Nathan had tried to break a window by flinging his body against it.

The window hadn't smashed into slivers of glass. Nathan hadn't plummeted to the street below. Instead, he had bounced off the window and landed on the apartment floor. Nothing the family did had any effect. Their violent attacks on the apartment hadn't produced a single crack or splinter.

Beating on the walls and flinging their bodies against the window should have raised a ruckus, but the walls absorbed the sound. When the awful truth sank in that they were trapped, and that there was no way to escape, panic seized them and the screaming began. They screamed until their throats were raw. They clung to one another and begged God to save them. When it became obvious that HaShem wasn't going to rescue them, they fell into a stunned silence and stared at the walls. Finally, they began moving around again. They continued to try to escape because there was nothing else to do.

Jacob paused to rub his arm. His face should have been shiny with sweat, but their bodies no longer perspired. They were neither hot or cold, hungry nor thirsty. No one needed to use the water closet. Sadie supposed that was a good thing since they could no longer leave the apartment. She was beginning to treasure anything that could be called good.

The hands on the mantle clock stayed frozen at 10:45. Papa had only paid the meter in the kitchen for a week's worth of gas, but the lights continued to shine. Papa called the never-ending source of gas a miracle on the same level as Hanukkah's eight days of oil.

Clouds covered the windows making it impossible to know if it was day or night. Though their bodies didn't need sleep, the family would grow tired of thinking and fall asleep. But when they woke up, they had no way of knowing how long they had slumbered. Though there didn't seem to be any way to measure the hours, Sadie was determined to find one.

Mama provided Sadie with the answer. While Papa was the head of the family, Mama was the *balaboosta*, the head of the home. Before their imprisonment, Mama had run the family's three-room apartment on a strict schedule. Every morning, she rose before the rest of the family to prepare breakfast. While Papa and the boys had made dresses, Mama had daily and weekly routines that included grocery shopping, cleaning, and laundry. She had started dinner at the same time every day so that hot food would be waiting for her family when their workday was done.

At first, Mama reacted to their imprisonment the same as the rest of the family. She tried to find a way to escape the apartment. When nothing worked and there was nothing else to do, Mama began to follow her daily routines again. They were so deeply ingrained that she continued them even though the reasons for them had ceased.

Mama's internal clock told her when to lie down and when to rise, when to stand in the kitchen and when to sit in the living room. She reminded Sadie of a chalet cuckoo clock that she had seen at Macy's magnificent store in Herald Square. It was first and only time that Papa had taken the family to the store. Nathan and Jacob had acted as if it were no big deal. For Sadie, the visit was an exciting adventure.

The store was enormous and packed full of busy people. Sadie had held tight to Mama's hand for fear of getting lost. She'd never seen so many gentiles in one location. The women smelled like flowers. As Papa led his family through the store, Sadie felt like an army general inspecting troops of dresses, hats, gloves, handkerchiefs, dolls, doll carriages, skates, shoes, table spreads, and sewing machines.

The family had lingered at the clock department while Papa purchased the mantle clock that now sat above the fireplace. Sadie had wished that her father had selected one of the cuckoo clocks hanging on the wall, specifically the one with carvings of leaves and birds. When the hour struck, a flock of mechanical birds popped out of the cuckoo clocks. Sadie and her brothers had jumped back in surprise. The bonging, clanging, and cuckooing was deafening. Along with cuckoo birds, the chalet cuckoo clocks had figurines careening out of doorways. One of the clocks had a milkmaid wearing a white head scarf and apron. Carrying a pail in one hand, she waddled over to a cow and dipped her pail toward the cow's teats before retreating inside the clock.

Mama became Sadie's cuckoo clock milkmaid. She watched her mother carefully and when her internal clock told her it was time to lie down to sleep, Sadie would mark a slash on the wall with a piece of coal. So far, there were forty-two black slashes. The slashes didn't include the days before Sadie came up with her system. She had no way of knowing how many days or months had passed since their imprisonment began.

Mama emerged from the bedroom, passed through the kitchen, and into the front room. The dining table was exactly as it had been the night the clock had stopped and the clouds descended on them. There were six Haggadas on the table waiting for the Passover service to resume with the *Birkat Ha-mazon*. Six wine glasses waited to be filled for the third cup of wine. In the center of the table were the seder plate, the box of matzo, and the bottle of wine.

Sadie sighed as her mother began to clear the table. Cleaning was another habit Mama couldn't relinquish. Yet as soon as Mama moved everything into the kitchen, everything would appear back in its place on the dining table. She never even got a chance to wipe away the crumbs.

This time, Mama tried something new. She ignored the Haggadas, the seder plate, and the wine glasses, and only put the matzo and the wine on the shelf in the kitchen. Sadie shook her head and gazed out the window.

Normally, the clouds were as static as a wall, but they began to billow. Sadie's eyes widened as the clouds parted and sunlight streamed in. Sadie grabbed Jacob's arm. His mouth dropped open. They could see outside the window.

"Papa. Mama," Sadie said. "Come quick."

They hurried to the window. Nathan joined the rest of the family. The street below was filled with merchants, mothers, and children. As Sadie searched the crowd for familiar faces, a sensation tickled her ears. Like apples and honey eaten once a year during Rosh Hashanah, it was a delight that was both strange and familiar.

She looked over her shoulder at Papa. "I can hear them. I can hear the people outside talking."

Papa squeezed her shoulder. "Then surely they can hear us." Papa shouted and banged his fists on the windowpanes. Nathan and Jacob joined him.

No one looked up.

"If the clouds have parted," Nathan asked, "then why can't they hear us? Why doesn't the glass shatter?"

Jacob ran to the front door and threw it open. He leaned against the doorframe for a moment before slowly closing the door.

"The clouds are still there."

He trudged back to the window. The family stared at Orchard Street's flow of humanity as if they were watching a holiday window display.

"Look." Sadie pointed at a girl with curly brown hair. "There's Bertha Rose. Bertha! Bertha! I wish you could hear me."

Bertha looked up. She held her hand on her forehead to shield her eyes from the sun. Hope spread through Sadie.

"She can see us!"

The family waved frantically and shouted at the young girl. She turned to her mother who was haggling with the owner of a vegetable cart. She tugged on her mother's dress until she got her attention.

After a brief conversation, Bertha's mother glanced at the building before returning to her conversation with the vegetable cart owner. Bertha struggled to regain her mother's attention.

"Bertha Rose saw us," Papa said. "She'll convince her mother to save us."

"How will they get in?" Jacob asked. "Clouds are blocking the door."

The dark clouds billowed and covered the window, blotting out the sun and cutting off the outside noise. The family tried to stare through the clouds, but they were too thick. Sadie turned away from the window. The hope she had felt earlier had drained out of her. She wasn't surprised to see that the seder plate, the matzo, and the wine had returned to the center of the dining table.

"Did you notice the snow on the street?" Nathan said. "Everyone was wearing their heavy coats. It's winter out there. In here, it's nothing."

"Don't worry," Papa said. "Sadie's little friend saw us. She'll bring help. They'll be here soon."

It wasn't until Sadie added twenty-three more slashes on the wall that Papa finally admitted that Bertha Rose wasn't bringing anyone to save them.

CHAPTER SIX

Meir showed Yetta where he kept Alice's food, her snacks, her catnip, and the location of the litter box. Alice trotted beside them to make sure Meir got everything right.

"If you run out of anything, let me know, and I'll Venmo you the money to get her whatever she needs," Meir said.

"Don't worry," Yetta said. "I'll come by twice a day except on the Sabbath of course. I'll bring with me at least one of the boys."

Meir was glad to hear about the boys. Whenever Yetta's sons visited his condo, they always played with Alice. And when they left, they always asked Yetta for their own cat. Meir wondered how she and Sidney had managed to delay the inevitable feline that would live in their home.

"I really appreciate you doing this," Meir said, "especially considering I have no idea how long I'll be away."

Yetta playfully punched Meir's arm. "Stop it," she said. "It's no trouble at all."

"Are you sure I can't pay you?" Meir asked.

"Your money's no good with me," Yetta said. "Besides, I owe you."

Meir glanced at Yetta. "What do you mean?"

Yetta bent and scratched Alice's head. "Let's have some coffee and talk. That is, if you have the time."

Meir was mostly packed and his flight to New York wasn't until later that day. They went to the kitchen. While the coffee brewed,

Meir set out sugar and milk for Yetta. He drank his black. Once the coffee was ready, they sat at the table in the breakfast nook.

Yetta sipped her coffee. "Do you have any cookies?" she asked.

"Sorry," Meir said. "I'm fresh out."

She waved her hand. "That's okay. I should stick with just coffee."

"You said you owed me," Meir said. "For what?"

"For introducing you to Nona at the seder. I'm sorry, Meir. I really thought you two would hit it off. You're both sweet, warm, intuitive people."

Meir cupped his hands around the warm mug. "I don't mind that you tried to set me up, I just wish you had let me know ahead of time."

"What I should have done was make sure Nona understood what it is you do."

"It's okay."

"It's not okay."

"When I first met you and Sidney, you didn't understand about kishef machers. Not at first."

"That's behind us now." Yetta patted Meir's hand. "This job you're doing in New York. Is it dangerous?"

Meir laughed. "You sound like my mother."

Alice snaked through their legs before going to her food dish. Meir was going to miss her.

"How did your parents react when you told them you were going to be a kishef macher?" Yetta asked.

Meir sipped his coffee. "Not thrilled."

At least, he didn't have to explain kishef machers to his parents.

They already knew. Meir's great great grandfather, Rabbi Lev Poppers had been a kishef macher. Nobody had become one since Lev died and Meir's parents had hoped that he was the last. But then, Meir picked up the Jewish magic family tradition.

Meir narrowed his eyes at Yetta. "I have a question about the seder," he said. "Did you invite Sylvia Solomon in case things didn't work out with me and Nona?"

"What are you talking about?" Yetta asked. Her eyes grew wide. "Wait a minute. Did Sylvia try to get you to hire her?"

"So, you didn't ask her to talk to me?"

"I swear I didn't. I invited her because she's our friend." Yetta laughed. "You hired her, didn't you?

Meir blushed. "I admit it. I did hire her."

Yetta clapped, making Meir blush even more.

"Yay!" Yetta said. "If anyone can find the right person for a kishef macher, it's her."

CHAPTER SEVEN

Meir and Esther's shadows stretched out before them as they walked along Delancey Street. It was six o'clock and people were heading home. Over his shoulder, Meir carried a satchel filled with sacred books, potions, and amulets—the tools of a kishef macher.

He hadn't been to New York in over a year, and he took a moment to relish the sights and smells that he'd come to associate with the city, like riding the subway with an international cast of characters and walking on busy sidewalks while savoring the smell of roasting chestnuts, burning rubber, and the skunky scent of marijuana. Even the sharp tang of urine brought back pleasant memories of times he had spent in the city.

They stopped at the corner of Delancey and Orchard in front of an eyewear store. Across the street was the Tenement Museum's gift shop. Esther nodded at the brownstone further down on Orchard.

"Stan Jolly will show you Sadie's apartment."

"You're not coming with us?" Meir asked.

"This is as close to the museum as I'll get."

Meir leaned close to Esther. "See the *frummie* over there?"

He nodded toward a painfully thin man with a gray beard standing in front of a shop two doors down from them. He appeared to be somewhere in age between sixty-five and death. He was dressed in the ultra-Orthodox Jewish fashion of black suit and white buttoned shirt. Instead of a *shtreimel*, fedora, or kippah, he wore a black fisherman's cap.

"I think he's staring at us," Esther said.

"He is. Do you recognize him?"

"No, but I've seen those fisherman's caps before." Esther crossed her arms. "I have a confession to make, Meir."

Meir grinned. "Let me guess. I wasn't the first kishef macher you tried to hire."

"How did you know?"

"There's a prominent kishef macher sect here in New York. I figured the only reason you would go all the way to Atlanta to see me was if the Worms had turned you down."

Esther frowned. "They were rude, but I don't think that's any reason to call them names."

Meir laughed. "They're called Worms because their sect originated in Worms, Germany."

Esther stared daggers at the old man. "They told me to leave before I could get their official name."

"You're not Jewish and you're a woman. In their world, you don't exist."

Esther glared at the Worms. "If they wouldn't help me before, then why is he here now? They had their chance."

"He's here because of me," Meir said. "I'm a Falk named for our founder, Rabbi Reuben Falk. He was a Worms until he left to start his own sect. There's been bad blood between the Worms and the Falks ever since."

"Are the Worms and the Falks like the Sharks and the Jets?"

Meir chuckled. "Except for the singing and dancing. The Worms consider New York City their turf."

Esther grabbed Meir's arm. "Wait a minute," she said. "New

York is a huge city. How do the Worms even know you're here?"

"The Worms have a magical border around the city."

"Like an *eruv*? Is this an eruv kishef?"

"Exactly. Crossing the eruv kishef alerts them when an outside kishef macher enters their territory. They knew I was here the second my plane landed."

"They can't stop you from being here." Worry creased Esther's forehead. "Can they?"

"It's a free country. They just want me to know that they know I'm here."

Meir waved at the Worms. He didn't wave back.

"Why is he wearing a fisherman's cap?" Esther asked.

"Not sure how kishef machers in Germany adopted a cap that originated in Greece," Meir said, "but stranger things have happened."

"Okay. Fisherman's caps are a mystery." Esther pointed at Meir's Trilby hat. "How did the Falks ended up wearing Leonard Cohen hats?"

Meir adjusted the rim of his hat. "Falks cover their heads to honor God, but how we cover our heads is a personal choice. We have members who wear kippahs, baseball caps, and in the case of one of our members, a cowboy hat. I chose this hat because it looks good on me."

The lights in the Tenement Museum's gift shop went out. Fifteen minutes later, people filed out of the museum's side entrance. Esther faced the eyewear store's display window as if she had taken a great interest in their sale on sunglasses.

"I don't want anyone from the museum to see me," Esther said.

"I'm sure they either hate me or think I've lost my mind."

A woman with frizzy hair almost made it past them when she did a double take. "Esther? Is that you?"

Esther blushed. "Hey, Rita. How are you?"

Rita hugged Esther. "I'm so glad to see you! We've missed you so much. How have you been?"

Before Esther could answer, another museum employee spotted Esther and stopped to hug her. And then a third employee joined the group. They inquired about Gus, asked what Esther was doing lately, and wanted to know if there was any chance she would be coming back to work for the museum. Esther gave vague answers and caught up with the latest museum gossip before the employees said goodbye and went on their way.

"I can see they really hate you," Meir said.

Esther glared at Meir. "Shut up. By the way, your friend is gone."

Meir looked around. The Worm had slithered away. Meir took a silver amulet from his satchel and handed it to Esther.

"Since the Worms know that I'm working for you," Meir said, "I want you to wear this."

Esther held the metal amulet in the palm of her hand. It was square with rounded corners and had three symbols on it. Two of the symbols were crude drawings of birds and the third look like a walking Hebrew letter Bet.

"I've seen this before," Esther said.

"You have?" Meir asked.

"It's Senoy, Sansenoy, and Semangelof. The three angels that protect babies and their mothers."

"They protect everyone in all situations."

"I can pick up one of these at any Judaica store in the city."

"Yes, but this amulet really works. Please. Put it on."

"Seriously?"

"If anyone tries to hurt you, this will protect you."

Esther put the amulet around her neck. It hung next to her silver cross.

"Why did you decide to become a kishef macher?" she asked.

"I suppose it chose me," Meir said. "Like you, I didn't know kishef machers and Jewish magic existed until I was thirteen. That's when I found out that I was Moses *mishpocha*."

Esther snorted. "You don't mean that literally."

"Yes. I do."

Esther waved her hands. "Whoa. Whoa. Whoa. Are you seriously claiming that you're related to Moses."

"All kishef machers are descendants of Moses, the original kishef macher."

Esther crossed her arms. "Let me get this straight. When you were thirteen, you started doing Jewish magic because you discovered that Moses was your great-great-great-great-great-granddaddy."

Meir laughed. "It wasn't that simple. In a way, kishef machers are like musicians and artists. We're born with talent, but we still have to learn our craft. I showed signs that I had the ability to do Jewish magic, but I had to attend Falk Yeshiva to learn how to harness that ability."

"That actually makes sense."

As the sun sank behind the buildings and the city's lights came on, New York took on a different character, one that was more relaxed. Even the traffic seemed more subdued and less hectic. A tall man with wavy blond hair and no jacket came out of the museum's side entrance. He waved as he walked toward them.

"That's Stan Jolly," Esther said. "He'll take you inside."

CHAPTER EIGHT

1940

Sadie had covered half the fireplace wall with slash marks before the other family members finally asked her for an explanation.

"Even though we can't tell day from night, Mama still sleeps and rises like always," Sadie said. "Each time she goes to sleep marks a new day."

"Some habits never die," Papa said.

"Why do it when she sleeps instead of when she rises?" Nathan asked.

"I'm using the Hebrew calendar method," Sadie said. "A new day begins when the sun goes down."

"I'm wondering why it took us so long to ask Sadie why she was writing on the walls," Jacob said.

"I thought it was her way of dealing with being trapped," Papa said.

Rather than feeling spied on, Mama was pleased to have found a way to serve her family again.

"You'll be the family timekeeper," Mama said.

"Sadie is much too young for such an important task," Nathan said. "I have the maturity she lacks. I'll take over now."

"But I'm the one who figured out how to keep track of the days," Sadie said.

"We would have found a way sooner or later," Jacob said. "Nathan's right. You're too young. But I'm old enough to help Nathan."

Sadie punched Jacob's arm. "You're only three years older than me."

"She's right," Nathan said. "You're both too young. I'll keep the calendar on my own."

"But I need something to do," Jacob said. "Otherwise, I'll go crazy."

The three siblings glared at each other. Papa stepped in between them.

"That's enough! I am still your father, so I'll decide, and you will abide by my decision whether you like it or not." He stood up straight and looked down at his children. "I didn't notice what Rebekah was doing and I'm her husband. But Sadie did. She's earned the right to be the family timekeeper."

"But, Papa," Jacob said.

"I have made my decision."

Jacob stared at the floor. "Yes, Papa."

For ten days straight, Sadie's older brothers refused to speak to her. They sneered at her each time Mama headed for the bedroom and Sadie made a new mark on the wall. After the ten days, it was if they had forgotten to be angry with her, and they stopped treating her as if she had done something terribly wrong to them.

Rather than have Sadie redecorate the walls, Mama found other material for Sadie to use as her calendars. Presently, Sadie was working her way through a Hebrew schoolbook.

Jacob pointed at the schoolbook. "What's the count?"

"Eight thousand three hundred and ninety-five," Sadie said.

"How many years is that?"

"Twenty-three."

"I would have been thirty-six. I would have been married with a family."

Sadie rubbed the graphite on her fingers. She wished Jacob had gotten married and that his wife had given birth to a daughter. Surely, she would have inherited her father's curly hair and beautiful blue eyes. As her aunt, Sadie would have given her dolls to play with and candy to spoil her appetite.

"I would have been to Coney Island so many times, I would have been sick of going," Sadie said.

"If I would have been thirty-six, you would have been thirty-two," Jacob said.

Sadie smoothed the hem of her dress. "I wouldn't be trapped in this little girl body. I would have breasts and a husband. And God willing, I would have had children of my own."

Papa sat by the window and stared at the dark clouds. Of all the family members, Papa was the most depressed. He couldn't sell dresses trapped inside the apartment. He was no longer the boss of his growing dress business. His dream of opening a clothing store had evaporated. Though she didn't miss the work, Sadie missed his determination to make their lives better, one completed dress at a time.

Mama came to Papa and put her hand on his shoulder.

"I'm going to bed now."

"And a new day begins," Papa said.

"Why don't you join me?"

"Not right now. You go ahead."

As Mama headed for the bedroom, Sadie opened the schoolbook and made a slash mark with a stubby pencil. She used her Coney Island postcard to bookmark the page.

"Poor Papa," Sadie said.

"Poor all of us," Jacob said.

"He no longer goes to bed with Mama. Whenever he sold a lot of dresses, I would hear them in the bedroom when he got home."

Jacob scratched his arm. "I never even had a chance to learn how to *shtup*."

Esther smacked Jacob's arm. "Don't use words like that around me."

Jacob scowled. "You're over thirty. You're too old to be offended."

"We don't eat, we don't drink, we don't pee," Sadie said. "I'm not even sure we're still breathing air, and you're worried about sex?"

"I also miss being hungry."

Sadie nudged Jacob. "How can you miss being hungry? Hunger is about the only thing I don't miss."

"Not the hunger itself. The joy of eating that ends the hunger."

Sadie chuckled. She was about to continue their conversation but was distracted by Nathan banging on the kitchen wall.

Over his clothes, Nathan wore the dress that the family had been working on before the clock stopped. He had taken the dress apart and sewed it back together over a dozen times before he decided to try it on. It hung loosely on his thin frame and the hem ended at his knees.

He was trying to break into the airshaft. Everyone, including Nathan, knew that he'd never get through, but no one would tell him that it was a waste of time. When time stood still, there was no way to waste it.

The banging stopped. Nathan leaned against the doorway to the front room. He held a pair of scissors in his hand. He pointed them at Papa.

"This is your fault," Nathan said.

Papa didn't look at Nathan. Instead, he continued to stare at the impenetrable clouds. This wasn't the first time Nathan had accused Papa of causing their strange predicament.

"You got it all figured out?" Papa asked.

"I do! You caused this to happen to us."

"You think you're so smart. If I got us trapped, then tell me how I can set us free?"

Sadie cringed. She hated arguments and did her best to avoid them. Crammed so close together, they were inescapable. Some were like summer storms, nothing more than a brief shower, and others were heavy thunderstorms full of lightning strikes and battering rain. This particular argument had been brewing for days and threatened to develop into a deluge.

"We died," Nathan said. "And now we're in *Gehenna*."

"Really?" Papa said. "I don't remember dying."

"Still making jokes after all this time trapped in this tiny box."

"I'm not joking. I'm not convinced we're dead. If we died, then why don't we remember dying?"

Nathan thumped his head against the doorway. "I'm getting to where the only thing I remember are these walls."

"Maybe Nathan is right," Jacob said. "Maybe a burning piece of coal fell out of the stove and set the place on fire."

"Or maybe that red-headed beggar Papa brought home slit our

throats," Nathan said. "And God has mercifully erased our memories."

Papa placed his hand against a windowpane. "Even if what you say was true, when souls go to Gehenna, they're only there for twelve months and then they either go on to *Olam Ha-Ba* or their souls dissolve. We haven't done either one."

Nathan pressed the tip of the scissors against the doorframe. "A wicked soul can remain in Gehenna for eternity."

"Why am I here?" Jacob asked. "I was too young to have done anything wicked enough to deserve this."

"Neither have I or Sadie. It's father's fault. He did something so evil that God punished not only him but his family as well."

Mama entered the living room. "Nathan! How could you say that? Apologize to your father."

Papa pointed at Mama and said, "See what you've done, Nathan. You woke your mother."

Sensing that the argument was about to turn uglier than it already was, Sadie dived under the table. Jacob joined her. She took the Coney Island postcard out of the schoolbook. She did this whenever she felt the walls closing in on her. She stared at the postcard and pretended she was standing outside the entrance to Luna Park waiting to meet a young man. Sometimes his name was Herschel, but sometimes he didn't have a name.

"I will not apologize," Nathan said. "Tell us, Papa. What did you do? Confess your sin. We deserve to know."

Papa clenched his fists. "I have nothing to confess. I am a good man. I worked hard to provide for my family."

"Liar!"

Nathan lunged at Papa and drove the scissors into his chest. Mama shrieked as father and son tumbled to the floor. Nathan straddled Papa and pummeled him with his fists. Papa held up his arms to deflect the blows.

Jacob scrambled out from under the table and grabbed Nathan's right arm. Mama grabbed his left. Together, they dragged Nathan off Papa. They bumped into the table, toppling it over. Glasses and plates crashed to the floor sending broken shards everywhere. The Haggadas and the box of matzo joined the debris. Sadie squeezed her eyes shut and curled into a ball.

Nathan kicked and screamed like a wild animal as Mama and Jacob struggled to hold onto him. Papa lay on the floor and wept.

Sadie opened one eye, and then the other. She pointed at the window.

"Look! The clouds have parted again."

Everyone stopped. Sunshine streamed through the panes.

"Who cares?" Mama said. "Papa has been stabbed."

"It's okay," Papa said. "I'm fine. See?"

Mama turned to Papa and gasped. The scissors weren't sticking out of Papa's chest. Nor was there blood. Papa unbuttoned his shirt and checked his skin. There was no puncture wound. Sadie found the scissors on the floor. They were clean and shiny.

The family gathered at the window. There were hardly any sidewalk vendors and even fewer horse-drawn carts. Clunky motor vehicles, some with wood paneling on the sides, filled the streets. On the sidewalks, some men wore short ties with their baggy suits and fedoras. Women wore hats that were too small for their heads and dresses with wide belts, big buttons, and squared shoulders.

Papa put his arm around Mama's waist and pointed at a woman in a bright yellow dress. The hem floated about her knees as she walked.

"What do you think?" Papa asked. "Would you wear something like that?"

Mama blushed and then pointed at a man in a dark suit. "The boys would look quite handsome in something like that."

For five minutes, they watched the street before the clouds returned. When they turned back to the apartment, they found the dining room table was standing again. The plates and glasses were unbroken and in their place. The Haggadas and the box of matzo had returned as well. They hung their heads. Nathan slipped the dress off and let it drop to the floor.

"I'm sorry I stabbed you, Papa," he said.

Nathan's attempt to kill Papa made Sadie wonder why one of them hadn't tried to do it before now or why one of them hadn't tried to kill themselves. She wondered why she hadn't tried. Was it the will to live no matter what the circumstances?

Seeing that he was unhurt, Mama hugged Papa. He hugged her back and they shared a long kiss. Papa smiled at Mama and then faced the children.

"Though Nathan's attack frightened me and hurt me emotionally, I felt no physical pain when he stabbed me. Nor did I feel his fists when he struck me. Nathan is correct. We are dead, and we're trapped in Gehenna."

"It can't be true," Mama said. "We're good people. All of us. God wouldn't punish us this way."

Papa held up his hand. "We can't know all the ways of HaShem.

For some reason, He has put us here."

"Maybe He's testing us," Jacob said. "Like He tested Job."

"Whatever the reason, we must not lose faith. Job never lost faith, and neither shall we."

Papa went to a chest of drawers and took out two books, a *siddur* and the Pentateuch. He held them up. "With this prayer book and the five books of Moses, we will prove to our Lord that despite our suffering, we have not lost our way."

"Is that how we're going to get out of here?" Nathan asked. "We're going to pray our way out?"

"No. We're going to pray, because even after death, we are Jews who believe in God."

The family gathered around Papa. He opened the siddur to the first page.

"Let us begin."

CHAPTER NINE

"Stan Jolly," Esther said, "This is Rabbi Poppers. Rabbi Poppers. Stan Jolly."

"Nice to meet you," Meir said. He offered his hand. Stan hesitated before taking it.

"I would have been here sooner," Stan said, "but I had to wait until everybody had gone home for the day."

"I still don't understand why I have to sneak in," Meir said.

Stan scowled. "The board of trustees would freak if they found out I let a mystic go ghost hunting in the building."

Meir was tempted to explain that a kishef macher could also be a mystic, but a mystic wasn't always a kishef macher. Instead, he said nothing because he was eager to get inside.

"Sadie isn't a ghost," Esther said.

Stan ran his hand through his hair. "Doesn't matter. I'm not supposed to do anything inside the building that isn't strictly about the immigrant experience in a historical context."

"In a way, this is an immigrant experience," Esther said.

"Whatever. Let's get this over with."

Meir glanced at Esther. If she noticed Stan's petulance, she didn't show it.

"There's a coffee shop on the next block," Esther said. "You know the one, right, Stan?"

"Yeah, I know the one."

"I'll wait for you guys there."

After Esther left, Stan led Meir around the block to the back of the museum. A chain link fence kept unwanted guests from entering. Stan looked around before unlocking the gate. He used another key to get inside the building and then turned on the hallway lights. Inside, the city's voice was muffled, and the prominent sound was the squeaking of ancient floorboards as Stan and Meir climbed the stairs.

Stan glanced over his shoulder. "I've worked here for four years. I've never seen a ghost."

"Esther believes that Sadie isn't a ghost," Meir said.

"Okay. It's not a ghost. The point is, I've never seen anything out of the ordinary."

On the fourth floor, Meir caught a whiff of *schmaltz*, the spread made from chicken fat and onions. Meir only smelled schmaltz in certain places: Jewish homes, Jewish delis, and where someone had created Jewish magic. Stan stopped at the end of the hallway.

"This is the apartment where Esther thinks she saw Sadie Rosenfeld."

"You don't believe her, do you?"

Stan put his hands on his hips. "I don't think she really saw anybody. I'm only letting you do this because she's my friend."

"I take it you also don't believe I'm a kishef macher."

"Not only do I not believe you're a whatever it is you call yourself, I don't believe you're a rabbi."

Meir shrugged. "It's a hazard of my profession."

"So far, the only thing I do believe about you is that you have good taste in hats."

Meir adjusted the brim of his Trilby hat. "Thank you."

"How much did Esther pay you to come here?"

"That's between us."

Stan glared at Meir. "One-time payment?"

"I really don't see how it's any of your business."

"It's bad enough that you've gotten her hopes up, you're ripping her off too."

Meir smiled. He liked that Stan was as protective of Esther as Gus.

Stan reached for the door.

"Stop!" Meir said.

Stan drew his hand away from the doorknob. "Why? What's wrong?"

"You can't see it, can you?"

"See what?"

"Step back and I'll make it visible."

Stan rolled his eyes. "You don't have to put on a magic act for me."

"Humor me."

Stan moved aside. Meir placed his hand on the hardwood door, lowered his head, and said a few words in Hebrew. Dark red swipes appeared on the doorframe. The sloppy painting looked like the work of a drunken painter.

"Whoa!" Stan said. "How'd you do that?"

"I'm a kishef macher," Meir said. "With God's help, I make Jewish magic."

Stan ran his hand along the door frame. "Is this supposed to be some kind of magic paint?"

"It's not paint. It's lamb's blood."

Stan wiped his hand on his pants. "How very biblical."

"It's a bit old school but effective. Whoever cursed this apartment wanted time to pass over it the same way the Angel of Death passed over the homes of Jews in Egypt. You can open the door now."

Stan and Meir used the flashlights on their phones to light their way into the apartment. They could see the outline of the footprints Esther and Stan had left in the dust during their visit to the apartment in January.

Meir stood in the parlor, closed his eyes, and in Hebrew said, "Lord, reveal what is hidden."

He opened his eyes and swung his flashlight around the room. The apartment was the same. There was no girl with a yellow bow in her hair standing by the window, but the smell of schmaltz was so strong he could taste it. An annoying pain burrowed in between Meir's shoulder blades. Esther had been right. This was no ghost story.

"Let's move back to the hallway," Meir said.

They filed out of the apartment. Meir stood in the doorway and repeated his request to God. The room filled with yellow light, illuminating two adults and three children in early twentieth-century clothing. Their lips moved but Meir couldn't hear them.

"What am I looking at?" Stan stammered. He was wide-eyed and pale.

"This must be the Rosenfeld family," Meir said.

Meir reasoned that the older man was Baruch. He rocked back and forth as he read from a prayer book cradled in his hand. In front of Baruch two boys, Nathan and Jacob, sat in straight back chairs. A woman and a young girl, Rebekah and Sadie, were perched on the edge of the windowsill. Sadie had a bow in her hair. She looked exactly like Bertha Rose's illustration.

When Meir visited the museum years before, he remembered seeing a renovated apartment on the floor below them, filled with antique furniture and dress-making tools that were almost identical to what he observed now in this apartment. Though the building blocks of daily life in the renovated apartment were in excellent condition and handled with great care, they were still dull and rusted with age.

In the Rosenfeld home, brass still shined and the labels on boxes were brand new. Except for an unfortunate wine stain, the tablecloth was a bright white and the flowery wallpaper had not begun to wilt. Even the bow in Sadie's hair was a sunny yellow.

"Can they see us?" Stan asked.

"If they could, they would have noticed us by now," Meir said.

"I feel like we're spying on them."

"Me too," Meir said.

He closed the apartment door. His running shoes squeaked on the hallway's polished floor as he walked back to the staircase. He sat on the stairs and placed his satchel in his lap. Stan followed Meir.

"You really are a kishef macher, aren't you?" Stan asked.

"I've dedicated my life to Jewish magic."

"I'm sorry I said you weren't a rabbi."

Meir waved his hand. "It's okay."

Stan nodded toward the apartment. "What did we just see?"

Meir sighed. "The Rosenfelds are in a time bubble."

"I don't understand what that means."

"The rest of the world moves forward, but they don't. They can move, think, and feel emotions, but they don't need food and water because they haven't aged a minute since the bubble was created."

"You can save them, right?"

Meir scratched his beard. "I studied this kind of thing in yeshiva. Time bubbles are tricky things."

"Tricky? What does that mean?"

Meir stayed seated. "Rabbi Sadikoff was one of our teachers at Falk Yeshiva, but he spent most of his time writing commentaries of our sacred books. He wrote them in Hebrew by hand. His handwriting was very neat and meticulous. He was working on a commentary of the *Charba de Moshe,* the Sword of Moses, but he was having a hard time. He claimed constant interruptions from students and rabbis were making it impossible for him to get anything done. I'm sure his complaint was legitimate. When he wasn't writing a commentary, Rabbi Sadikoff was a pleasant man who wore a cowboy hat and told amusing stories about his early life in Tennessee. Everyone loved being around him.

"His solution to avoid interruptions was to create a time bubble in his study. Once inside, no one could distract him. Since time was at a standstill, he wouldn't need to stop to eat or sleep. He could devote his entire attention to his writing. And that's what he did. For a year, no one saw Rabbi Sadikoff. His study door was always closed. One day, I peeked inside. Except for a few cobwebs, the room was empty. Rabbi Sadikoff's desk, ink pens, papers, and books had gone into the time bubble with him.

"At the end of the year, a student was walking by his door when she thought she heard someone calling for help, but the voice sounded like it was coming from far away."

Stan held up his hand. "Hold up. She? The student was a woman?"

"As far as I know, she still is. Her name is Barbara."

"I thought women weren't allowed to go to yeshivas."

Meir shrugged. "The Falks are different from most other kishef macher sects. Since women can be Moses mishpocha, the Falks believe they deserve to attend Falk Yeshiva."

"I didn't understand half of what you just said, but I'll take your word for it. What happened to the rabbi?"

"Barbara looked inside Rabbi Sadikoff's study. His desk and writing supplies were back. So was Rabbi Sadikoff. He was lying on the floor barely able to move. He had sounded far away because his voice was weak. His hair and his beard had grown down to his knees. He had black circles around his eyes. His fingernails and toenails were long ugly spirals. Though Barbara was shocked by the sight of him, she managed to remain calm and called the medical staff to take poor Rabbi Sadikoff to the infirmary. He was bedridden for three months before he was fully recuperated."

"What went wrong?" Stan said.

"Nothing. The spell worked like it was supposed to. However, to release the spell, Rabbi Sadikoff had to essentially pop the time bubble. When he did that, the time he'd held at bay came rushing in. Rabbi Sadikoff aged a year in seconds. Our bodies aren't used to aging that rapidly. Back in the study, the teachers found Rabbi Sadikoff's completed manuscript neatly stacked on his desk. The teachers all agreed it was his best work. But living in the time bubble for a year almost killed him. He was forty-six when he went in and he was forty-seven when he came out, but he looked like he was sixty."

Stan leaned against the wall and stared at the ceiling. It didn't take him long to do the math.

"The Rosenfelds have been in their apartment for a hundred years."

"If I pop the bubble," Meir said, "time will rush in. It will take less than a minute for them to age a decade, then add nine more decades. They'll be dead before their bodies finish catching up to the present."

"Aren't there any other options?"

Meir nodded. "I can crush the bubble. It sounds gruesome because it is. They'll be turned to dust, but they'll die instantly."

Stan pointed an accusing finger at Meir.

"That's murder!"

Meir calmly faced Stan.

"Would you rather I leave them where they are? Trapped in the apartment for eternity?"

Stan stared at the floor. "I can't allow you to just kill them."

"I'm not asking your permission, Stan. This is my decision."

"This is insane. I'm not even sure I believe this is happening."

"If you have a better idea, I'm all ears."

Stan ran his fingers through his hair. "Let's ask Esther. She started this whole thing."

Meir stood up straight. "And she hired me to make this decision for her."

Stan went to the apartment door. He reached for the doorknob but changed his mind. He came back to Meir.

"Okay. Do what you have to do."

"It takes time to prepare and execute the spell. I prefer to do it alone. Wait for me downstairs. I'll join you when I'm done."

Relief flooded Stan's face. He raced down the stairs.

Meir squared his shoulders and walked to the Rosenfelds' apartment. There were many parts to the spell, and he had to get them in the proper order. He didn't need to open the door to cast the spell. He didn't think he could bear to look at the family again.

He opened his satchel and took out his tallit. It was dark blue with black fringe. He recited the tallit prayer and kissed the edges before draping it over his head and shoulders. He took out his worn copy of the *Sefer HaRazim*, the Book of Secrets. He flipped through the pages until he found the passage he wanted.

Meir was about to begin the incantation when his phone rang. He had forgotten to turn it off. He checked the number and saw it was the shadchanit. He thought about letting the call go to voicemail, but he had a feeling she'd just keep calling back.

"Ms. Solomon?"

"Rabbi. I'm so glad I caught you."

"Sylvia, I can't talk right now. I'll call you back later."

"Don't hang up! This is very important. I have one quick question and then I'll let you go."

Meir sighed. "Okay. One question."

"Are you Orthodox, Modern Orthodox, Hasidic, Conservative, Reform, Reconstructionist, or Secular-Humanist? To me, Secular-Humanist is like Coke Zero. I call it Jew Zero."

"I don't understand how this is important."

"It's okay if I arrange a date with a Modern Orthodox and a Conservative, but a Hasidic Jew doesn't want anything to do with a Reform. And vice versa. You see what I mean?"

Meir was annoyed at the interruption, but he also saw her point. Because he had a beard and often wore black, people assumed that he was Orthodox. But he wasn't, and the women he would meet through Sylvia would want to know his affiliation.

"I'm an UnOrthodox Jew," Meir said. "I've studied Torah and Talmud and I know all the secrets of Judaism, but I pick and choose which traditions to follow."

"I get it," Sylvia said. "You're Jewish Renewal. I thought that died out in the seventies."

"I'm not Jewish Renewal."

"Can you think of a better category for what you just described?"

Meir thought for a moment. "No. I really can't."

"Okay, I can work with this. I'll let you get back to whatever it is you're doing. You're not on a date, are you?"

"Definitely not. Goodnight, Sylvia."

Meir hung up and turned off the phone to make sure he wouldn't be interrupted again.

For the next fifteen minutes, he prepared the spell that would crush the Rosenfeld family. More than once during the process, he almost backed out. He had no right to be their executioner. But this was the most merciful thing he could do.

He recited prayers that included HaShem's secret name and the names of His angels. He took spices from his satchel and sprinkled them on the floor in front of the door. When the door glowed an eerie blue and the smell of ozone burned Meir's nostrils, he knew the spell was ready.

He rocked back and forth in front of the door as he chanted the last prayer. There was no sound. The floorboards trembled, and dust motes floated about him. The blue glow faded away.

Meir opened the apartment door. After a minute, he slowly

closed it.

He found Stan in the building's courtyard next to the outhouses that had provided the only toilets for the tenement until the early 1900s. Stan was smoking a cigarette. Meir was tempted to ask him for one. It might help settle his nerves. But he didn't smoke and didn't feel like starting now. Upon seeing Meir, Stan dropped the cigarette and ground it out with his shoe.

"So that's it?" Stan asked. "They're dust?"

"No," Meir said. "The spell didn't work. The Rosenfelds are still trapped in a time bubble."

CHAPTER TEN

1945

Jacob stared at the cracks in the ceiling. He'd long memorized them and had moved on to creating patterns in the lines that meandered like streams across a plain. Hard to believe that he'd been a fidgeter. Never able to sit still. Now, he could stay perfectly motionless for hours.

His mind continued to fidget. His hands ached for a task but found none.

He looked over at the dress they had been working on before Passover. The last dress they would ever work on. Nathan had gone through a phase where he took it apart and put it back together. Once he grew tired of that activity, he wore the dress for a while. After Nathan had tried to kill Papa, those phases had passed.

Jacob never told anyone, but he hated making dresses. He didn't dare tell Papa. Dresses put food on the table and a roof over their heads. But he was a boy. Boys weren't supposed to make dresses. The boys in the neighborhood teased him about it. Called him a *faigeleh*.

The thing that worried Jacob the most was that he was good at making dresses. He had a natural talent for stitching. He could see the parts of the dress and envision how they would fit together into a whole. When he stitched, the needle and thread singing in his hands, his mind wandered and a wandering mind was a mind freed.

Jacob flexed his fingers, but it didn't relieve the ache. The ache was too deep. He needed to stitch something. Not a dress. Something else. Moving quietly to avoid waking Nathan, he went to the sewing supplies.

Using scraps, he stitched two pieces of fabric together. The action felt good. Some of the ache dissipated. He squinted at the stitched fabric. The two pieces looked like wings. Wings belonged on a bird. He worked for hours, and when he was done, he had created a bird. Crude, but recognizable.

He heard Nathan stirring. In a panic, he quickly hid the bird under a stack of scraps and scurried back to his makeshift bed. He didn't want anyone to know what he'd done. He wasn't ashamed of the bird. He needed the secret as much as he needed to use his hands.

The next night, he was ready to stitch again. But no more birds. Nothing against birds, but he felt he'd already outgrown them. He wanted a bigger project. One that would occupy him for a long time. He decided on a subject he could observe every day without anyone knowing he was studying them.

A family portrait.

The next night he started working, using his blanket as his canvas. As he stitched, his mind wandered, and for a few precious hours flew free of the apartment.

CHAPTER ELEVEN

The smell of burnt coffee greeted Esther as she entered the coffee shop. She ordered coffee with soy milk and splurged on a slice of carrot zucchini bread. People on laptops dominated the available space, but she managed to secure a table against the wall under a bulletin board filled with flyers for neighborhood events. Esther wished she had brought a book to read since she had no idea how long she might be waiting.

As she sipped her coffee and nibbled on her carrot zucchini bread, she considered texting Gus to give him an update but killed that idea immediately. Esther's friends had often told her how lucky she was to have a husband who was quiet and laid back. That wasn't the real Gus. He was only quiet and laid back around people he didn't know.

When Esther and Gus went to Atlanta, Gus didn't say a word during the entire meeting with Meir. But after they left Meir's apartment, she couldn't get him to shut up.

"I can't believe you gave money to that *bambalán*," Gus said. "You need to cancel that check before he deposits it."

"Give Rabbi Poppers a chance. Besides, I didn't give him that much."

"That's how guys like him operate. They milk you for a little bit at a time and before you know it, they've cleaned you out."

"I don't think he's like that. I got a good feeling about him."

"All that means is that he's a slick con man. I wouldn't be surprised if he wasn't a real rabbi."

"I have to trust somebody or else I'll never find out about Sadie."

At the mention of Sadie's name, Gus stopped arguing. Even if he didn't believe Sadie existed, he accepted the fact that Esther did, and he didn't want to stand in the way of her quest to find the girl she'd seen in the window.

Esther finished eating and used a napkin to wipe the crumbs off her hands. She checked her watch. Stan and Rabbi Poppers had been in the museum for close to an hour. The bread felt heavy in her stomach. There was no way of knowing how much time the rabbi needed, but with each passing minute, Esther's doubts about the self-proclaimed kishef macher were growing.

Maybe Gus's distrust of the rabbi had finally rubbed off on her. She had to wonder what sort of mystical creator of magic had a website. He had yet to do anything to prove he was capable of creating real magic. And she still hadn't forgiven him for feeding her that disgusting clove bubblegum popcorn.

Esther took a deep breath. There was no need to freak out. If Rabbi Poppers ended up being a fake, she would be disappointed, but not devastated. She would be out fifty dollars, which would bother Gus more than her. While Esther didn't entirely trust the rabbi, she did trust Stan Jolly. When the two of them joined her at the coffee shop, Esther would take Stan aside and get the truth about Rabbi Poppers. Stan would be able to tell her if the rabbi was what he claimed to be or if he was putting on an act. If Stan said he was a bambalán, then she would thank Rabbi Poppers for his time and send him back to Atlanta. Once he was gone, she would continue her search for someone who could find Sadie.

Satisfied with her decision, Esther was about to get a refill on her coffee when Stan and Rabbi Poppers entered the coffee shop. They spotted her and headed toward the table. Esther could tell from the expression on their faces that something had gone wrong. Rabbi Poppers was dark and gloomy while Stan was pale and shell-shocked. Stan plopped down into a chair opposite Esther. She leaned forward and studied his pasty face.

"Are you okay?" Esther asked. "You look like you're about to have a stroke."

"I need a drink," Stan said. "Desperately."

Esther knitted her brow and turned to Rabbi Poppers.

"We have a lot to talk about," Meir said.

They left the coffee shop and found a bar that wasn't too crowded, and the jukebox wasn't playing too loudly. They sat on a row of barstools, with Esther in the middle. Stan ordered a shot of tequila with a beer chaser, Esther ordered white wine, and Meir asked for hot tea with a shot of bourbon. After the bartender served their drinks, Esther watched wide-eyed as Stan quickly swallowed the tequila and asked for another shot.

"Somebody tell me what the hell happened," Esther said.

"We saw them," Stan said.

Esther grabbed his arm. "You saw her? You saw Sadie?"

"Not just Sadie. The whole family. Mother, father, sister, brother, brother. They're all trapped in there."

"The whole family? I just saw Sadie."

"That was a coincidence," Meir said. "You happened to look when Sadie was at the window. It could have just as easily been Nathan or Jacob."

"They had lamb's blood on the door," Stan said. "Tell Esther about the lamb's blood."

"It's on the doorframe, not the door," Meir said.

"Like in the Passover story?" Esther said.

"Exactly. Except in this case, someone made Time pass over the Rosenfelds. They didn't run off in the middle of the night. They never left the apartment."

Esther gulped her wine and ordered another glass. Stan drank his beer and Meir sipped his tea.

"I don't understand," Esther said. "Are they alive or dead?"

"Rabbi Poppers tried to kill them," Stan said. "But they're still alive."

Esther grabbed Meir's arm. "You tried to kill them?" she asked.

"Imagine the Rosenfelds are inside a balloon on the bottom of the ocean," Meir said. He cupped his hands together to form a hollow ball. "If you pop the balloon, it will fill with water and drown them. The water is time." He closed his hands into fists.

Stan nudged Esther. "Have you noticed how rabbis make everything sound like a parable?" Stan asked.

"The Rosenfelds can't be saved," Meir said. "I tried to give them a quick and painless death, but I failed. The bubble is very tricky. I've never seen one like it."

"So that's it?" Esther asked. "You're just going to leave them in there?"

"I promised you that I would use all the resources at my disposal to solve your dilemma. I'm going to call one of my former teachers at Falk Yeshiva. Hopefully, he'll know what to do." Meir sipped his tea. "And I'm going to try and talk to the Worms."

Esther narrowed her eyes at Meir. "How's that going to happen? Aren't you and the Worms like the Sharks and the Jets?"

Meir chuckled. "More like clashing cousins. We're all Moses mishpocha which means we are literally distant relatives."

Stan leaned against the bar. "I missed this one. Who are the Worms? And who is Moses mishpocha?"

"The Worms are a kishef macher sect here in New York," Esther said. "I asked them to help me, but since I'm a shiksa, they turned me away. That's when I turned to Meir."

"No Jewish magic happens in the city without them knowing about it," Meir said. "They should know about the Rosenfelds."

"Will they talk to you?"

Meir held up his forefinger. "There is one Worms who will speak to me."

Meir excused himself and went to the bathroom. Once she was sure he was gone, Esther turned to Stan who was ordering another shot of tequila. She hadn't seen him drink this much tequila since the museum's holiday party.

"Did you actually see Rabbi Poppers perform magic?" Esther asked.

Stan nodded vigorously. He drained the last of his beer and stared at his empty glass.

"Honestly, when you told me that you hired a Jewish wizard, I thought you'd gone mental. But I didn't say anything. I felt it was something you had to do to process whatever it was that was really upsetting you."

"You and Gus worry too much about me. I'm stronger than you think."

The bartender brought Stan his shot of tequila.

"I figured I'd show the rabbi the apartment, he'd do some kind of lame hocus pocus, and then after he was gone, I'd call Gus and insist that he make you see a therapist."

Esther smiled. She knew that she could trust Stan to tell her the truth.

"Rabbi Poppers is the real deal?" Esther asked. "Really?"

"He made a believer out of me," Stan said. Then he drank his shot.

A shiver of excitement ran down Esther's spine. "I can't wait to tell Gus he was wrong."

CHAPTER TWELVE

1967

Everyone but Jacob stood by the windows. At Papa's signal, Jacob plucked the box of matzos off the dining table. The dark clouds melted away and the family pressed their faces against the glass panes. Jacob joined his family watching the street.

"Look at those two with the long hair," Nathan said pointing at a couple wearing bell bottom jeans and fringe vests. "I can't tell the boy from the girl."

"The one that might be the boy is waving at us," Papa said.

"He's holding up two fingers."

"Two? What does it mean? Two boys? Two girls?"

It was Jacob who figured out that moving the box of Manischewitz's matzos would temporarily clear away the clouds that covered the windows. He joked that it only took him thirty years to make the connection between the two.

The box always returned to the table on its own, even if someone was holding it tightly. Nathan and Jacob worked for days trying to figure out exactly how the trick worked. They removed the matzos and took the box apart. The box returned to the table intact with the matzos inside. They crushed the matzos and tore the box into pieces. It returned to the table whole with the matzos unbroken. When the box returned so did the clouds covering the windows. Jacob counted the seconds between removal and return and determined that exactly five minutes passed.

"Look at that car," Mama said. "It's purple."

"I'm sorry to see the shoe store went out of business," Sadie said. "Just like the cars and the clothes, the stores are always changing."

Jacob peered down the block.

"Moscot Eyewear is still on the corner. It hasn't changed since they moved in."

"People always need eyeglasses." Sadie turned to Mama. "Remind me, Mama. Where is Coney Island?"

"You can't see it from here," Mama said.

"Tell me anyway."

Mama pointed south. "That way."

"I want to know every detail you can remember."

Mama put her arm around Sadie's shoulder.

"Your father only took me courting there a couple of times. I've told you everything I can remember."

They watched the street traffic until five minutes had passed and then the box of matzos went back to its place on the table and the clouds returned. Everyone moved away from the window. Jacob and Sadie sat on the floor and leaned against the wall. Sadie checked her calendar.

"Fifty years and we're not a minute older."

Jacob shrugged. "Moscot is not the only thing that never changes."

Sadie continued to rely on Mama's circadian rhythm to track the days, months, years, and decades, but Nathan and Jacob had used the box of matzo to prove its accuracy. They had waited for their mother to go to bed. When she rose, they moved the box, looked out the window, and saw that the sun was rising.

Ever since the day Nathan had tried to bury a pair of scissors into Papa's chest, Papa had been leading daily *Shacharis*, *Mincha*, and *Maariv* prayer. In between Shacharis and Mincha, every family member took turns reciting passages from the Pentateuch. Between Mincha and Maariv, they often discussed the passages recited that day. These daily rituals had done much to make their imprisonment more bearable.

The daily rituals had also helped the family develop the same circadian rhythm as Mama, sleeping and rising along with her. Since they couldn't control the ever-burning gas lights in the front room and the kitchen, they covered them at night with strips of fabric that would have been used to make dresses. The back bedroom was always dark as a tomb.

The immersion into prayer and study established a sense of purpose to their days. By embracing God's words, they were able to transcend their enslavement. Not entirely, but prayer made their suffering more tolerable.

After Micha, they moved the box to see a few minutes of the world outside the apartment. During those precious minutes, spread out over fifty years, they had witnessed the evolution of stores, vehicles, and fashion. Horses disappeared from the street. The Jews left 97 Orchard Street and other immigrants took their place. One immigrant group after another made the building their home. But then one day, the waves of immigrants dried up. A group left and another didn't take its place, leaving the Rosenfelds the sole tenants.

After Maariv, they played games of their own invention. For eighteen years, their favorite was a biblical guessing game. A family member would pick a character from the Bible and then each member of the family would ask ten questions to figure out who they chose. Winning was easy if it was someone like Moses' wife Zipporah. The real challenge was guessing the identity of someone less well known, like Korah, whom God punished for rebelling against Moses by having the earth open her mouth and swallow him.

When it was time to sleep, Papa and Mama went to their small bedroom. Nathan and Jacob arranged the chairs in the front room to act as their beds. Sadie curled up on a stack of blankets in the kitchen.

While the rest of the family quickly fell asleep, Sadie often stayed awake for hours. Listening to the sound of her father snoring, she would take out her Coney Island postcard, and looking at the blurred message on the back, she would imagine that in clear writing her suitor invited her to spend the day with him.

As the years rolled by, the message from her suitor changed and her fantasy dates grew more elaborate.

Her imaginary suitor was no longer occasionally nameless. He was always Herschel. Tall, dark, and handsome, Hershel came from a good Jewish family. Sometimes he took her to Luna Park to ride the carousel and the roller coaster. Whenever they rode in the Tunnel of Love, he would steal a kiss from her. On cloudy afternoons, they strolled along the Riegelmann Boardwalk and ate lunch at a restaurant.

On sunny days, they went to the beach and swam in the ocean. Sadie had seen the ocean but had never stepped foot on a beach before. She tried to imagine how sand felt on bare toes, and the salty taste of the ocean.

They didn't always go to Coney Island. Sometimes he took her to Macy's and waited patiently as she tried on the dresses that she saw women wearing on Orchard Street. On one very special date, he took her to meet his parents to discuss their intention to marry.

Unable to sleep, Sadie took out her Coney Island postcard and fantasized about a date with Herschel. In Sadie's fantasy, she was not trapped in a nine-year-old's body. She was twenty-one with womanly hips.

There was a knock at the door. Sadie rushed to open it before anyone else because she knew it was Herschel. She was expecting him. Opening the door, she beamed at the tall handsome man.

"Hello, Sadie."

"Hello, Herschel. Come in."

"I brought you a gift."

Herschel handed Sadie a book. It was a novel about a woman who travels to far off places to have adventures. Sadie hugged it to her chest. Something new to read was a precious gift. She wouldn't be marking days on the pages of this book.

Papa and Mama chatted with Herschel while Sadie gathered her handbag and put on her hat.

"Where are you going today?" Papa asked.

"Coney Island," Herschel replied.

"Again? Aren't you tired of going there?"

"Never," Sadie said. "It's the most wonderful place."

The young couple left the apartment building and walked arm in arm on the sidewalk. Despite the parade of fashion that Sadie had witnessed over the decades from her fourth-floor window, everyone was dressed in the same early twentieth century fashion that she had seen on the street before her imprisonment.

Stopping in front of Moscot Eyewear, Herschel hailed a Ford Model T taxi and instructed the driver to take them to Coney Island. As the taxi chugged along, Sadie gazed out the window at the big shiny city full of people going places and doing things whenever and wherever they pleased.

"I'm very fond of you," Herschel said.

"I know," Sadie said.

"Someday we shall be married."

Sadie smiled at Hercshel. "I know," she said.

The taxi drove beyond the tall buildings and busy streets until they were alone on a two-lane road cutting across a flat sandy plain. Far away, Sadie could see the blinking lights of Coney Island. There was nothing else out there. The wonderland had the coastline to itself. Sadie was filled with the delicious anticipation of desperately wanting something and knowing she was about to have it.

When the taxi arrived at the entrance to Luna Park, Sadie almost leaped out before the car stopped. The park was full of happy people and amazing sights. Sadie and Herschel went on the Kiss Waltz and the Turkey Trot. They rode braying burros and danced in the dance pavilion. Whenever possible, Herschel put his arm around Sadie's waist. She felt safe in his strong hands.

"Are you hungry?" Herschel asked.

Famished," Sadie said.

They ate in a restaurant with tablecloths and fine dishes. Sadie blushed at the way Herschel watched her every move. She couldn't believe how lucky she was to have such a wonderful man in love with her.

After their meal, they left the park and strolled on the beach.

Sitting on the sand, they held hands as they watched the sunset. The sound of the waves lapping on the shore mixed with the sounds of people and music coming from the park. Luna Park's multiple lights came on creating a wonderland that competed with twinkling stars.

A brass band began to play rousing music and fireworks exploded over the ocean casting blue and red reflections on the water.

"Are you cold?" Herschel asked.

"A little," Sadie said.

He put his arm around her shoulder, and she nuzzled next to him. Leaning close, he pressed his lips against hers. Sadie had never kissed anyone in real life but had practiced by kissing the back of her hand. That was how Herschel's kiss felt.

She might have imagined making love to Herschel if she had any idea how. There was no chance of her asking Mama what she did with Papa. After all these years, there were still some things she couldn't discuss with her mother. And really, she didn't need to find out. Kissing Hershel in her dream world was enough.

The fantasy ended with Herschel bringing Sadie home. Sadie gave the back of her hand a final goodnight kiss and went to sleep on her pile of blankets in the kitchen.

CHAPTER THIRTEEN

Meir bought two tickets for seats near the Met's dugout. He was fortunate to find such outstanding seats considering he got them the day of the game. The tickets were expensive, but Meir didn't mind. He could afford it, and his mentor and former teacher, Rabbi Zelig Fruman, was a diehard New York Mets fan. Meir wanted Zelig to have the best view possible.

The Mets were playing the Phillies. It promised to be a good game. As a favor to Zelig, Meir would root for the Mets even though he was a Minnesota Twins fan. He had fond memories of going to Twins games with his father and his brother.

Meir texted the seat numbers to Zelig. He put one of the tickets in his back pocket and handed the other to the Citi Field gatekeeper. He bought a bag of peanuts and a soda before finding his seat. The weather was pleasantly cool and only a few clouds meandered in the sky. A perfect day for baseball. Meir was glad he thought to wear a light jacket. Instead of his Trilby hat, he wore his Minnesota Twins ballcap. Nobody seemed to mind that he was wearing it in Mets' territory. He tore open his bag of peanuts. He loved the sound of the shells cracking open before popping the oily seeds into his mouth. He rubbed the bits of shell off his fingers.

The game started and there was no sign of Zelig. Meir would have called to see what was holding him up, but he knew the rabbi wouldn't answer. All Meir could do at the moment was watch the game and wait.

The Mets had a runner on first base. He tried leading off the base a few steps only to have the Phillies' pitcher throw the ball to the first baseman to hold the runner on base. This went on a few times before the pitcher resumed pitching to the batter.

Meir thought about how for Jews like the Rosenfelds, immigration was like a baseball game. For them, leaving Europe, coming to America, living in a cramped tenement apartment, and finding a job, any job, was getting to first base. Becoming successful enough to buy a home and send your children to school was second base. Armed with a good education, your children get better jobs than their parents. This is third base. The Jewish immigrants and their children are successful members of American society. They are free, comfortable, and happy. They have made it home. But not the Rosenfelds. They never made it past first base.

The Phillies' pitcher turned his attention back to the batter. As soon as he pitched to the batter, the runner ran for second base. The batter swung and missed. The ball smacked into the catcher's mitt, and he quickly threw it to second base. The second baseman caught the ball and tagged the runner out, ending the inning.

As the Phillies' players trotted off the field, Meir saw Zelig making his way up the ballpark stairs. He had on a New York Rangers jersey and a New York Mets baseball cap. His long white hair was tied into a ponytail.

Zelig spotted Meir and waved. A hot dog vendor blocked his path. The vendor was calling out for potential customers and didn't notice someone was behind him. Rather than ask the vendor to move aside, Zelig passed through his body like a ghost slipping through a wall. The vendor did a double take but continued to hawk his hot dogs.

Zelig walked through the legs of the people seated in Meir's row. A few of them glanced at their legs and then at Zelig before turning their attention back to the game.

"Rabbi Poppers," Zelig said as he hovered in a seated position over the seat next to Meir.

"Rabbi Fruman," Meir said. "Thank you for coming, but why didn't you bring your body? You could have taken the Short Line bus into the city and then caught a cab to the ballpark."

Physically, Zelig was in his bed at Falk Yeshiva. His spirit had traveled to New York City by astral projection.

"Don't ask," Zelig said. He looked around the stadium. "I can't tell how cold it is. Is that jacket warm enough for you? I wouldn't want you to catch a chill."

"I'm quite comfortable. Thank you for asking."

"These are good seats." The rabbi studied the scoreboard. "The Phillies have already scored. Why am I not surprised?"

The Mets scored two runs which put Zelig in a slightly better mood.

Five years had passed since Meir had last seen his former teacher. Zelig hadn't changed a bit. His weather-beaten skin had ruddy patches and his nose was constantly peeling. He could hide an entire bagel in his flowing white beard. "It was nice of the Worms to assign you a chaperone," Zelig said.

Meir scanned the stands until he spotted the Worms spy. He was the same skinny man with the gray beard whom Meir had seen outside the Tenement Museum. His somber black fisherman's cap stood in contrast to the festive baseball caps around him. He was seated many rows behind Meir and Zelig.

"He's been following me ever since I arrived in town," Meir said.

Zelig stroked his beard. "And you've been here how many days?"

"Three."

Zelig glanced back at the Worms. "When did you first notice him?"

"On the sidewalk outside the Tenement Museum."

"Tell me in detail what you found inside the museum."

Meir told Zelig about the Rosenfeld family's predicament.

"You're sure it was lamb's blood on the doorframe?" Zelig asked.

"I scraped some off and tested it later in my hotel room."

"Lamb's blood is only used for special occasions. I wonder what was so special about the Rosenfelds?"

"That's something I hope to find out."

"And you say they were conducting a seder?"

"Not when I observed them. It was evening, so I assumed they were doing the maariv. But the table was set for a seder in such a way that they were either at the beginning of the service or the middle."

Zelig crossed his arms. "Either way, they've had a hundred years to finish. They should have put the seder plate and the Haggadot away by now."

A Mets player struck the ball, and it sailed high toward the wall. It looked like a home run, but the ball didn't have quite enough power behind it and dropped into an outfielder's glove. Rabbi Fruman groaned.

"You can't save the family," Zelig said. "Crush the bubble. Put them out of their misery."

"I know. I tried," Meir said. "The bubble wouldn't pop."

Zelig frowned at Meir's hands.

"Now I wish I had come in my physical form. Those peanuts you're eating—they look so good. There's nothing better than eating salted peanuts and drinking a beer at a ball game on a beautiful day."

Meir cracked open a shell and popped the contents into his mouth. He chewed slowly. "What should I do about the Rosenfelds? I can't leave them in the bubble."

Zelig turned back to the game. "Did you pack a copy of *Charba de Moshe* and *Sefer Raziel HaMalakh*?"

"Yes, Rabbi."

"What about the *Sixth* and *Seventh Book of Moses*?"

"I downloaded all of them onto my tablet."

Zelig nodded. "Good. Good."

"What exactly am I looking for?" Meir asked.

"The fact that you couldn't crush the bubble means this isn't simply a time bubble. It's a time bubble curse. The cursed must complete a task to pop the bubble."

Meir nodded. "Of course. A time bubble with a puzzle attached to it. But why?"

"My guess is the kishef macher wanted to teach the family a lesson."

"Seems more like a punishment than a lesson."

Zelig stroked his beard. "Tell me, Meir. Why does a Jew punish another Jew?"

This reminded Meir of his yeshiva days when Zelig would ask students leading questions rather than simply giving them the answers. Citi Field wasn't a classroom. Meir would have preferred that

Zelig had gone straight to the information he needed, but he knew from experience that there was no way he could get the tzadik to do it.

"A Jew punishes another Jew," Meir said, "for not being a proper Jew."

"What's a proper Jew?"

"Depends on which Jew you're asking."

Zelig pointed at Meir. "Exactly. Finding out why this particular kishef macher trapped the Rosenfelds will help you figure out how to free them."

"But after all these years, the kishef macher is probably dead."

Zelig shrugged. "Nobody said this job was easy."

Meir dropped the bag of peanuts. They rolled in all directions. "The time bubble is a prison. Prisons have doors and doors have keys."

Zelig picked up his train of thought. "The lesson is the key. It's highly likely that the Rosenfelds have had the key to their freedom all along, but never realized it."

Meir was already feeling pity for the unfortunate family, but a new wave of grief washed over him.

"When I saw the family, they were praying together. They seemed calm. After a hundred years, I wouldn't have been that calm."

"Actually, you probably would be," Zelig said. "The passing years would have drained away your anger. And your joy."

They watched the game in silence until the seventh inning stretch.

"You do realize that finding the key won't save the Rosenfelds," Zelig said.

"After a hundred years, nothing can save them," Meir said. "But isn't death better than being trapped for eternity?"

Zelig sighed. "I can only answer that question for myself. I am not the Rosenfelds."

The Mets flubbed an easy pop fly, putting a Phillies' player in scoring position. Three plays later, the Phillies scored, making it two to two. The game went into extra innings before the Mets lost. Zelig was disappointed, but not surprised. People trudged toward the exits.

"Thank you for coming," Meir said. "I'm sorry your team lost."

Zelig waved his hand.

"It was a nice day and I got to see one of my best students." He leaned close to Meir. If he had been there physically, Meir would have felt the bristles of Zelig's beard. "Are you planning on going into the bubble?"

"If that's the only way to get the Rosenfelds out, then I'll have to go in."

"What about the nice lady who hired you?"

"Esther Luna? What about her?"

"Are you going to take her with you into the time bubble?"

Meir paled. "Absolutely not."

"Have you discussed it with her?"

Meir waited for spectators to inch past them.

"I think it's better if I don't give her a choice," he said.

"Maybe you shouldn't go either," Zelig said.

"I can't leave them in there. It wouldn't be right."

"The time bubble blocks astral projection. You won't be able to come to me for help and I won't be able to come to you."

Meir rubbed bits of peanut shells off his hands. "I know, Rabbi."

"Getting inside the time bubble will be the easy part. Getting out? Not so much. You'll be trapped in there with them until you find the key. Do you understand what I'm saying?"

Meir looked up at the beautiful blue sky. He felt a chill despite his comfy jacket.

"I could be trapped inside the bubble for a hundred years. I could be trapped forever. I must have faith that I will find the key. I have to believe that I can free the Rosenfelds."

CHAPTER FOURTEEN

1982

Sadie couldn't sleep. She tossed and turned on her blankets. Her clothes itched. Her nose itched. She tried thinking of Hershel while staring at her Coney Island postcard, but even he couldn't lure her to slumber. Finally, she got up and went into the front room, moving quietly so as not to wake her brothers.

She couldn't remember when the family had stopped picking up the matzo box. It was a daily ritual that gradually dwindled away. A day was skipped here and there. Then many days in a row passed without anyone gazing out of the window for five precious minutes. And then they stopped completely. It was if the family had lost interest in a world that they couldn't touch. Instead, they had turned inward.

Except for Sadie. Her imagination always carried her outside the window. To feed that imagination, she needed to see what was out there. She would pick up the box of matzos in the middle of the night, and then sit on the windowsill. The clouds parted. A bright full moon sat in the center of the sky. A car drove by, but otherwise Orchard Street was deprived of human activity.

Nathan joined her at the windowsill.

"Did I wake you?" Sadie asked.

"You're not the only one who has trouble sleeping. Like you, I watch the street."

"It's empty tonight. There's nothing to see."

"Not entirely. Look."

Nathan pointed at the building directly across the street. At first, Sadie saw no one, but then she noticed a plume of smoke and followed it down to a woman sitting on the stoop. The woman rested her arms on her knees as she puffed on her cigarette. The sleeves had been roughly torn from her shirt and her pants had multiple rips. She wore men's boots and black leather bracelets with rows of shiny studs. Her hair was black except for a yellow streak down the middle.

Sadie had seen people dressed like this lately. At first, she thought they were beggars, but then she noticed them entering shops on the street and leaving with bulging bags. Also, their boots were shiny. Beggars didn't shine their shoes.

The woman dropped her cigarette and ground it out with the heel of her boot. She started to light another cigarette but got to her feet instead. A man ambled toward her. He was dressed identically to her except he had a chain around his neck. Sadie had seen this before too and had figured out that the latest fashion included wearing a dog's leash as a necklace. The woman ran to the man, threw her arms around his neck, and kissed him.

Sadie put her fingers on her lips.

The man draped his arm around the woman's shoulder, and she put her arm around his waist. They walked toward Delancey Street. Shortly after they passed out of sight, the clouds returned to cover the window. Nathan and Sadie remained seated on the sill.

"Do you ever think about Edna?" Sadie asked.

Nathan gaped at her.

"How did you know about Edna?"

Sadie grinned. "Did you really think you could keep her a secret forever?"

Nathan chuckled and then sighed.

"I used to think about her all the time. It drove me crazy at first. Since I was trapped in here, I couldn't stop her from seeing other boys. But then, I worried that she wouldn't find someone else."

Sadie wrinkled her nose. "You want Edna to be with someone else?"

Nathan shrugged his bony shoulders.

"My sweet Edna would be eighty years old by now. It would break my heart if she was an old maid who never stopped waiting for me to return. I prefer to believe that she fell in love with a good man, got married, and was blessed with lots of children and grand-children."

Jacob began to snore, loudly and with great gusto. It always amazed Sadie that such a small body could create such a large noise. Nathan lifted the box of matzo. The clouds parted. They gazed at the moon.

"I don't believe Papa trapped us here," Nathan said. "I only blamed him because I didn't want to admit that it's my fault."

Sadie stared at Nathan. She could tell from the way his forehead knotted that he wasn't joking. "It couldn't possibly be your fault," she said.

"Yes, it is. It happened the day we brought the beggar home for the seder. The day the apartment became our prison. Papa and I were coming home from Macy's. They had bought Papa's dresses and wanted more. Papa was so happy. I was in a foul temper because I didn't have the nerve to tell him that I planned to move out at the end of Pesach."

"I thought you were going to leave, but I didn't realize it was going to be that soon."

"Edna's aunt and uncle agreed to let me live with them and I had a job waiting for me at a bakery. I wanted to tell Papa and couldn't. Then he put me in a worse mood when he stopped to talk to the beggar."

"Oh yes. Eli, the beggar. I forgot about him."

"He was sitting in mud. His cupped hand was empty as people hurried past him. Papa glared at them and said, 'How can they ignore a fellow Jew?' I told Papa that Eli was a schnorrer and if we give him our money, then we'll be schnorrers. But Papa didn't listen. He invited the beggar to come join us for the seder."

Sadie could picture Papa marching up to the beggar and insisting that he come to the apartment.

"Papa was always doing things like that. No matter how little we had, he always found a way to give to those with even less."

"Yes," Nathan said. "He's a good man. A good Jew. But I tried to get Papa to ignore Eli. I was going to leave, which meant Papa was going to lose a worker. He couldn't afford to be generous to beggars. He was going to need every penny he had. But really, I was only thinking of myself. I was selfish. I was the one who sinned. God didn't punish Papa. He punished me. That's why we're here."

The clouds returned. Sadie quickly lifted the matzo box.

"How can you call yourself selfish?" she asked. "You thought you were trying to help Papa. And even if you could call what you did selfish, I don't think it was such a great sin to merit such harsh punishment."

"Then why is God punishing us? What did we do wrong?"

Sadie rubbed her nose. Never before had she and her older brother talked like this. It had taken them long enough to get around to it.

"I don't think we did anything wrong." Sadie paused. "If I tell you something, do you promise not to laugh?"

Nathan pressed his hand against a windowpane. "I don't, Sadie. I haven't had a good laugh in a long time."

"Okay. Laugh if you want to. I think this is a mistake."

Nathan didn't laugh. "A mistake?"

"I can see no reason for all of us to be trapped here," Sadie said. "So, it must be a mistake."

"How do we correct the mistake?"

"If I knew that, we would have gotten out of here a long time ago."

Nathan looked like he was brooding, but then he always looked that way. Maybe that was what attracted Edna to him. He would have been a serious husband.

"Do you know why you and Papa fought so much?" Sadie asked.

"Because he was stubborn and wouldn't listen to anyone else's opinion?"

Sadie giggled. "No. Because you were both stubborn. You still are. You favor Papa the most too."

Nathan furrowed his brow. "You think so?"

"You don't see it? You inherited his dark hair and sharp cheek-bones. You probably can't tell because of Papa's beard."

"You're right. I can't."

"Jacob inherited Mama's curly hair and fair skin, but he also got

Papa's blue eyes."

Nathan nodded at Sadie. "You also have Mama's fair skin and Papa's blue eyes. But where did you get that thick golden-brown hair?"

Sadie ran her hand through her hair. "Mama once told me that I have Bubbe Bessie's hair."

"It was a nice gift she gave you."

Sadie blushed. "Thank you."

They watched the moon until the clouds returned. Nathan bid Sadie good night and went to his bed of chairs. Sadie went to the kitchen and lay on her blankets.

Sadie thought about Herschel. Since he was an imaginary lover, he would never leave her for another woman. He would never grow old. Like Sadie, Herschel was trapped in time.

CHAPTER FIFTEEN

El Plato de Oro sat between a beauty supply store and a phone store. Gus Ramos's parents owned the East Harlem restaurant with its lunch counter and back room crammed with four-top tables and plastic chairs. An outsider might look at the cheap wood paneling, the dull tile floors, the wobbly tables, and the faded Puerto Rico travel posters on the walls and think that this place was a crumbling, outdated dump. To the restaurant's loyal customers, the Puerto Rican comfort food they served was as precious as *oro*.

Over the years, Gus had worked as a busboy, a dishwasher, a cashier, and a cook. Five years earlier, he'd become manager when his parents retired. He met Esther in El Plato de Oro. She used to come in for lunch every Tuesday with her friends. When Gus saw Esther, it was love at first sight. Esther had to look at Gus a few more times before she fell in love with him.

Behind the lunch counter, under the cracked menu sign, were family photos yellowing with age. There were baby pictures of Gus, his two sisters, and Gus's nieces and nephews. Gus hoped to add a few baby pictures of his progeny once Esther was ready to try again.

Gus was at the cash register counting out a customer's change when Camilla hurried to his side, crossed her arms, and tapped her foot. Gus ignored Camilla as he handed the customer his change and thanked him for coming. Once he was gone, Gus acknowledged Camilla.

"What?" he asked.

"Got some customers in the back complaining about their order," Camilla said. "They want to talk to the manager."

Gus could feel the acid in his stomach churning. Other than replacing worn-out equipment and starting a website, he hadn't changed anything since taking control of the restaurant. That included his employees. They were like family, and in his cousin Camilla's case, they were family. The menu, which featured his mother's recipes that she got from her mother who got them from her mother, hadn't changed since the restaurant opened forty-one years ago. Complaining about the food was an insult to his family.

Gus put his fists on his hips. "Who's complaining?"

She leaned in close enough for Gus to smell her lemony perfume and pointed toward the back room.

"Table in the corner," she said. "The black hats."

"I didn't see them come in."

"I don't see how you missed them."

Camilla had a tendency to be sarcastic. The place was packed with the lunchtime crowd. Keeping track of any particular customer would have been a chore.

"Why would Orthodox Jews be here?" Gus asked. "We don't serve kosher food. Hell, our specialty is roast pork."

"They ordered the chicken," Camilla said.

Gus leaned over the counter and squinted at the crowd. The only hats he saw were baseball caps, mostly with Yankees logos.

"Table in the corner?"

"Yeah," Camilla said. "Near the bathrooms."

"Take over the cash register. I'll talk to them."

Gus went around the lunch counter and said hello to a few regulars as he squeezed between tables on his way to the back of the restaurant. He spotted the three men, could see the disappointment on their faces, and was not impressed. Over the years he'd faced dozens of whiny customers. Based on his experience, the problem was never the food, but the customer's unrealistic expectations.

He thought he knew all the different black hats worn by Orthodox Jews, but he didn't remember ever seeing the fisherman's caps worn by these guys. Two of the men looked to be in their late sixties. One was very thin, and the other was very fat. The third man looked to be in his thirties. He had red hair and an equally red beard. He was obviously the boss. He wore a black suit like the others, but his fit better because it was tailor made. He sat still with a quiet authority while the older men fidgeted and glanced at him nervously. Gus was surprised that the ginger Jew was the leader. Most Orthodox Jewish leaders were ancient fossils with long white beards and wrinkly faces.

Gus stood at their table. "I'm the manager. What seems to be the problem?"

The thin man pointed at his plate. "The chicken is no good."

On the table were three *medio pollo asado con arroz y habichuelas*, half roasted chicken with yellow rice and beans. It was the lunch special of the day. The chicken on the thin man's plate had been torn into and partially devoured. The rice and beans appeared to be untouched.

"We're not a kosher restaurant," Gus said. "If you were expecting kosher chicken then you came to the wrong place."

"The chicken is no good," the thin man repeated.

"There's nothing wrong with the chicken. We make the best roast chicken in El Barrio."

"Taste it. It's no good."

Every table was occupied. People were waiting to be seated. If these guys weren't happy with their meal, they should leave, because Gus needed the table for customers who knew a non-kosher restaurant when they saw one.

"I'm sorry you're not happy with your meal," Gus said. "There's no charge. Have a nice day."

The man put his fists on either side of his plate and glared at Gus.

"I'm not leaving until you taste the chicken."

"Why?" Gus asked. "You said it was no good."

"To prove to you that it's no good."

Gus leaned over and put his hands on the edge of the table. "I gave you a free meal. But I'm not going to play 'taste the chicken.' Besides, you already ate some. I'm not going to eat food that's been touched by a stranger."

The man's eyes grew wide. "Are you saying I'm unclean?"

"I'm saying you have to leave," Gus said. "You've wasted enough of my time already."

The thin man crossed his arms. The fat man did the same. The red-haired man did nothing.

"We're not leaving until you taste the chicken," the thin man said.

Gus pointed at the door. "Leave my restaurant."

"Taste the chicken."

"Get the hell out of here."

"Taste the chicken."

Gus's anger boiled over. He stabbed his thick fingers into the man's plate and tore off a chunk of chicken. He stuffed the succulent meat into his mouth and chewed.

"Tastes great. I told you. We make the best roast chicken in El Barrio."

The thin man and the fat man glanced at the red-haired man. He nodded. All three grinned at Gus.

"If you say so," the thin man said.

They stood and snaked their way through the tables and out of the restaurant. Gus motioned for the busboy to clear the table. He went back to the front counter.

"What was the problem?" Camilla asked.

"They said the chicken was no good."

"That's crazy. We make the best roast chicken in El Barrio."

"That's what I told them."

Gus rang up customers, asked them if they enjoyed their meal, and thanked them for coming. Things were going smoothly. There was plenty of business. He didn't want the black hats to ruin his day, but he couldn't get them out of his mind. Especially the boss. The ginger Jew. Something about his attitude bothered Gus. As if the whole thing had been a game.

"How's Esther?" Camilla asked.

"She's fine," Gus said.

"She still looking for ghosts with her magic Jew?"

Gus felt a stab of pain in his gut. He had been certain that Esther would have come to her senses by now and realized that Rabbi Poppers had no more magic than the Zoltar fortune-telling machine that used to be in Coney Island. Instead, she had become even more convinced that Poppers had powers, amazing powers.

"You got customers waiting for you," Gus said.

Camilla went back to waiting tables. Gus's stomach growled, but he didn't feel hungry. The room spun, and he had to hang onto the register to keep from falling. He hadn't felt dizzy since he had the flu last year. He wiped sweat from his forehead with a white cloth. He looked at the cloth. His sweat had left a yellow stain. He felt hot and sticky. He didn't notice that Camilla had returned to his side until she spoke.

"You okay, Gus?" Camilla asked. "You look terrible."

"I'm fine."

Gus's stomach gurgled, and he farted. He blushed. The gas had built up inside him too quickly for him to block it. Camilla wrinkled her nose at the stench but didn't move away.

"Are you sure you're okay?"

Gus's tongue felt thick in his mouth. "Feelth funny. Thomach hurths."

Camilla felt his forehead. "You're burning up. You should sit down. I'll cover the cash register."

Gus agreed. He turned to leave and collapsed. His face hit the floor, but he didn't feel it. He could hear Camilla shouting, but she sounded like she was miles away.

CHAPTER SIXTEEN

In Meir's opinion, fall couldn't arrive soon enough. With the sun beating down and heat rising from the sidewalk, he regretted his decision to walk the thirteen blocks from his hotel to Midtown Comics. The short trek might have been easier if he'd worn a T-shirt and shorts instead of his usual black Trilby hat, black sport coat, black jeans, and white dress shirt. Sweat plastered the shirt to his back. He was a block from the store when his phone rang.

"Hello?"

"Rabbi. It's Sylvia Solomon. Can you talk?"

Meir glanced at his watch.

"I have a minute. How are you, Sylvia?"

"Don't ask. I have so many aches and pains, it would take days to tell you all about them. But forget about that. I've got good news. I found the perfect woman for you."

"So soon?"

"I don't mess around. She's beautiful. She's a little older than you, but you can't tell by looking at her. I'll text you her phone number. She's waiting on your call."

Meir dug a handkerchief out of his back pocket and mopped his forehead. "That might be a problem. I'm not sure how long I'll be in New York."

"Can you give me an estimate?"

"It could be a few days or a few years."

Meir could hear her tapping something. The tapping sounded

angry. "She's going to think you don't want to meet her because she's too old," Sylvia said.

Meir stuffed his handkerchief back into his pocket. "I'm sorry, Sylvia. My job can be unpredictable."

"Can't you give me some idea of when you can meet her?"

"No, I can't. If she won't wait, then there's no reason for us to meet."

Meir hated that he lost his temper. It was this blasted heat. The sun was baking his brain.

"Well, since you put it that way," Sylvia said.

"I'm sorry. I didn't mean to be a *putz*."

"I have to go. I have another call." Sylvia hung up.

As Meir put his phone away, he gazed at the people walking by. No one looked at him. This was New York City. Nobody cared if he had an argument with someone on the phone.

The Midtown Comics near Times Square occupied the top two floors of a corner building. Meir climbed the stairs and entered the store. The air conditioning brought instant relief to the sticky heat. A galaxy of heroes and villains greeted him on the covers of the comics in the newsstands that lined the walls. The front counter clerk's attention was glued to a comic book.

"Are back issues still upstairs?" Meir asked.

The clerk nodded without looking away from his comic book. Meir went through the aisles to the stairwell that led to the top floor.

Along with a vast army of action figures were tables that held rows of long cardboard boxes filled with back issues of comic books. A Worms stood hunched over a box, rifling through the comics. He was younger than the Worms spy who had followed Meir around town. In fact, he was the same age as Meir.

He looked up and then glanced at his watch. "You're early."

Meir nodded at the boxes. "We both had the same idea."

"Since we're both early, I suggest we take some time to do what we came here to do; look at comics before we discuss whatever it is you asked me here to discuss."

"Good idea."

Meir sifted through the box nearest to him. He loved the aged paper smell of old comic books. To anyone seeing these two young men in their dark suits and beards, one wearing a Trilby hat and the other a fisherman's cap, both carrying satchels, they would have been mistaken for guys trying to hide their geekiness with trendy fashion. No one would have guessed they were Jewish magicians capable of performing feats as amazing as those of comic book characters.

Fifteen minutes later, Meir turned to the Worms. "What'd you find?" he asked.

The Worms showed Meir his stack of *Doctor Strange*, *Hellblazer*, and *The Occult Files of Doctor Spektor*.

"Nice," Meir said. "Here are mine." He spread out back issues of *The Phantom Stranger*, *Moon Knight*, and *Doctor Fate*.

"It's no surprise that we're attracted to heroes with supernatural powers," the Worms said. "We can relate to them."

"Thank you for agreeing to meet with me, Richie," Meir said.

The Worms wrinkled his nose. "Beryl," he said.

"That's right. You changed your name."

"I didn't change it. His holiness, Rabbi Chaim, anointed me with my proper Hebrew name."

Rabbi Chaim was the spiritual leader of the Worms. He had

inherited his position from his father, who had inherited it from his father, who inherited it from his father, who inherited it from the rebbe who founded the kishef macher dynasty in Worms, Germany.

"Leaving the Falks to join the Worms was the wisest decision I ever made," Beryl said. "You should have come with me."

"You should have stayed," Meir said.

In what seemed like a different lifetime, Richie Stein had been Meir's best friend at the Falk Yeshiva. They had done everything together, including making regular trips to Manhattan to buy comic books. Meir missed Richie. He didn't care much for Beryl Stein.

Beryl studied his stack of comic books, each one sealed in a plastic bag. "Perhaps now would be a good time for you to tell me why you asked me here."

"A Worms has been following me since the day I arrived. One day is standard operating procedure. But every day?"

Beryl shrugged. "Rabbi Chaim felt it necessary."

"Why?"

"You'll have to ask him yourself. I don't question his decisions."

They paused their conversation until after a teenager in an oversized hoodie squeezed past them.

"Do the Worms know why I'm here?" Meir asked.

"Of course we do," Beryl said. He glared at Meir. "You want me to say it? Fine. You're here because Esther Luna hired you and you discovered a time bubble in the Tenement Museum."

"Inside that bubble are the Rosenfelds. How long have the Worms known about them?"

Beryl crossed his arms. "What are you implying?"

"I'm not implying anything. I'm just trying to figure out why

Rabbi Chaim decided to keep an eye on me. Is it because he doesn't want me doing magic on what he considers his turf? Or is he worried I'll find out something he doesn't want me to know?"

Beryl looked around the store. Despite their past relationship, Meir braced himself for a possible attack.

"I don't like these questions," Beryl said.

"Then you really won't like the ones I'm about to ask," Meir said. "If the Worms know about the Rosenfelds, why haven't they rescued them?"

"Maybe there was a good reason why they were cursed and that's why they're still in a time bubble."

"I can understand why a Jewish magician might have felt justi-fied in cursing Baruch Rosenfeld or even his wife, Rebekah. But why would anybody in their right mind curse three children, the youngest only nine years old?"

Surprise flickered in Beryl's eyes before he regained his compo-sure. "You have no idea what you're talking about."

"Sadie Rosenfeld was nine when the family was cursed," Meir said.

Beryl was about to respond, but then stared at the ceiling. Meir recognized his expression. It was like the dazed expression a cat gets when it's playing and suddenly stops to stare off into the distance. In Beryl's case, it meant he was receiving a telepathic message. After a minute, he nodded and then smirked at Meir.

"Go back to Atlanta," Beryl said. "You no longer have any rea-son to be here."

"Is that a threat?"

Beryl gathered his stack of comic books.

"Call Esther Luna. I'm sure she'll tell you that your services are no longer wanted."

A chill ran down Meir's spine. "If you did anything to Esther, I'll turn your sorry ass into a pig."

"Oooh, I'm so scared." Beryl shook in mock fear. "We didn't do anything to Esther. Directly."

"What did you do?"

"In sickness and in health. Till death do us part."

Meir took out his phone and called Esther. The call went to voicemail. He hung up and called again. Again, the call went to voicemail. The third time Esther answered.

"I can't talk right now."

"Where are you?" Meir asked.

"The hospital. Something happened to Gustavo. He's very sick." Esther began sobbing. "He's dying."

"Which hospital?"

"Metropolitan."

"I'm on my way."

Meir bounded down the stairs and out of the store.

As soon as Beryl left the air-conditioned comic book store, the hot sun bore down on him and sweat beaded on his forehead. He didn't mind. He was originally from Miami Beach and was accustomed to heat and humidity. Joining the parade of pedestrians on West 40th Street, he walked to the subway entrance on Broadway where a fellow Worms was waiting for him.

"Reb Feintuch," Beryl said. "What are you doing here?"

"Rabbi Chaim asked me to keep you company on the ride

home," Feintuch said.

A feeling of guilt took root in Beryl's stomach. Had he done something wrong and that was why Rabbi Chaim sent Feintuch to keep an eye on him? Beryl shook his head. This was ridiculous. He'd done exactly what Rabbi Chaim had instructed him to do and had nothing to worry about.

"Good," Beryl said. "I could use the company."

The two Worms went down the stairs and waited on the platform for the N train. Feintuch leaned his skinny body against an iron girder.

"What a week I've had," Feintuch groused. "My feet are killing me from following that pisher, Poppers, around the city. But I don't have to do that no more."

Beryl had volunteered to tail Meir around New York, but Rabbi Chaim had assigned the task to Feintuch instead.

"Despite his misguided attempt to get involved in something that doesn't concern him," Beryl said, "I still consider Meir my friend."

Feintuch scowled. "Why?" he asked.

Beryl was trying to formulate a reply that wouldn't lead to an argument when their train arrived. The car wasn't crowded, and they were able to sit together. Even after years of living in New York, Beryl still enjoyed the rocking of a subway car. It reminded him of ocean waves.

"What's in the bag?" Feintuch said. He pointed at the plastic bag Beryl held in his hand.

"It's not much of a mystery," Beryl said. "There's a Midtown Comics logo on the bag."

"Comic books?" Feintuch asked.

"Yes. Comic books."

"Are they kosher?"

Beryl still struggled with a feeling of guilt. But it wasn't due to any imagined dereliction of duty to Rabbi Chaim. He worried that he had somehow betrayed Meir.

"What potion did you give to Esther Luna's husband?" Beryl asked.

Feintuch ignored his question. "Remember Rabbi Chaim's warnings about the evils of assimilation," he said, pointing at the plastic bag. "Even something seemingly innocent like a comic book that isn't about *haredi* life can be a bad influence."

Beryl studied Feintuch. "You were at the restaurant," he said. "You sent me the telepathic message that you had successfully given Esther Luna's husband the potion."

"You don't want Rabbi Chaim to find you with those comic books," Feintuch said. "You should throw them in the garbage."

Beryl groaned in frustration. "Just tell me what you gave him? Rabbi Chaim said it was only going to make him a little sick. Is that true? Or did you give him something worse?"

Feintuch looked away from Beryl.

"I did as Rabbi Chaim instructed me," he said. "When the *mashiach* tells you to do something, you don't ask questions."

Beryl thought Rabbi Chaim was a great man, but he didn't think he was the Messiah. However, he knew better than to argue the point with fellow Worms who did believe it.

"I'm going to find out what you gave him eventually," Beryl said. "You might as well tell me now."

Feintuch shrugged. "Then you'll find out eventually."

Beryl glared at him. "You know what, Reb Feintuch?"

"I'm dying to hear what you have to say," Feintuch said.

"I was wrong when I said I could use the company."

CHAPTER SEVENTEEN

1990

Sadie woke the moment she felt a hand on her shoulder. Her first thought was that she had overslept, and Papa was rousing her to join the family for the morning prayers. But it wasn't Papa. Jacob knelt next to her bed in the kitchen. Sadie was about to speak when Jacob held his finger to his lips.

"I want to show you something," he whispered, "but only you."

Sadie sat up and rubbed her eyes. She couldn't imagine what Jacob could possibly show her in their three-room world that she hadn't already seen.

"Well? What is it?"

Jacob left the kitchen and came back immediately. He held a neatly folded blanket. "Promise not to tell anyone?"

Sadie put her hand over her heart. "I promise."

He held the blanket to his chest.

She sensed that he was about to change his mind. "You know you can trust me," she said.

Jacob looked lovingly at the blanket in his hands before unfolding it. He gripped the edges and held it up. Sadie gasped. Using strips of red, yellow, blue, black, and white fabric, Jacob had stitched together a family portrait. Sadie was amazed at the amount of detail. She could easily identify every member. There was Nathan's thick eyebrows, Papa's heavy beard, Mama's long nose, and Jacob's curly hair. He had even included the yellow bow in Sadie's hair.

"I didn't know you were such a good artist," Sadie said.

"My first attempts were terrible. But I had plenty of time to practice."

"How long did it take you to do this?"

Jacob shrugged. "I put it aside from time to time, so I'm not exactly sure."

"Come on. Certainly, you have some idea."

Jacob gazed down at his masterpiece. He allowed himself a little smile of pride. "Twenty or thirty years."

"It's magnificent."

"I'm not done yet."

Sadie would have loved for Jacob to show this to the rest of the family. Mama and Papa would have been so proud of him. They would have insisted on hanging it above the mantle so that it would have been seen and appreciated every day. Maybe someday Jacob would show it to them, but Sadie understood that for now it had to be his secret. With no privacy or escape from the other members of the family, a secret was a rare and precious thing. And what a wonderful secret.

"How did you manage to create this without any of us knowing?" Sadie asked.

"I didn't touch the dress on the mannequin," Jacob said. "If I had, Papa would have suspected right away that I was working on something. Instead, I used the scrap pile. Since tools and supplies are kept in the sewing machine drawers, I didn't worry about anyone noticing that I was using the spools of thread. But five years ago, I ran out."

Sadie's eyes widened. "What did you do?"

Jacob grinned.

"I took apart my coat. Obviously, I don't need it since I can't go out into the cold even if I wanted to, so I dismantled mine for the thread. And for extra bits of fabric."

Sadie still couldn't understand how Jacob managed to keep anyone from discovering this amazing thing bursting with color and artistry. It covered one side of the blanket entirely.

"It hasn't been easy," Jacob said. "I wait until everyone is asleep and then I only work a few hours. Luckily, Nathan is a heavy sleeper. But then, there are times when someone can't sleep, and they sit by the window. That's usually either you or Mama. I pretend to be asleep until you go back to bed. Sometimes when we're praying, I'm really thinking about what I want to work on next."

"But where do you hide it?"

Jacob turned the blanket around. The opposite side was the same dull brown blanket that he used to cover himself every night.

"I hide it in plain sight. The art is against my body where no one can see it. When I get up in the morning, I fold the blanket so that the art is on the inside. We've grown accustomed to using the same things every day so I'm not worried that Nathan might use my blanket by mistake."

Sadie tousled Jacob's hair. "Thank you for sharing your secret with me."

Jacob folded the blanket. "Our first years trapped in here were the hardest for me. I desperately needed something to keep my hands busy. You had the calendar. Mama had her daily routines. Papa and Nathan would argue. But I had nothing."

"When Nathan went through that stage, where he took the dress apart and put it back together, I was surprised you didn't help him."

Jacob glanced toward the front room. "He wouldn't have let me. It was something he had to do on his own."

Jacob patted the blanket. Sadie was tempted to pat the blanket too, but it was his creation. It seemed too intimate for her to touch.

"I have a secret," Sadie said.

"You don't have to tell me."

"It's only fair. You told me yours. Though mine is not nearly as impressive as yours. I pretend that I have a boyfriend. His name is Herschel. We go to Coney Island."

Jacob carefully folded the blanket. "Is he Jewish?"

"Does it matter? He's only make believe."

"I suppose not. I was just curious."

"Yes. He's Jewish."

"When the two of you go to Coney Island, do you meet there, or does he come here to pick you up?"

Talking about Herschel as if he were a real person gave Sadie an odd sense of pleasure.

"He picks me up here," Sadie said.

Jacob nodded. "The next time he comes to visit, ask him to stop by the store on the way and get me some spools of thread."

CHAPTER EIGHTEEN

Meir entered Gus Ramos's hospital room. He took out his handkerchief and held it over his nose in a vain attempt to avoid the smell of rotting fish. The bed closest to the door was empty. The sheets were tangled, indicating that the bed had been recently occupied. The privacy curtain between the beds was pulled across the room.

Wheezing could be heard on the other side of the curtain. The wheezing was punctuated by a loud fart, which added the smell of rotten eggs to the already putrid stench in the room. Meir pulled the curtain aside. Gus was in the bed with his eyes shut and his mouth open. His face glistened with sweat.

"You don't look so good," Meir said, even though he knew Gus couldn't hear him.

Esther entered the room looking like a bandit, with a scarf tied over her face just above her nose.

"Meir? How did you get in here?"

"I didn't use magic if that's what you're thinking. I asked the nurse which room Gus Ramos was in."

Esther took an ice chip from a plastic cup next to Gus's bed and placed it in his mouth. She mopped his head with a hand towel. His sweat left splotches of yellow on the fabric.

"The smell drove everybody out of the room," Esther said. "There was an old man in the other bed, but he demanded that the hospital move him. Nobody will come in here but me and the nurse."

"Gus was given a nasty potion," Meir said. "My guess is that it was slipped into something he was drinking."

"We think it was put on a chicken breast."

"A chicken breast? How did they manage to get it into his food?"

"Three Worms came to El Plato de Oro. They all ordered the chicken special and then one of them told Gus that his chicken was no good. For some reason that I still don't understand, Gus ate the chicken."

"Are you sure they were Worms?"

"They wore black fisherman's caps."

"They put the potion on a chicken breast. That's wrong on so many levels."

"The chicken is in toxicology to determine what kind of poison they used."

"They won't find anything. Magic potions are undetectable by science."

Gus farted again.

"I love Gus, but I can only stay in here for a few minutes at a time," Esther said as she waved her hand.

"Let's get some air. My eyes are burning."

They left the room. Esther pulled down her scarf. Family members and close friends were gathered in the waiting room.

"Everybody," Esther said, "this is Rabbi Meir Poppers."

Worried faces glanced up briefly and acknowledged his presence. One family member, a muscular woman with big brown eyes, joined Esther and Meir.

"So, you're the magic Jew?" she asked.

"This is Gus's cousin, Camilla," Esther said. "She was raised in a barn."

"I can make an antidote for Gus," Meir said. "But I need to do it soon before the potion causes any permanent damage."

"What kind of permanent damage?"

"To his internal organs. He could die if we wait too long."

Esther paled. "Thank you for offering, but I think we should let the doctors take care of Gus."

Meir put his hand on Esther's shoulder. "The doctors can't cure a magic potion. I'm the only one who can save him."

Esther gnawed on her knuckle. "This is Gus's life we're talking about. I'm supposed to trust magic over modern medicine?"

"Let me try. I'll bring the antidote here."

She gazed at her family's worried faces. "Okay. You can try."

"I need access to a kitchen."

Esther shook her head. "I can't leave the hospital. I have to stay here with Gus."

"He can use the restaurant's kitchen," Camilla said.

"I'll need to get a few things first," Meir said.

"The restaurant's van is in the hospital parking lot. I'll take you wherever you want to go."

Meir faced Esther. "I'll be back soon," he said.

CHAPTER NINETEEN

Camilla led the way to the hospital parking lot where she had parked the van with the words *El Plato de Oro* in gold letters painted on the side. In a normal social situation, Meir would have felt self-conscious being alone in a van with a beautiful woman, but he was too busy trying to save a man's life to worry about it.

"Where to?" Camilla asked as she started the engine.

"Lavi Glatt," Meir said.

"Who?"

"Not who. What. It's a kosher grocery store at 805 Avenue U."

Camilla glared at Meir. "I thought we were in a hurry."

"We are."

"You want to go from East Harlem to Brooklyn during rush hour traffic? We won't get there until midnight."

"It's okay. I know a shortcut."

Camilla swore in Spanish. She drove out of the parking lot and into bumper-to-bumper traffic. They crawled a block before Meir held up his hand and mumbled a few words in Hebrew. The world shimmered. Camilla frantically looked left and right, and then slammed on the brakes. Drivers honked and shouted rude things as they drove around the van.

"Where are we?" Camilla asked.

"At our first destination."

The van was in front of the kosher grocery store, Lavi Glatt, in

Brooklyn. They had traveled sixteen miles through New York City rush hour traffic in less than a minute.

"How did we get here?" Camilla asked.

"I did a spell called *kefitzat ha-derekh,* the shortening of the way," Meir said. "Can you park?"

Camilla craned her neck in search of an open space along the curb. "Somewhere, but nowhere near the store."

"I'll get what I need while you drive around the block." Meir hopped out of the van.

The store smelled like the inside of a refrigerator that hadn't been cleaned since Reagan was president. Half of the labels of the items on the shelves were in Hebrew. The industrial fan mounted to the ceiling made a steady clicking noise. Orthodox Jewish women in their wigs and long dresses wandered the aisles. Meir hurried past them on his way to the frozen meat section.

Meir picked out a vacuum-packed whole kosher chicken cut into eight pieces. He then went to the spice section for a box of kosher salt. He carried his items to the front counter and stood behind an elderly woman. With achingly slow deliberation, she placed coins on the counter to pay for a jar of borscht and a bottle of orange juice. Glaciers were melting faster than her movements, so Meir mumbled a spell that shortened the old woman's way out of the store. Meir paid for the chicken and salt, then he hurried out to the sidewalk.

Meir heard a car horn blaring. Camilla waved as she inched the El Plato de Oro van toward him. He dashed to her. She stopped and he hopped in.

"Where to now?" Camilla asked.

"Lin Sister Herb."

"Who is she?"

"Again, not who. What. It's a Chinese herbal supply store on Bowery."

As they eased into traffic, Camilla glanced at the bag at Meir's feet and then at Meir.

"What are you?" she asked.

"I keep telling people I'm a kishef macher. With God's help, I create traditional Jewish magic. But no one ever believes me."

Camilla grinned. "The way you jumped past traffic just now made a believer out of me."

Meir grinned. He twisted around to look in the back of the van. Other than a hand truck, it was empty. "Is this what you do for Gus's restaurant?" he asked. "Drive the van?"

Camilla laughed. She had a full-bodied laugh. "No. I'm a waitress. I used the van to take Gus to the hospital."

"You didn't call an ambulance?"

"Ambulances take too long."

"Did you use the hand truck to get Gus into the van?"

"No. I carried him."

"By yourself?"

Camilla flexed her arm in a weightlifting pose. Her bicep bulged. Meir wondered if she crushed her lovers in moments of passion. Then he wondered if they died happy. He knew he shouldn't think such thoughts, especially when he should direct all his attention to saving Gus, but she was close enough for him to smell her lemony perfume again, and to see how tightly her shirt clung to her body.

Meir recited the kefitzat ha-derekh. Though she had previously experienced the shortening of the way, Camilla gasped when the van instantly traveled fifteen miles to Chinatown. She was even more shocked to find a parking space in front of the store.

"Can I come with you?" Camilla asked.

"Sure."

Lin Sister Herb's overworked air conditioner made the store as frigid as a meat locker. Tourists in T-shirts and cargo shorts took cell-phone photos of the bins filled with twisty roots that looked like dried octopus arms. Meir ignored the barrels of sandals, bowls of smooth stones, trays of incense, and shelves jam-packed with boxes of tea and bottles of pills. He went directly to the front counter on which decorative trays were filled with dried plants. He ignored those as well.

"Excuse me," Meir said to the salesclerk. "I need some specific herbs."

The clerk was a twenty-something Asian woman wearing a white lab coat. She leaned on the counter. "Whatever it is, we probably have it."

Counting on his fingers, Meir gave her the names of the four herbs that he required. The clerk's eyes widened.

"Wow. Only old Chinese doctors who still practice traditional Chinese medicine ever ask for those herbs. How did you even know about them?"

Camilla put her arm around Meir's waist. Her closeness sent a delicious shiver through him.

"He's a Jewish magician," Camilla said. "He makes Jewish magic."

Camilla's comment made Meir's pride swell.

"With God's help," Meir added.

The clerk turned to the wooden file cabinets behind the counter. They reminded Meir of old library card catalogs. The clerk trailed her finger along them until she found the right drawers. Soon, she had four small plastic bags piled on the counter, each filled with dried herbs. Meir paid her, and she placed them in a paper sack.

Meir and Camilla returned to the van.

"Where to now?" Camilla asked.

"Gus's restaurant so that I can make the potion that will cure him."

"Let's use my apartment instead. We won't have to work around the cooks."

"The restaurant is still open?"

Camilla nodded. "Gus would be furious if we closed because he was sick."

Despite the urgency of his mission, the prospect of being alone with Camilla in her apartment thrilled Meir. She gave Meir her address as they pulled into traffic. He cast his spell and ten seconds later they had covered the eight miles to Camilla's apartment building.

She lived on the fourth floor. The elevator was broken so Camilla led the way up the stairs. Meir caught himself watching her plump butt and quickly looked away. As soon as they entered, she turned on the window air conditioner. The apartment smelled comfortable and spicy at the same time. The kitchen was spotless.

"What do you need?" Camilla asked.

"A large pot, a cutting board, a kitchen knife, and a ladle."

As Camilla gathered the things Meir requested, he placed the items he'd purchased on the counter. He took off his jacket and rolled up his sleeves before filling the pot with water from the sink. He put the pot on the stove and turned on the burner. He washed the chicken and rubbed kosher salt into all eight pieces. As Meir waited for the water to boil, he watched Camilla straighten up the already tidy apartment. She caught him watching her and his face burned with embarrassment. She came into the kitchen and leaned on the counter. He glanced at her cleavage and then turned his attention to the stove.

"Did you see the men who gave Gus the potion?" Meir asked.

"I waited on them."

"What did they look like?"

Camilla described the three men. Meir's stomach dropped.

"Your description of the thin man fits the Worms who was following me."

"Worms? You call them worms?"

"It's the name of their kishef macher sect. I'm a Falk after our founder, Rabbi Falk. They're named after Worms, Germany because that's where they started."

Camilla took out her phone and got on the internet. "What do you know? There really is a city in Germany called Worms.

"The Worms with red hair had to be Rabbi Chaim," Meir said.

"Is he a big deal?" Camilla asked.

"He's the leader. I'm surprised he was there."

"You mean like when a gang leader sends his guys out to do a hit? He never goes himself unless it's super important and he wants to make sure there are no screw ups."

"That's a good analogy."

The water began to boil. Meir dropped the chicken into the pot.

"What's so super important about Gus?" Camilla asked.

"Poisoning him was a warning. Stay away or bad things will happen."

Camilla grabbed Meir's arm and squeezed. He winced. She really was strong.

"What did Gus ever do to them?"

Meir patted Camilla's hand and she let go.

"Not a damn thing," Meir said. "They went after Gus because they couldn't get to Esther. I gave her an amulet that protects her from their magic. I was stupid not to give one to Gus as well." He glanced at Camilla. "And now that you've helped me, I should probably give you an amulet, too."

Meir chopped the herbs into separate piles. He said a prayer over each herb before sprinkling it into the pot. The herbs made soft popping sounds when they hit the boiling water.

"What's so super important that they're willing to poison Gus to scare you away?" Camilla asked.

"Do you know about the family trapped in the Tenement Museum?"

"Gus told me. He thought Esther imagined the whole thing, but she told him that you proved she was right. Gus still wasn't convinced."

"What do you think?" Meir asked.

"After that shortening our way through traffic trick, I'm a believer."

Meir grinned. "The Rosenfelds are real. For some reason, Rabbi Chaim doesn't want me to free them."

"I'm getting to where I really don't like this guy."

"Yeah. He's getting on my last nerve."

Meir recited more prayers as he stirred the ingredients together. Chicken fat rose to the surface and changed from dull yellow to fluorescent orange. Thick clouds of steam filled the kitchen. Camilla opened the kitchen window.

"I've never seen chicken soup glow like that," she said. "It looks radioactive."

After five more minutes of stirring the pot, Meir announced that the antidote was ready and had Camilla get him a plastic container. He filled the container and pressed a lid on top. He put the container into a bag, and then put on his jacket.

"Let's go to the hospital."

"What about the rest of the soup?" Camilla asked.

"Wait for it to cool down. It will become thick enough that you can scoop it into a garbage bag. Then scour the pot with bleach and scalding hot water. Be sure to wear rubber gloves. And whatever you do, don't eat it, not even a drop."

Camilla wrinkled her nose. "I wasn't planning on it."

Meir and Camilla returned to the hospital. They were close enough that Meir didn't have to use the shortening of the way.

At the hospital, they found Gus and Esther's family in the lobby, gathered around Esther. She sobbed on her mother's shoulder. Meir tried to get her attention to let her know that he had the antidote, but she was too distraught to talk to him. Esther's father led Meir away and explained that Gus's condition had gotten worse, and the doctors had no idea what was making him sick. Meir pulled Camilla aside.

"We're running out of time. Will you help me?"

"I've been with you this far," Camilla said. "Lead the way."

They hurried to Gus's room. Before going in, Meir looked in

both directions to make sure no one was around. Gus's wheezing had become weaker, and his skin was the color of rancid chicken fat. As Meir and Camilla approached him, he farted.

"I forgot how bad he smelled," Camilla said, fanning the air.

"It's the magic potion. It's called Black Fly Potion and we need to get it out of his system as soon as possible."

Meir checked the bathroom.

"There's only a shower," he said. "I was hoping there would be a tub. No matter. The shower will do."

He handed Camilla the bag with the antidote, got his arms around Gus, and tried to lift him out of the bed. He didn't get very far.

Camilla put her hand on Meir's shoulder. "Allow me," she said as she handed the bag back to him.

Camilla picked Gus up as if he were a sack of potatoes. Meir opened the bathroom door and had Camilla place Gus on the shower floor. She grabbed a towel off a rack and wiped his orange sweat off her arms. Meir took the plastic container out of the bag and pried the lid off.

"I have to warn you," Meir said. "This is going to be really gross."

Gus farted again.

"How can it be any worse than this?" Camilla asked.

"You haven't seen anything yet."

"Just do it!"

"Hold his mouth open."

Camilla pried Gus's mouth open. Meir poured the soup down his throat. Some of it dribbled out of his mouth and onto his chest.

Meir didn't stop until the container was empty and then he moved back. Camilla moved back with him.

A nurse appeared at the bathroom door. "Who are you?" she asked. "What are you doing in here?"

"I'm a kishef macher and I'm saving this man's life," Meir said.

"You can't be in here. Get away from that patient."

"You're right about that. No one should go near him right now."

"I'm calling security."

Esther and her family arrived and crowded the doorway.

"Why is Gus in the shower?" Esther asked.

"I gave him the antidote," Meir said. "We should be seeing results any second now."

"Did you tell the doctor?"

"There wasn't time."

"You should have told the doctor. Put Gus back in bed."

Gus's eyes popped open.

"Not a good idea right now," Meir said. "Everybody stand back."

Gus's cheeks puffed out. He leaned to the side and a thick black substance gushed out of his mouth and splashed on the shower's tile floor. The smell of spoiled fish and rotten eggs was nowhere near as bad as the putrid odor of the black goo he expelled. Everyone watched in horror as more and more poured out. The shower's drain couldn't handle the onslaught and the goo bubbled around Gus, soaking his hospital gown.

"It's an exorcism!" shouted Esther's mother. "He's driving the devil out of Gustavo."

Gus spit out the last bit of goo and rested his head against the tile wall.

"Gus?" Esther asked. "Are you okay?"

Gus burped. "Whoo! I feel much better."

"Chicken soup really does cure everything," Camilla said.

Gus's cheeks puffed out again and he grabbed his stomach. He leaned his head back and opened his mouth wide. A swarm of black flies flew out. Esther's family shrieked and fled the room. The nurse fainted. Camilla caught her before she hit the floor. When the last of the flies exited Gus's mouth, Esther kneeled next to the shower and wrapped her arms around her husband.

"Now I get the name," Camilla said. "Black flies. Black Fly Potion."

"I was going to warn everybody about them," Meir said, "but I didn't think they'd believe me."

CHAPTER TWENTY

Worms' headquarters occupied all six floors of the Trachtenberg Building, an unremarkable red brick structure that sat on the edge of Borough Park. Rabbi Chaim's office looked like a storage room for a Jewish history museum. The bookcases that lined the wall were on the verge of collapsing from the weight of the musty books on the shelves. Scattered about the room were incantation bowls, ancient menorahs, and faded tapestries.

Rabbi Chaim's door was open, but Beryl Stein knocked anyway. Chaim looked up from the book he was reading and waved him in. Beryl sat in a visitor's chair.

"I received an update on Gustavo Ramos," Beryl said. "He'll make a full recovery."

Chaim narrowed his eyes at Beryl. "Who?" Chaim asked.

"Esther Luna's husband. The restaurant owner. You had Feintuch give him the Black Fly Potion."

"You said he'll make a full recovery?"

"Yes. Meir was able to cure him in time."

Chaim turned his attention back to his book. "Don't worry," he said. "The woman who started this trouble, the man's wife, what was her name again?"

"Esther," Beryl said. "Esther Luna."

"Esther got the message loud and clear. She'll fire Meir and he'll have no choice but to leave New York immediately."

Beryl shifted in his chair. He was having trouble getting comfortable in this situation.

"I thought we were going to give her husband something that would make him sick but only enough to scare her. Not something as deadly as a Black Fly Potion."

"Do you have a problem with my choice of potions?" Chaim asked.

"Ramos could have died."

"As my papa would say, '*A fremdeh tsoreh iz kain tsibeleh nit vert.*' The troubles of a stranger aren't worth an onion."

"I don't think that applies here since we poisoned him."

Chaim closed his book, leaned back in his leather executive chair, and steepled his fingers. "I think it's time you got married."

Beryl gaped at Chaim. "Is now really the time to discuss this?"

"Why not? You're not getting any younger."

"Rabbi Chaim, please."

"What could be more important than finding a proper Jewish woman to bear you many children?"

"I was hoping we could discuss the people trapped in the time bubble."

"What is there to discuss?"

Beryl swallowed his frustration. "Rabbi Chaim. The other Worms follow you with blind devotion, but you have always encouraged me to challenge you if I felt it necessary."

Chaim came around his desk and sat in a chair next to Beryl. "Do you truly feel this is necessary?"

"Yes, Rabbi."

"Then speak."

"Before I met with Meir, you told me about Baruch and Rebekah Rosenfeld."

Chaim wagged his finger. "An evil couple and very dangerous."

"That's what you told me."

Chaim glared at Beryl. "You doubt me?"

Beryl held up his hands. "No. Never would I doubt you."

"I told you what happened. A revered kishef macher trapped them in an eternal time bubble because their crimes against Jews and humanity justified their extreme punishment."

"Who was the kishef macher?"

Chaim stroked his red beard. "I don't remember. My *zayde* told me the revered kishef macher's name, but that was a long time ago and I've forgotten it."

"Usually, men who are revered have names that are remembered," Beryl said.

Chaim shook his head. "His name doesn't matter. Only his actions. He did what was necessary for the safety of all Jews. This is why we had to stop Rabbi Poppers. He doesn't understand what's at stake. He's like a child with a hand grenade."

Beryl walked to the window and looked at the street below. "Do you know what atrocities the Rosenfelds committed?"

"I didn't feel the need to ask. Zayde's word was good enough. Do you not agree?"

"Yes, of course, Rabbi."

"Good!" Chaim clapped his hands. "We can put this silly discussion aside and start on the road to finding a nice Jewish girl to be your wife."

Beryl faced Chaim. "It's a good thing only Baruch and Rebekah are trapped in the bubble and no one else."

Chaim went back to his desk. "Is this another one of your challenges?" he asked.

"I need to know," Beryl said. "Are Baruch and Rebekah alone?"

"Yes, they're alone."

"What about Sadie Rosenfeld?"

"Who?"

"Meir said she is one of Baruch and Rebekah's three children trapped in the bubble with their parents."

Chaim laughed and picked up the book he'd been reading when Beryl entered his office.

"Meir is lying. There are no children. There is no Sadie Rosenfeld."

CHAPTER TWENTY-ONE

Esther and Gus's cat Flan kept Meir company as he studied the titles of the books on Esther's bookshelf. There were Stephen King novels, Harry Potter books, Pura Belpré Award winning books, and chef memoirs. One shelf was dedicated to Jewish history books.

"Tell me, Flan," Meir said. "How many of these books were required reading for graduate school and how many did Esther acquire out of curiosity?"

Flan rubbed his face on the bookshelf. Meir had just met the caramel-colored cat, so he wasn't sure what the feline was trying to tell him.

Meir found a battered paperback of Jewish Folk Tales between two academic hardbacks. He grinned as he flipped through the pages. When Meir was ten, his zayde gifted him the same book on the fifth night of Hanukkah.

He was sitting in an easy chair reading the paperback when Esther entered the living room. She plopped down on the sofa opposite Meir. She wore a sweatshirt and yoga pants, had dark circles under her eyes, and her hair was uncombed. Gus had been released from the hospital but was still weak from the effects of the magic potions.

"I'm thankful for the love and support of my family and Gus's family," Esther said, "but I can't tell you how happy I am to finally get them out of the apartment. All their fussing was wearing poor Gus out."

"Seems to me they wore you out too," Meir said.

Esther scratched her nose. The apartment was messy. An empty gallon tin of Poppers jalapeño cheddar popcorn sat on the coffee table.

"Is it that obvious?"

"Only in your voice. You should get some rest yourself."

Esther waved away Meir's concern. "I'm fine. I'm so relieved to have my Gus back." Esther leveled her eyes at Meir. "I'm sorry I doubted you."

Meir scratched his beard. "Did you? I don't remember that happening."

Esther stared at her knees. "I didn't say it out loud."

Meir laughed, which made Esther giggle, and whatever tension had been between them melted away.

"I'm the one who should apologize," Meir said. "I only gave you protection. I should have also given Gus an amulet."

"He wouldn't have worn it. And what if the Worms couldn't get to Gus? They would have gone after somebody else close to me."

"I still feel responsible."

Esther stood. "I'm going to make hot tea. Would you like a cup?"

"I would love some."

Esther went to the kitchen to make the tea. Flan followed her, perhaps hoping she'd give him something to eat. Meir went back to reading the paperback. He knew there was something important about the story he was reading, but he couldn't put his finger on it. When Esther returned with two steaming cups, he held up the paperback.

"May I borrow this?"

"You saved my husband's life," Esther said. "You can keep it."

Meir slipped the book into his satchel and took out an amulet. He placed it on the coffee table next to the empty popcorn can.

"I know this is closing the barn door after the horse has gone, but make sure Gus wears this."

Esther sipped her tea and then stood up abruptly. "I can't believe I forgot. I'll be right back."

She hurried into the kitchen and came back with an El Plato de Oro business card. On the back, written in feminine handwriting, was Camilla's name and phone number.

"Camilla made me promise that I'd give you this," Esther said. "You made quite an impression on her."

Meir put the card in his coat pocket. "You really think so?"

"Meir! You gave her jewelry."

"Actually, it was an amulet. Did she say whether she liked it or not?"

"Ask her yourself."

As Meir sipped his tea, he looked out the window. He couldn't see the moon. There were too many buildings in the way. But he could feel it out there, watching over the city. He turned to face Esther.

"The Worms poisoned Gus to scare you into telling me to leave New York and forget about the Rosenfelds. I was lucky I saved Gus before it was too late. I may not be so lucky next time."

Esther picked up her teacup and then put it down again. "I don't want to leave that poor family in their apartment forever. But I don't want anyone I care about getting hurt. Is that selfish of me?"

"Not at all."

Esther stared at her hands. "So, that's it? We just give up?"

"I'm leaving New York in the morning. When I get to Atlanta, I'll refund your money."

Gus lumbered into the living room. He wore gray sweatpants and a white tank top undershirt. Esther rushed to his side.

"You shouldn't be up. Come back to bed."

Gus held up his hand and walked past her. He gritted his teeth as he lowered himself into the chair Esther had vacated.

"I hear my wife talking to a strange man in my living room and you expect me to stay in bed?"

"How do you feel?" Meir asked.

"Hungry. Esther. Could you bring me something from the kitchen?"

"Of course," she said. "What would you like?"

"Anything but chicken."

Esther hurried to the kitchen. Gus pointed at Meir.

"You're not leaving New York. You're going to rescue that family."

"But Gus," Meir said. "They almost killed you."

Gus snatched the amulet off the table and put it around his neck. "I don't know how they do things where you come from, but here in El Barrio, if a man tries to kill you and doesn't finish the job, then it is your duty to go find him and kick that *mamabicho* in the balls."

Esther brought an unopened gallon tin of Poppers jalapeño cheddar popcorn and a can of soda. Flan followed her from the kitchen and rubbed against Gus's leg. He scratched the cat's head.

"I've lived in El Barrio my entire life," Esther said. "I don't remember ever hearing that. Are you sure that's how we do things here?"

She pried the lid off the tin and placed it on the table in front of Gus. She popped open the soda and placed it next to the popcorn. Gus grabbed Esther's hand and kissed it.

"Trust me," he said. "That's what we do here."

Gus grabbed a handful of popcorn and stuffed it into his mouth. He closed his eyes as he chewed. Then he pet the cat some more. Esther ate some popcorn and offered the tin to Meir. He declined. Despite its popularity, he'd never cared for that flavor.

"No," Esther said firmly.

Meir and Gus gawked at her.

"He's got to," Gus said. "We can't let them get away with this."

"It's not that," Esther said. She leveled her eyes at Meir. "The Worms used a potion that almost killed Gus. Isn't there a potion that will save the Rosenfelds? Something that will make them younger?"

"There are no potions to reverse aging," Meir said. "But there are potions that slow down aging."

Esther's face lit up. "Do that. Give them that potion."

Meir frowned. "It wouldn't work quickly enough to counteract the rush of time."

"Is there nothing you can do?"

"I'll contact my potions teacher at Falk Yeshiva. Nobody knows more about potions than her."

"Then that's what I want you to do," Esther said. "You can't leave, Rabbi Poppers. Not until you kick the Worms in the balls. And the best way to do that is for you to save the Rosenfelds."

CHAPTER TWENTY-TWO

2013

For years, only Sadie continued to lift the matzo box and peer at the world below. But the family joined her when she told them about construction crews arriving at their building. They watched them coming and going and listened to banging and sawing below them. Then, moving trucks brought boxes of all sizes.

After the workers left, Jacob was the one who figured out that 97 Orchard Street had become a form of entertainment. He noticed that groups of people gathered at the stoop at regular times throughout the day. A guide then spoke to the group and gestured at the building before leading the group inside.

"I'm inclined to agree," Sadie said. "But what kind of entertainment?"

"Maybe they're looking for ghosts," Jacob said.

"Maybe they're looking for us," Nathan said.

Sadie scowled at her brothers. "Be serious. I'm very curious as to why these people are coming into our building."

The family had just finished afternoon prayers and were gathered at the window.

"I don't believe it's a nickelodeon," Papa said. "You don't need a guide for that."

"Or an amusement park," Mama added.

"Whatever it is they're coming to see," Nathan said, "it must be very exciting because people are here every day."

The clouds returned.

"Somebody pick up the matzo box," Baruch said.

Jacob lifted the box. The clouds parted. Over time, the family had come to recognize the faces of the guides. They even named them. Sadie had two favorites, a tall man with blond hair they called Roland and a woman with black hair and a round face they called Alma.

Alma was down there now, talking to a group of people.

Once when Sadie couldn't sleep, she fantasized about going for a walk with Roland, but she was immediately overcome with guilt. She felt like she was cheating on Herschel. Instead, she fantasized that she was on a double date, she with Herschel and Alma with Roland.

Sometimes, Sadie fantasized that she and Alma spent the day without the men. They gossiped about their suitors' best attributes. Roland was athletic, and Hershel had a lovely singing voice. Sadie enjoyed this fantasy immensely. She hadn't had a close friend since Bertha Rose.

Bertha Rose. Sadie hadn't thought of her childhood companion in years. According to her calendar, the family had been trapped in the apartment for ninety-six years. Certainly, Bertha had died by now. Sadness washed over Sadie. Everyone she knew was probably dead.

As Alma led the latest group of entertainment-seekers indoors, the five minutes elapsed, and the clouds returned to cover the window. Sadie wondered if she would watch Alma grow older and older, until one day, she didn't return.

CHAPTER TWENTY-THREE

Meir entered the Russian Tea Room and froze. He had heard about the lavish décor, the old paintings on the wall, and dominant use of red, but he hadn't expected the diners to be dressed up for afternoon tea. Maybe some, but not all of them. And here was Meir in his black Trilby hat, black sport coat, black jeans, white dress shirt, and black Adidas sneakers. He didn't wear nicer clothes because he didn't think he'd need them. Glancing at his watch, he wondered if he had time to run to a men's clothing store for a tie and a pair of dress shoes.

The maître d' approached Meir before he could escape.

"How many in your party?" he asked.

"I'm expecting someone," Meir said. "They should be here soon."

As the maître d' led him to a booth, Meir felt the other diners were staring at him with disapproval. Once seated, he hid behind his menu.

Falk Yeshiva's potions professor, Rabbi Rhea Katzerman, had chosen the Russian Tea Room. Meir had been too grateful that she had agreed to meet with him to suggest an alternative location. Rabbi Katzerman's knowledge of ancient potions was unparalleled. If a potion existed that could save the Rosenfelds, she would find it.

As Meir marveled at the sparkling chandeliers and a magnificent glass bear sculpture, he wished he was here to catch up with an old friend. This was the perfect place for such an occasion. But he and Rabbi Katzerman had grim business to discuss, and recent events had made his mission even more urgent.

The day before, Stan Jolly had informed Esther and Meir that the Tenement Museum was planning to close 97 Orchard Street for a year to do renovations. Walls, floors, and the roof would get long-needed repairs.

Once 97 Orchard Street was closed, only construction workers would have access to the building. Stan wouldn't be able to get Meir inside until they were done. Meir either had to try and release the Rosenfelds from the time bubble before the museum closed or wait a year until the museum reopened.

What Meir learned from Rabbi Katzerman today would help decide his course of action. If no potion existed, then the merciful thing to do would be to pop the time bubble as soon as possible. If there was a potion, then he might wait until the museum reopened and Stan could get him inside.

Meir's thoughts were interrupted by Rabbi Katzerman's arrival. To his relief, she was dressed casually. Her head covering of choice was a black beret and she carried her kishef macher supplies in a canvas messenger bag. She was in her seventies with gray hair and hazel eyes. She had the type of beauty that improved with age. Meir had had a teenage crush on her that had evolved into deep respect.

"Rabbi Poppers," she said as she seated herself across from him. "So good to see you again."

"Rabbi Katzerman," Meir said. "Thank you for coming."

"Okay, now that we've said our official greetings, we can address each other by our first names."

"I'd like that, Rhea."

She gestured at the dining room. "Have you ever been here before?"

"This is my first time."

She grinned, "Afternoon tea is such a decadent delight. Do you mind if I order for both of us?"

"Go right ahead," Meir said, secretly relieved. He was completely out of his depth here.

Rhea ordered tea sandwiches, blinis, scones, and pastries. She let Meir choose his own tea.

"Thank you for coming in person," Meir said. "When I met with Rabbi Fruman, he had to come by astral projection."

Rhea shrugged. "That's because he's an administrator. It's harder for him to get away."

The food arrived on a three-tiered tray. They stuck to small talk while they ate. Meir bit into a smoked salmon and cream cheese tea sandwich. He would have preferred it on a bagel instead of thin slices of bread, but the salmon was just salty enough and had the perfect amount of chewiness. The pastries gave him intense sugar rushes. Once they finished off the caviar blinis, they discussed Meir's situation while sipping tea.

"You certainly found an interesting problem," Rhea said. "Everyone at yeshiva has been talking about it."

His former teachers were talking about him. As if Meir didn't feel enough pressure already.

"Did they offer any advice?" Meir asked.

"We didn't feel it wise," Rhea said. "Best to let you find your own way to a solution."

"Not quite a vote of confidence," Meir said. "But I'll take it as one."

Rhea patted Meir's hand. "You're doing fine."

"Thank you, Rabbi. I mean, Rhea."

"I still can't figure out how the Falks missed a time bubble in the middle of New York? Despite what the Worms believe, this is as much our home as theirs."

"I have some theories that I shared with one of the Worms."

Rhea grinned. "I assume you mean Richie. How is he doing?"

"He's going by Beryl now. He looks good."

Rhea leaned forward. "I have good news and bad news. After much searching, I found a potion that slows down aging."

"I'm surprised it's not better known considering how much people want to stay young," Meir said.

"The reason nobody uses the potion is that the way it slows down the body's natural aging can potentially cause long term health defects."

"Is that the bad news? Because if it is, I see no problem giving the potion to the Rosenfelds. At least they would be alive."

Rhea shook her head. "Sorry. The bad news is no potion is strong enough to save the family. If they'd only been in the bubble for fifty years, they might have had a chance. A very slim chance. After a hundred, it's impossible."

Meir sighed. "So, there's no hope."

Rhea sipped her tea. "The potion can't save them, but it would make their deaths less painful."

"How so?"

"It would alleviate some of the discomfort of rapid aging, making their deaths a little less painful. Really, it's all we can do for them."

Rhea rummaged in her bag, took out an index card, and handed it to Meir. The potion's recipe was handwritten in Rhea's precise penmanship.

"They have to drink the potion," Rhea said. "It's the only way to get it into their systems. Theoretically, consuming gallons of potion would slow their aging down enough to survive. But they wouldn't be able to drink it fast enough and they'd be in too much pain to do it if they could."

Meir studied the potion. He could get the ingredients at Lin Sister Herb.

"How much potion do you suggest I make?" Meir asked.

Rhea looked up at the chandeliers. "Let's see. There's five of them and you."

Meir gawked at Rhea. "Me?"

"You'll need it if you get stuck in the bubble for a long time. Of course, you might end up with kidney failure, but you'll be alive."

"I'll keep that in mind."

"In fact, that's why I chose the tea room for our meeting. I wanted to give you a treat before you went into the bubble. It might be a while before you have another chance to do something fun."

Meir took a moment to take in the diners' pleasant chatter, the clink of spoons on teacups, the aroma of tea, and the fishy smell of caviar. Rhea was right. Once inside the bubble, discovering new delights would be denied to him. But then, the Rosenfelds had been denied new smells and tastes for a century.

"As for how much potion to make," Rhea said. "I suggest you make a liter. Enough to fill a wine bottle. The potion will not have any effect on them until they start aging again, so have them drink it the moment the bubble bursts."

Meir rubbed his finger over the index card. "Just out of curiosity. What if I gave it all to Sadie?"

"That's the youngest, right? The girl?"

"Yes. She was nine when this started."

"And now she's a hundred and nine."

"Granted. But what if she drank all of it? The whole liter?"

Rhea crossed her arms. "You'd have to force it down her throat. She might survive a few hours. Maybe even a whole day. But Meir, would she want that?"

"A day of freedom after a hundred years in prison. If it were me, the answer is yes."

"You can't speak for her. And what about her family? What do you tell them? 'Sorry. I can only save her.'"

Meir sighed. "You're right. They've been through enough without adding this kind of *tsuris*." He tapped his spoon on the table. "The museum is going to be closing soon."

Rhea stared at Meir. "How soon is soon?"

"The renovations are scheduled to begin two months from now."

Rhea refilled her teacup. "Will you still be able to get inside?"

Meir shook his head. "Not while they're working on it."

"How long will the renovations take?"

"A year. I'm wondering if I shouldn't wait until they're done."

Rhea scowled. "I wouldn't wait. Every year adds more weight to the flood of time. Soon, no amount of potion will lessen their pain. Also, you'd be giving the Worms a year to find a way to keep you from ever getting to the Rosenfelds."

Rhea reached into her bag and handed Meir another index card with another handwritten potion on it. Meir studied the card.

"Black Fly Potion?" he asked.

"In case the Worms try to mess with you again. Fight fire with fire. A good thing about this potion is that it only has to come in contact with the victim's skin. You don't have to pour it onto a piece of chicken."

Rhea pulled a face. Apparently, she was as appalled as Meir that the Worms had put Black Fly Potion on a perfectly good piece of roast chicken.

Meir put the cards in his satchel. "I can't thank you enough for this," he said.

Rhea paused before handing Meir a third card. "I have one more potion for you," she said.

The look of sadness on her face concerned Meir. The drawing of a skull and crossbones at the top of the card and the words "HANDLE WITH CARE" at the bottom worried him even more.

"I remember this potion from when I was in your class," Meir said. "It would kill the Rosenfelds instantly."

"You're no longer my student," Rhea said. "We can talk as kishef macher to kishef macher. The reason you're going into the time bubble is to end their lives."

Meir shook his head. "I can't do this. It's too much."

"I brought the anti-aging potion because you asked for it. But this potion is more merciful. It's painless. They won't suffer."

"I understand. It's a euthanasia potion. But I feel like it would be an assassination."

Rhea motioned to the waiter to bring the check.

"It's your choice, Meir."

Meir stared at the card. "If I do make it, and I'm not saying I will, how much should I make?"

"A quarter pint. You won't need that much but just to make sure everyone gets enough to do the job."

Meir put the card with the others in his satchel. Not only had she provided him with the potions he needed, she'd given him a lot to think about.

"Thank you, Rhea," he said. "For everything."

CHAPTER TWENTY-FOUR

2017

The family had finished their morning davening. Mama was busy rearranging items in the kitchen and Papa had retreated to the bedroom. Nathan and Jacob were having a contest to see who could balance a chair on the palm of his hand the longest. Nathan usually won this game, but Jacob was getting better at it. Sadie lifted the box of matzos, sat on the windowsill, and watched the street below. Though the seasons never touched the Rosenfelds, Sadie could tell from the pedestrians' heavy coats and the puffs of steam coming from their mouths that it was a cold wintry day.

She spotted Alma walking toward the building. "Alma has arrived."

Jacob gave Sadie a sideways glance. "How does she look?"

"She's wearing a lovely coat."

Sadie had memorized Alma's routine. Every morning, she walked past 97 Orchard and entered the building on the corner. Later, she returned with a group of people behind her.

Today was different.

Alma happened to glance at Sadie's window. She took a few more steps, stopped, and turned back. She stared directly at Sadie. Sadie was excited. People usually stared at the ground or straight ahead as they trudged past the building. They rarely looked up, and of all people, it was Alma who looked. Forgetting that they weren't actually friends, Sadie waved. To her delight, Alma waved back. Then she ran down the street.

"I waved at Alma," Sadie said.

"She saw you?" Nathan asked.

"Yes."

Nathan never took his eyes off the chair in his palm, which might be why he always won. "Maybe she'll come rescue us."

"Don't make sport of me. We all know no one is coming."

"Sorry, Sadie. How did Alma react?"

"She ran away. Do you think I scared her?"

"No. She probably thinks she's having a vision as a result of heavy drinking."

Sadie stared at the street. "Alma is not a drunkard."

Nathan shrugged. "Perhaps she suddenly became ill and needed to get to a privy?"

The clouds returned to cover the window.

Sadie picked up a cookbook sitting on top of a stack of books. It was her latest tome to use as a calendar. She flipped to a clean page and marked down the new day with the nub of a pencil. According to Sadie's records, they were closing in on a hundred years trapped in their apartment. It was a milestone that the family would not be celebrating.

Jacob lost control of the chair he was balancing. As it fell to the floor, the chair knocked over Sadie's stack of calendar books.

"Sorry about that," Jacob said.

"It's okay. Picking them up gives me something to do."

Sadie stacked the books in a corner away from her brothers. She wasn't sure what she would run out of first, books to use as calendars or pencils to mark the days. If it was books, she didn't know what she would do. She couldn't mark the pages of Papa's prayer books. They held the word of God.

After she completed her task, Sadie picked up the box of matzos and watched the people on the street. With two minutes left before the clouds would return, Alma exited Sadie's building.

"Alma was in our building," Sadie said.

"I thought you said she went to the other building," Nathan said.

"She did. I guess she came back."

"She's very busy today."

Alma ran across the street. Sadie gasped when she was almost hit by an automobile. From the frantic way she moved, Sadie could tell that something had frightened her.

She looked directly at Sadie. Their eyes met. There was fear etched on Alma's face.

Alma screamed.

Sadie felt a stab of pain between her eyes and a deeper pain in her chest. Alma wasn't her friend. The only place they'd met was in Sadie's imagination. She was relieved when the clouds returned. She couldn't bear to frighten Alma for another second.

CHAPTER TWENTY-FIVE

Meir wore a bathrobe and nothing else. He didn't normally wear a bathrobe, but the robes provided by New York Hilton Midtown hotel were incredibly comfortable. It was one of many reasons why he always stayed here when he was in the city.

Packets of herbs from Lin Sister Herb and a plastic bag from Duane Reade Pharmacy sat on the bathroom countertop. The index card with the ingredients for Black Fly Potion written in Rabbi Katzerman's neat handwriting was propped up on the counter. Meir handled the herbs as if they might explode at any moment. He filled a drinking glass with water from the tap and poured the liquid into the hotel's tiny coffeemaker. While he waited for the coffeemaker to heat the water, he picked up his cellphone and called his parents. When his mother picked up, Meir turned on the speaker and laid the phone on the countertop.

"Hello? Who's calling?" His mother's words were muffled.

"Hey, Mom. It's Meir."

"Meir?"

"Sorry I woke you up. I forgot that it's an hour earlier there in Minneapolis. I can call back later."

"That's okay. Howard is already up. I keep telling him he doesn't have to get up so early, but I guess it's a habit."

Meir heard the phone being fumbled about and his mother calling his father to pick up the other phone. Soon, his parents, Howard and Rona, were both on the line.

"Is everything okay?" Howard asked.

"I'm good, Dad," Meir said. "How are you guys?"

"We're good. Couldn't be better."

"Are you in Atlanta?" Rona asked.

"No. I'm in New York."

"New York? Are you visiting your old school?"

"No, Mom. I'm here on business."

Hot water dripped from the coffeemaker into the drinking glass. Steam rose from the water and fogged the bathroom mirror. Meir reached into the plastic bag and took out a box of latex gloves. He stretched a pair onto his hands.

"Hey, Dad," Meir said. "What did you decide about the clove bubblegum popcorn?"

"You were right," Howard said. "It stinks. I'm dropping it."

Meir carefully added the herbs to the hot water. He used the wooden stir stick that came with the coffeemaker to mix the herbs together. The water turned green, and the earthy scent of deep woods filled the bathroom.

"Howard, tell Meir what you're working on now," Rona said.

"You know I'm always looking for the perfect combination of sweet and sour," Howard said.

"It's been your obsession for years," Meir said.

"There're a hundred variations of sweet and salty popcorn, but sweet and sour is still a relatively untapped market. And then I thought, why re-invent the wheel? Why not just put sweet and sour sauce on the popcorn?"

"Like Chinese food?"

"You got it. If there's sweet and sour chicken, why not sweet and sour popcorn? In fact, I put a batch in the mail for you yesterday. I want to know what you think."

Meir added the powder from one of the vials into the glass. He mumbled a prayer. The water changed from green to fluorescent orange. The smell of rotten fish overtook the smell of deep woods.

"You might want to move ahead without my input," Meir said. "I may be in New York for a while."

"Is there something you're not telling us?" Rona asked.

"I don't want to worry you." Meir used his forearm to rub his nose, to avoid touching his face with his gloved hand. "But this job I'm doing, it involves very strong magic. It's potentially dangerous."

"Maybe you shouldn't do this job. Ask that teacher you like so much. What's his name?"

"Rabbi Fruman."

"Ask Fruman to do it for you."

"No, Mom. It's my responsibility."

"But you said it was dangerous."

"Potentially dangerous. Everything I do as a kishef macher is potentially dangerous."

Howard stepped in, as he often did, whenever Meir and Rona argued about Meir's chosen profession.

"Let the boy be," Howard said. "Did Moses's mother tell him not to save the Israelites?"

"Only because she wasn't there," Rona said. "If Moses's mother had been around, he wouldn't have gotten lost in the desert for forty years."

"Mom," Meir said. "This is why I went to Falk Yeshiva, to solve this kind of problem."

Rona sighed. "Promise me that you'll be extra careful."

Meir added the powder from the second vial into the glass and stirred the contents. He mumbled another prayer. The contents changed from fluorescent orange to a clear liquid. It gave off no smell at all. He took a travel size plastic spray bottle he'd gotten at the drug store and poured the contents into it. He pointed the bottle at the toilet and squeezed the handle until liquid sprayed into the bowl. The liquid left no color or scent.

"Don't worry, Mom," Meir said. "I'm taking every precaution."

CHAPTER TWENTY-SIX

Meir said goodbye to his parents, put the herbs and powders back into his satchel, cleaned the countertop, and flushed the toilet. He peeled off the latex gloves and dropped them in a wastebasket. He carried his things out of the bathroom and packed everything but the travel spray bottle into his satchel. He made sure the liter bottle of anti-aging potion he'd made the day before was securely sealed, and put the spray bottle in the breast pocket of his jacket.

The morning sun streamed through the hotel room blinds. He took off his robe and tossed it on a chair. He got into the bed, climbed under the covers, and slipped his arm around the sleeping woman. She stirred and kissed him. Her naked body warmed him as he tasted her morning breath. She was the perfect combination of sweet and sour.

"*Buenos días*," Camilla said.

"Good morning," Meir said. "Should I order us some breakfast?"

Camilla stretched and yawned. Her amulet was nestled between her breasts. "Let's go out. I know a good place nearby."

"Okay, but I need coffee first."

Meir called room service and ordered a pot of coffee while Camilla went to take a shower. He admired her firm body as she strolled to the bathroom. Inspired by his visit to the Russian Tea Room and Rabbi Katzerman's comment that she'd had Meir met her there so that he could do something fun before entering the time bubble, he had devoted a few days to doing other fun activities.

He had eaten a pastrami sandwich and a slice of cheesecake at Katz's Delicatessen. He had seen a Broadway musical based on a popular movie. He had visited the Empire State Building's 86th Floor Observatory for his favorite view of New York.

And Meir had gotten up the courage to ask Camilla on a date with the expectation that they would go to dinner and maybe see live music. The fact that the date ended in his hotel room was beyond anything he'd expected.

Once Meir heard the shower water running, he took out his phone. There was a text message from Yetta Burd with photos of her boys playing with Alice.

Meir texted Yetta. *Thank you for the photos. I hope Alice is behaving herself.*

A minute later, Yetta texted back. *Are u kidding? She's great. The boys love visiting her.*

After a few false starts, Meir finally found a way to ask Yetta the question that had to be asked. *If something, God forbid, happened to me, would you be willing to keep Alice permanently?*

He wasn't going to tell her that the something that might happen was getting trapped in a time bubble for a hundred years. He worried Alice would end up at a shelter where a cat her age would have little chance of being adopted.

Moments after Meir hit send, Yetta called. "What's wrong?" she asked.

"Nothing."

"Is it really nothing or do you just not want to tell me?"

"It's nothing."

"Then why ask me a creepy question like that?"

"I worry about these things. I won't be able to digest food properly until you answer my question."

"If God forbid anything happens to you, Alice will live a long, pampered life in the Burd home."

Meir smiled. "Thank you."

"Since I have you on the phone, there's something I was going to talk to you about later, but we might as well talk about it now."

"What's on your mind?"

"It's about Alice."

Meir sprang to his feet. "Is she sick? Her vet does house calls. I left you the number."

"There's nothing wrong with her," Yetta said. "She's eating and pooping like a champ. But I can tell from the way she clings to me and the boys when we come to see her that she's lonely."

Meir's stomach clenched. "I can't come home," he said. "I have a job to do."

"I understand. That's why I was going to wait until you got home. By the way, do you have an idea of when you'll be back?"

Meir rubbed his forehead. "I'm not sure. It could be a while. I hate to ask this…"

"Ask me anything, Meir."

"Could you keep her at your house? That way she'd have company all the time."

"Consider it done. However, you should consider getting a second cat. Especially, if you're going to have more assignments like this one that keep you away from home for a long time."

Meir imagined two cats running up and down the stairs of his condo, sleeping on the furniture, and filling the litter box twice as fast as Alice did now.

"I think it's a good idea," Meir said.

They said their goodbyes. Meir moved on to his email messages.

Sylvia Solomon had sent him the email address of the woman she'd found for him with a warning that if he didn't contact her for a date as soon as possible, someone else was going to be her *bashert* and he would kick himself for the rest of his life for waiting too long.

Meir considered having Sylvia tell the woman never mind, he'd met someone else. She was taking a shower in his bathroom right now. Even though he'd only been on one date with Camilla, they were obviously attracted to each other. Why else would they have made love last night unless they had fallen in love?

He started the email to Sylvia, stopped, and erased it. He should discuss this with Camilla first. She would help him find the right words to explain their newfound love to Sylvia.

Room service brought a carafe of coffee. After the waiter left, Camilla emerged from the bathroom with a towel wrapped around her chest and another wrapped in a turban for her wet hair. Meir poured the coffee. He took a sip before taking his shower. When he came out, Camilla was dressed in the clothes she'd worn on their date the night before, a tight shiny dress, high heels, and a denim jacket. Meir drank another cup of coffee as he dressed. Putting on his jacket, he patted his chest to make sure the spray bottle in the breast pocket hadn't fallen out.

When they stepped out of the hotel, Meir was pleased to find that the weather was cooler. Still warm, but not boiling like it had been. Camilla led the way to the side of the hotel. She joined the line of people waiting to be served at a red and yellow food cart.

"The Halal Guys?" Meir asked. "This is where you want to go for breakfast?"

"It's not typical breakfast food," Camilla said, "but I love their baba ghanoush."

"Eggplant for breakfast?"

"You ever have a bagel with lox and cream cheese for breakfast? That's fish first thing in the morning."

"Good point."

The Halal Guy servers prepared orders with grim efficiency. They perked up when Camilla got to the head of the line.

"Camilla!" the server said. "What the hell are you doing here?"

"I was in the neighborhood," she said.

The server pointed a metal spoon at Meir. "Who's your friend with the spiffy hat? You normally hang out with cooks. He don't look like no cook to me."

Camilla hooked her arm around Meir's. "Oh, he can cook," she said. "I watched him make chicken soup that brought the dead back to life."

Meir grinned and shrugged his shoulders. The server laughed.

Camilla got baba ghanoush and pita bread. Meir got the chicken platter. They sat on the base of a statue in front of an international investment bank and watched people hurry to work.

"I wasn't sure you would call me," Camilla said.

"I'm glad Esther gave me your number. Last night was amazing."

Camilla frowned. "It's not like I jump into bed with every guy I go out with."

"Neither do I. I mean with every girl I go out with. In fact, hard-ly ever."

Camilla bumped Meir. "I couldn't tell."

"I'd like to see you again."

"I'd like that too."

Meir's mouth went dry. "I think we shared something special last night. I'd like to see where it goes."

Camilla put her hand on Meir's shoulder. "I'm going to stop you right there. I've seen that lovesick puppy dog look before. You think that since we had sex one time, we should get married. Am I right?"

Meir's cheeks burned with embarrassment. "No. I wasn't thinking that at all."

Camilla looked him in the eyes. "Be honest, Meir."

Meir sighed. "I guess I did."

"I get it. It's like how a hammer sees everything as a nail."

"I'm sorry, what?"

Camilla chuckled. "You want to find someone and settle down. And so, you see every girl you go out with as a potential life partner. If you have sex with one of those girls, you think oh yeah, this has to be the one."

He gazed at Camilla. She had an earthy beauty and a natural smile. How could he not fall in love with her?

"You're right," Meir said. "I'm being ridiculous."

Camilla kissed his cheek. "Not at all. I'm very flattered."

But Meir did feel ridiculous. He probably wouldn't have called her for a date if he wasn't about to enter a time bubble. The possibil-ity of getting trapped for eternity had given him the nerve to ask her out. Even if they had fallen deeply in love, it wouldn't have been fair to ask her to wait for him. On the other hand, Meir was relieved that he didn't tell Sylvia Solomon to drop him as a client.

"I don't get it," Camilla said. "You're seriously cute. You're smart. You don't stink. Best of all, you can do magic, real magic. If I were looking for someone, and I'm not, I would definitely be interested. Why don't you have a girlfriend?"

Meir poked at his food. "I think magic is the main reason. If last night was the first time you'd met me, would you have believed me if I told you I was a kishef macher?"

Camilla shook her head. "I didn't believe it until I saw it with my own eyes."

"Jewish magic is sacred. It should only be done to help others. I can't do it just to impress somebody."

"I understand. I really do." Camilla put her arm around Meir's waist and pulled him to her. Her body was soft and firm at the same time.

"I was wondering the same thing about you," Meir said. "You're beautiful, sexy, brave, and smart. You know the best places to go for breakfast. Why don't you have a steady boyfriend?"

Camilla leaned her head against his shoulder. "I'm too much for most guys. Especially Latinos. It's one thing for a woman to speak her mind and work as hard as a man. They can deal with that. Barely. But I can bench press more than they can and have bigger muscles. That freaks them out. You know what they call me? And they don't even do it behind my back."

"What?" Meir asked.

"Camilla Gorilla."

Meir gasped. "That's terrible!"

"I don't care. I like lifting weights. I like being strong. I like speaking my mind. It's who I am. I'm not going to change just to make some insecure guy feel like a real man."

"You're perfect the way you are."

Camilla snuggled up next to Meir. He wondered if there was time to go back to the hotel room. But then, her smile turned into an angry scowl. She jabbed her finger in the direction of a sidewalk stand that was selling scarves and knit caps.

"I know that guy," Camilla said. "He was one of the black hats that poisoned Gus."

The Worms who had been following Meir around the city was doing a terrible job of pretending to be shopping for a cap.

"Are you sure?" Meir asked.

"He was the one who demanded I send Gus to their table."

Camilla put her container aside and started toward him. Meir grabbed her arm. He dragged him with her a few steps before she stopped.

"Let me go," she growled.

"He's an old man," Meir said.

"I don't care."

"You could get arrested."

"Doesn't matter. He's going down!"

"Let me take care of this. Kishef macher to kishef macher."

Camilla sat and crossed her arms. Meir took the spray bottle from his breast pocket and held it in the palm of his hand. He strolled over to the Worms. The thin man pretended to be very interested in a purple knit cap with a marijuana leaf symbol. Meir checked to see if he wore an amulet, and wasn't surprised to see that he didn't. He'd heard that the Worms never wore them because they believed no kishef macher had the nerve to attack them.

Meir smiled at the Worms. "We've never been properly introduced," he said. "I'm Rabbi Meir Poppers. And you are?"

"I know who you are," the Worms said. "Why are you still in New York?"

"You don't have a name?"

The Worms glowered at Meir. "Feintuch," he said. "Rabbi Shlomo Feintuch. And my feet are killing me from having to follow you around."

Meir stopped smiling. "You had a chance to sit yesterday," he said. "When you poisoned Gus Ramos."

"What happened to him is your fault," Feintuch said. "You shouldn't stick your nose where it doesn't belong."

"Tell Rabbi Chaim his plan failed. All he did was make me even more determined to free the Rosenfelds."

"I got better things to do than be your messenger pigeon."

Meir ran his finger over the top of the spray bottle hidden in his hand. "How did you do it?" Meir asked.

"Do what?" Feintuch asked.

"The chicken. How did you get the potion on the chicken?"

"I only have to follow you. I don't have to talk to you."

Meir inched closer to Feintuch. "Come on. Call it professional curiosity. Did you pour the Black Fly Potion onto the chicken, or did you spray it on?"

The Worms narrowed his eyes at Meir. "Spray? How can you spray a potion?"

"It's easy. Go to a drug store and buy a plastic spray bottle. Put the potion into the spray bottle. And then do this."

Meir sprayed potion into Feintuch's face. Feintuch's eyes rolled back, and his knees buckled. Meir caught his arm before he sank to the ground, then he hailed a taxi. He stuffed the Worms into the taxi and gave the driver the address of the Worms' headquarters. As Meir closed the car door, Feintuch farted loudly. The driver cursed and rolled down the windows before driving away.

Meir rejoined Camilla. She greeted him with a kiss.

"You gave him a taste of his own medicine," she said.

"I was tired of him following me around."

Camilla looked at her watch. "I've got to go. I have to get ready for work."

"Thank you for a lovely time," Meir said.

Camilla laughed. "That's what I was going to say."

CHAPTER TWENTY-SEVEN

Meir and Esther stood at the corner of Delancey and Orchard in front of Moscot Eyewear. Along with his satchel, Meir carried a Strand Bookstore shopping bag heavy with books he'd bought that afternoon.

"Are you sure you don't mind keeping my luggage at your apartment?" Meir said. "You might be stuck with them for a long time."

"Give me a break," Esther said. "I'm glad to do it. Besides I have faith in you, Rabbi Poppers. You're going to be back very soon."

Meir wished he felt as confident in his abilities as Esther did. He looked at the skyline. The sun would drop behind the buildings soon and Stan Jolly would come to let them into the Tenement Museum.

There was something Meir hadn't told Esther. In his short career as an independent kishef macher for hire, he'd gotten by more on luck than skill. Like the time he exorcised a nasty dybbuk that had taken possession of a young boy. Meir barely knew what he was doing, and the boy almost died. He wouldn't be able to rely on luck to rescue the Rosenfelds.

Meir's confidence had further been shaken by his mother practically begging him to let Rabbi Zelig Fruman take over his assignment, and by Zelig himself suggesting that Meir not go inside the bubble. Maybe they could see what his ego refused to acknowledge. Maybe he wasn't ready for something this big and treacherous.

Icy fear ran down his spine. He was crazy to think he could do this. He should tell Esther she was wrong to trust him and take the first flight back to Atlanta.

Then Meir thought about the moment he saw the Rosenfeld family sitting together and praying. He had attended Falk Yeshiva to learn Jewish magic so that he could help people in need, like them. Yes, he was inexperienced. Yes, this was his most dangerous assignment. But he couldn't help anyone if he ran away.

"Camilla told me all about your date," Esther said.

Meir stared at the sunglasses in Moscot's window display. "I don't usually do that on a first date."

Esther laughed. "She didn't tell me you slept together."

Meir blushed. "She didn't?"

"No, she did not. But she did tell me how you took revenge on one of the Worms who poisoned Gus."

Meir scratched his beard. "He had it coming."

Esther pointed at Meir's shopping bag. "What books did you get?"

Meir held the bag open, and Esther peered inside.

"Took me hours to decide what to get," Meir said. "But I think these will interest them."

In the bag were books on world history, New York City history, United States history, Israeli history, fashion history, and the evolution of the automobile. There were books by Jewish authors including Sholem Aleichem, Chaim Potok, Martin Buber, Sidney Malamud, Elie Wiesel, Leon Uris, Philip Roth, and Judy Blume.

"Maybe you shouldn't give these to the Rosenfelds," Esther said. "Is it fair to show them what they missed if they're never going to leave the apartment?"

"They're going to have a lot of questions. The books will provide some of the answers."

Esther took her copy of *The Orchard Street Mystery* by Bertha Rose from her purse and handed it to Meir. "This is for Sadie."

"Are you sure? You went to a lot of trouble to track this down. It's not like you can go out and buy another copy."

"I want Sadie to know Bertha didn't forget her."

Meir put the book into his satchel. Esther looked past him.

"Here comes Stan."

Stan Jolly joined them on the corner. He gave Esther a hug and shook hands with Meir.

"Everybody has left for the day," Stan said. "We can go in now."

He led the way with Meir and Esther close behind. Now that Esther knew who the girl in the window was, she wasn't frightened by her anymore. She wanted to be present when Meir entered the time bubble.

They climbed the stairs to the fourth floor and stood outside the Rosenfelds' apartment. Meir put his shopping bag on the floor and opened his satchel. He took out his tallit and his Sefer Raziel.

"Were you able to find a potion to save them?" Esther asked.

"Sadly, nothing can save the Rosenfelds. They'll be growing older too quickly." Meir opened his satchel and showed Esther a liter bottle filled with a pink liquid. "However, this anti-aging potion will make the pain a little more bearable."

Esther stared at the apartment door. "Poor Sadie. I wish I could have met her, if only for a moment."

Meir played with the fringe on his tallit. He was ready to begin.

He gestured at the floor.

"Clouds will appear around this area. Stay away from them. You could get sucked into the time bubble with me. Just to be on the safe side, stand back there."

Stan and Esther walked to the end of the hallway. Meir hoped they were far enough away. He had no way of telling how much space the clouds would cover. He flipped through his prayer book until he found the passage he needed. He looked at Stan and Esther. Even from down the hall, he could see the concern on Esther's face.

Meir's black athletic shoes squeaked on the hardwood floor as he walked toward them.

"What's wrong?" Esther asked.

"Do we need to get further away?" Stan said.

Meir put his hand on Stan's shoulder. "Do you mind giving me and Esther a moment alone? There's something I need to tell her."

Stan looked at Esther and then at Meir. "Sure. But let me know when you're ready to go into the bubble. I don't want to miss it."

Stan went down the stairwell. Once he was gone, Meir turned to Esther. "Do you remember when you and Gus came to see me in Atlanta?" Meir asked.

"Of course I do," Esther said.

"There was a moment during our meeting when you left me alone with Gus."

"Yeah. I went to wash out the taste of clove bubblegum popcorn. I still can't believe you let me eat that disgusting stuff without warning me first."

Meir had already made a mental promise to warn people before subjecting them to his father's latest experiment in popcorn flavor combinations.

"When Gus and I were alone, he told me that you invented Sadie Rosenfeld because you were still grieving over your miscarriage, and that had the child lived, she would have been named Sophia."

Esther covered her mouth with her hand. She dropped her hand and sighed. "He told you about Sophia?"

"He told me not to tell you. He said he'd kick my ass if I did."

"He still might."

"I thought you should know."

Esther ran her hand through her hair. "Gus is such an idiot. A lot of women lose the baby on their first pregnancy. I was devastated, but Gus took it a lot harder. I didn't make the connection between Sadie and Sophia. He did."

"I suppose he really wants to be a father."

Esther sighed. "Like you wouldn't believe."

He did believe. Gus wanted to be a father as much as he wanted to be a husband.

Meir called down the stairwell. "You can come back now, Stan. I'm ready."

Stan hurried up the stairs and stood with Esther while Meir went back to the Rosenfelds' apartment. Meir rocked back and forth as he recited the passage from the Sefer Raziel. Clouds leaked out from underneath the door. They rose and billowed around Meir. As he finished the passage, he glanced toward Esther and Stan, but couldn't see them through the dense fog.

Meir's wristwatch had stopped ticking. He couldn't hear the traffic outside, but now he heard chanting coming from inside the apartment. The smell of chicken schmaltz was mixed with the dusty scent of burnt coal. What he could see of the hallway had changed. The wallpaper on the wall was a design he'd only seen in history books. The sheep's blood on the doorframe was a shiny red as if it had just been slathered on. Standing in front of their door, steps away from them, Meir had entered the time bubble that held the Rosenfelds.

A moment of pride in his accomplishment was quickly extinguished by the memory of what Rabbi Fruman had told him about time bubbles. Entering one was easy. Getting out, not so much.

Whatever lack of confidence Meir had felt earlier had to be put aside. It wasn't courage that he felt now, but a determination to see this through. Besides, he had no other choice.

Meir took off his tallit, folded it, and put it in his satchel along with his Sefer Raziel. He picked up his shopping bag and knocked on the door. With the world shut out, his rapping seemed as loud as thunder. There was no answer, so he knocked again.

CHAPTER TWENTY-EIGHT

2017

Baruch was reciting the evening prayers when there was a knock at the door. He paused, shook his head, and picked up where he left off. There was another knock. The family looked at each other and then stared at the door.

"Did you hear that?" Jacob asked.

"That wasn't one of you?" Baruch asked.

The knock came again.

"There's someone at the door," Sadie said.

"That's impossible," Nathan said.

"Who could it be?" Rebekah asked.

"The Angel of Death has finally arrived to take us to Heaven," Jacob said. "Or it could be someone else."

"One of us should answer the door," Rebekah said.

"I'll do it," Sadie said.

"Wait," Baruch said.

But Sadie had already opened the door. A man wearing a black suit and a black hat stood in the hallway. He had a leather satchel over his shoulder and held a large paper sack. Clouds billowed behind him. He smiled and gave a short bow.

"Hello. My name is Rabbi Meir Poppers. May I come in?"

CHAPTER TWENTY-NINE

Beryl Stein entered Rabbi Chaim's office and sat in a visitor's chair.

"*Nu?*" Chaim said. "What do you know from Feintuch?"

"We were able to give him the Black Fly Potion antidote in time," Beryl said. "He'll need to stay in bed for a few days before he's fully recovered."

Chaim angrily waved his hand. "That's not what I'm asking. Before Poppers gave Feintuch the potion, did he find out where Poppers was going?"

Beryl held out his hands. "Rabbi," he said. "Feintuch is a pious man, a fellow kishef macher, and one of your most loyal followers. If his cab had gotten caught in traffic, he almost certainly would have died before we could give him the antidote."

There actually had been little chance of Feintuch dying. Shortly after Meir had loaded Feintuch into a cab, he had texted Beryl and informed him what he had done so that Beryl would have the antidote ready the minute Feintuch arrived at Worms headquarters. Beryl had stretched the truth and made Feintuch's predicament more dramatic than it was because he was caught off-guard by Rabbi Chaim's attitude. He had expected the Worms' spiritual leader to show more concern for the well-being of his disciples.

"Stop fussing," Chaim said. "I'll check on Feintuch soon enough. If you'll forgive me, I'm a little distracted because I'm worried about the safety of all Jews."

"I'm sorry, Rabbi," Beryl said. "I don't understand. According to what you told me, the Rosenfelds have been in the time bubble for a very long time. If Meir were to free them, wouldn't they die? How could they be a threat?"

Chaim leaned back in his chair and stroked his beard. "Perhaps you're right," he said. "Perhaps I'm getting worked up over nothing. Zayde told me about the Rosenfelds' evil ways when I was but a boy, and perhaps I've let the story grow out of proportion in my mind."

"They can't harm us," Beryl said. "We're the Worms."

Chaim raised his chin defiantly. "The greatest kishef macher sect of all time."

Beryl stood. "Good. I'll let Feintuch know you'll be around to see him soon."

Chaim waited until Beryl was at the office door before calling him back. "Satisfy my curiosity," Chaim said. "How exactly did Rabbi Poppers give Feintuch the potion?"

Beryl stood behind the visitor's chair. "Meir walked up to him on the street and sprayed him with the potion."

"Sprayed?" Chaim asked.

"Yes. Feintuch said he saw a small bottle in Meir's hand and the next thing he knew he felt something squirting onto his face."

Chaim stroked his beard. "Clever. Crude. But clever. Still, this has gone too far. We told Poppers to stay away and instead he attacks a good pious man. That young man needs to learn proper respect for the Worms. I'll contact Falk Yeshiva and insist they discipline him before he causes any more problems."

Beryl gripped the chair. He had hoped Rabbi Chaim would be so concerned about Feintuch that he could put off telling him about

Meir until later.

"It's too late for that," Beryl said. "Meir entered the time bubble today."

Chaim sprang to his feet. "Poppers is inside the bubble?"

"Yes, Rabbi."

Chaim paced his office muttering to himself. He stopped abruptly, grinned, and returned to his desk.

"Our problem is solved," Chaim said.

"What do you mean, *solved?*" Beryl asked.

"Meir Poppers has trapped himself inside the bubble with the Rosenfelds. He'll never escape. He'll spend eternity with them."

Beryl paled. "That can't be true. Meir is smart. He'll find a way out."

Chaim chuckled. "The time bubble is no ordinary bubble. It requires certain tasks to open it. Poppers may be clever, but he'll never figure them out."

"Then we have to help him. We can't leave him in there."

Chaim glared at Beryl. "I forbid you! Poppers got himself into this. He made his bed now he must lie in it. For eternity if God wills it."

Beryl's knees felt weak. "If you'll excuse me, Rabbi. I wish to get back to my studies."

Chaim flicked his hand. "Yes. Get back to your studies. But don't worry. I haven't forgotten about finding you a wife. We'll get to that soon."

Beryl left the Worms' headquarters, hailed a cab, and told the cab driver to take him to the Tenement Museum on Orchard Street. As he stared out the window at the traffic, he replayed in his head his conversation with Rabbi Chaim.

The rabbi had told Beryl earlier that he knew little about the Rosenfelds and the time bubble. He claimed he didn't know who made it. Then how could he know the bubble was no ordinary bubble and required certain tasks to open it? And why was there obvious pride in his voice when he told Beryl this?

Two things were now obvious to Beryl. Rabbi Chaim lied to him. And Meir Poppers was in great danger. Beryl couldn't decide which upset him more.

CHAPTER THIRTY

Meir had goosebumps as he entered the apartment. He had made it inside. It was if he was in a diorama of perfectly preserved artifacts. Other than a thin sheen of coal soot on the mantle clock, the apartment was spotless. There was no dust or peeling wallpaper. The floor tiles were shiny. The family's clothes were clean and pressed.

Meir was amazed by everything he saw. Judging by the expressions on the Rosenfelds' faces, they were equally amazed by him. Meir smiled at Sadie. She smiled back.

"Are you an angel?" she asked.

"No," Meir said. "I'm a kishef macher."

"A kishef macher?" Rebekah asked.

She glanced nervously at the other members of the family. They eased away from him. Meir felt like an idiot for not remembering that as much as Jews in the past depended on kishef machers for potions and predicting the future, they were also feared and mistrusted.

"It's okay," Meir said. "I'm here to help you."

Baruch took a brave step forward and put his hand on Meir's shoulder as if to see if he was solid or as vaporous as the clouds that covered their windows.

"Did God send you?" Baruch asked.

"Not directly," Meir said.

"You're not the Angel of Death?"

"No. I'm as human as you are."

"Are you dead?"

"I'm quite alive."

"Are we dead?"

Meir sighed. The painful revelations were about to begin.

"You're alive. You're trapped in a time bubble."

The family pelted Meir with a hundred years' worth of questions. They spoke over each other. Meir couldn't keep track.

"Please," Meir said. "One at a time."

They didn't listen. The questions that they had kept bottled up for so long had burst free. They didn't even wait for the answers. It was if the opportunity to ask was more important than the information to be gained.

What was a time bubble? How did he get into the apartment? If he got in, then certainly he can get them out, can't he? Did anyone try to find them? Who won the war? Was there another war? What kind of entertainment was happening below them? Were they being punished? Did he know Edna Oxenhandler? Did Jews still live in the building? Why were they trapped here? What did they do wrong? Why has it taken so long for someone to find them?

Baruch stood between Meir and his family. "Enough! Can't you see it's too much for the young man? I'm sure he will explain everything we want to know." Baruch glared at Meir. "Isn't that right?"

"I'll do the best I can," Meir said. "I brought history books that will fill you in on some of the things that have been going on outside your apartment for the last hundred years."

Every member of the family lunged for the Strand bookstore

shopping bag except for Baruch. He clapped his hands. The family members turned to him.

"We must finish the evening prayers first," Baruch said.

Meir felt a flush of embarrassment. "I'm sorry I interrupted your prayers. If I had known, I would have waited until you were done before I knocked on your door."

Baruch looked Meir over. "If you're a kishef macher, then you must be a Jew," Baruch said.

"Yes, I am."

"You may join us. If you like."

"I would like that very much."

Baruch picked up the prayer book from where he had left it on the mantle next to the frozen clock. Nathan and Jacob sat in chairs in front of Baruch. Rebekah and Sadie sat on the windowsill. Meir sat in a chair behind the boys.

"Where were we?" Baruch asked.

"We had just completed the *Shema*," Nathan said.

Baruch flipped through the prayer book's well-worn pages until he found the place he wanted. Starting with the *Amidah*, Baruch continued the service. The family had barely finished reciting the *Aleinu le-Shabbe'ah* when Sadie turned to Meir.

"What books did you bring us?"

Meir looked at Baruch. "Is it okay for the family to see them now?" Meir said.

Baruch smiled. "Yes. They can see them now."

Meir took the books out of the shopping bag and placed them on the windowsill. As each family member chose a book, Meir studied the thick clouds covering the windows. Soon, the Rosenfelds were seated and reading. Meir had tried to find books with lots of photos in case they only read Yiddish or in case the children couldn't read, but apparently, they could all read English. They kept interrupting each other to announce something they had discovered.

"There was another great war with Germany," Nathan said. "How can this be? Six million Jews slaughtered. Six million."

"Palestine is now Israel. The Jews have a homeland again!" Rebekah said. "When we get out of here, we should go live in Israel. We've been in New York long enough."

"How can it be that they've elected a Catholic president and a *schwartzer* president, but not a Jewish president?" Jacob asked.

"A man walked on the moon," Sadie said. "I'll never look at the moon the same way again."

"Mini skirt," Baruch said. "I always wondered what they called them. Such a bad idea. Once a woman bares her legs up to her tuckus she has no modesty left. No mystery."

"I have good news and bad news about New York," Nathan said. "The good news is that more than one Jew has been elected mayor. The bad news is the Dodgers left Brooklyn."

"Computer," Sadie said. She looked at Meir. "Am I saying that right?"

"Yes."

"Do you have one?"

"Almost everybody does. I have one with me."

Meir took out his smartphone.

"It's so small," Sadie said.

"They used to be bigger. Technology has advanced to a degree that everyone can carry a computer with them wherever they go."

The family stopped reading and gathered around him. They gawked as he added and divided numbers on his calculator, showed them photos of Alice, and played a Beatles' song.

"What about all these other symbols?" Sadie said, pointing to the other apps. "What do they do?"

"Phone, mail, weather reports," Meir said. "Various forms of communication and news."

"Show me."

"I'm afraid I can't. They don't work inside the bubble."

Meir wondered how he was going to explain the Internet, but the family glanced at the clouds outside the window.

"I'm not surprised," Nathan said. "Until you came along, nothing got in here."

The family turned away from Meir's smartphone and dove back into their books. He thought that they would have spent hours playing with it. But then again, he had presented them with a mountain of information. Perhaps the smartphone was just too much too soon. The books were easier to digest. Once they finished a book, they traded it for one they hadn't read yet. As they read, Meir moved about the three-room apartment.

He noted the dining table was set for the Passover Seder. The wine stain on the tablecloth was still wet. The clock on the mantle was frozen at 10:45, the moment the Rosenfelds became trapped in the bubble.

A wooden mannequin wore a red and white dress. Meir admired the craftsmanship. He studied a wall half-covered in black slash marks and rubbed his thumb on one of the slashes. They were made with coal. He picked up a book from a stack in the corner and found slash marks made with pencil on the pages inside.

He left the front room and moved into the kitchen. The pots and pans were put away. The dishes were clean, and the floor was swept. A stack of neatly folded blankets sat next to the wall. There wasn't much food; there wouldn't be in a pre-refrigerator apartment, but what little food remained was perfectly preserved. There was no stench of something spoiled or rotting away. What Meir did smell was schmaltz, the telltale sign of Jewish magic, just as he had in the hallway before he entered the apartment. The scent was strongest at the dining table in the front room.

Meir stood in the doorway to the back bedroom. He didn't go inside. This was most likely Baruch and Rebekah's bedroom and entering without their permission would have felt like an invasion of privacy.

He went back to the front room where the Rosenfelds were still catching up with the rest of the world. Meir sat on the windowsill next to Sadie. She glanced shyly at him before putting down the book on United States history she was reading.

"You look like someone I know," Sadie said.

"Someone who lived in the building before you were trapped?" Meir asked.

Sadie shook her head. "He doesn't live here. He comes to visit me."

Meir wrinkled his brow. "A man comes here? To the apartment? How does he get in?"

Sadie glanced over her shoulder at the clouds. "Would you like to look out the window?" she asked.

Meir felt a tingle at the base of his spine. Though he wanted to know who Sadie's visitor was, looking outside would answer one of his questions—how was Esther able to see Sadie in the window?

"Yes," Meir said. "I would love to look out the window."

"Jacob," Sadie said. "Lift the matzo box."

Jacob sat next to the dining room table. Without looking up from his book, he picked up the matzo box and placed it on the floor. The clouds outside the window parted. Meir gazed at the street below. A lone car drove by and a group of four young men sauntered along the sidewalk. A quarter moon hung above the buildings. He started to get up, but Sadie touched his hand. Her small hand was warm and calloused.

"Don't bother," she said.

"You don't know what I was about to do," Meir said.

"You were going to see if the clouds had parted in the hall-way."

"Yes. That's what I was going to do."

Sadie sighed. "Only the clouds at the window open up and only for five minutes."

"What happens after five minutes?" Meir asked.

"The clouds return, and the box goes back to where it was."

"If you move anything from the table, after five minutes, it goes back to where it was," Jacob said. "That's why the table is still set for the seder."

Sadie turned back to her book. "The clouds only part when you move the matzo box. After five minutes, if you want to keep watching the street, you'll have to pick up the box again."Sure enough, at the end of five minutes, the clouds returned, and the matzo box disappeared from the floor and reappeared on the dining room table.

Meir scratched his beard. Rabbi Fruman had been right. To break the curse, the Rosenfelds had to complete a task. Lifting the matzo box only broke part of the curse. There was no telling how many more tasks had to be completed before the curse was lifted.

Meir was eager to begin the search for those tasks. The Rosenfelds, not so much. They were content to keep reading even though Meir represented the possibility of escape. The time spent in this three-room prison had taught them infinite patience. Also, Meir had to remember that despite appearances, he was in the company of centenarians who were set in their ways.

This was going to be hardest with Sadie. Though she had the body of a nine-year-old, she was over seventy years older than him. While the rest of the family had their complete attention on their books, she kept stealing glances at him and smiling.

Meir would have to exercise patience. He sat on the floor with his back against the wall. Baruch shook Meir's shoulder and informed him that he'd been asleep for six hours.

"It's time for the morning prayers," Baruch said.

Meir couldn't believe he'd fallen asleep. He yawned and stretched his sore muscles. The family put down the books they were reading, picked up their prayer books, and took their places in front of Baruch. After the morning service, they returned to their books. The pile of books that everyone had read grew in the middle of the room.

To pass the time, Meir lifted the matzo box. It was an overcast morning. New Yorkers hurried past strolling tourists. Meir spotted Beryl standing across the street, his eyes glued to the fourth-floor window. Rabbi Chaim must have sent him to spy on them. Meir considered getting the Rosenfeld children to stand with him at the window so that Beryl could see that more than Baruch and Rebekah were trapped here, but he didn't want to interrupt them. Instead, Meir waved at Beryl. He didn't wave back.

When the family finished reading the history books, they moved on to the novels Meir brought them. He had considered bringing them classic novels from the last century but decided to bring only stories written by Jewish authors. He wanted them to see how the Jewish imagination had evolved.

Sadie picked up *Forever…* by Judy Blume and studied the cover.

"That's an excellent book," Meir said. "But you might like to read this one first."

He took *The Orchard Street Mystery* from his satchel and handed it to Sadie. Her eyes grew wide.

"Where did you get this?"

"My friend Esther found it in a bookstore," Meir said. "She wanted you to have it."

Sadie narrowed her eyes at Meir. "Who is this woman, Esther? And how does she know so much about me?"

"You waved at her from the window. At first, she was scared of you, but then she was determined to find out who you were. Esther is the reason I'm here. She hired me to help you."

Sadie grinned. "So, her name is Esther. We called her Alma. I was worried that I had upset her."

"She got over it."

"Tell me everything about her. Is she Jewish?"

Sadie lifted the matzo box. She gazed at the street as Meir told her about Esther Luna. When he was done, Sadie traced her finger over the drawing of her on the book's cover.

"Bertha was my best friend."

"She never forgot about you," Meir said.

Sadie rocked the book in her arms and cried. The family put down their books and rushed to her side.

"Did he hurt you?" Nathan scowled at Meir.

"Look at what he brought me," Sadie said.

She held up the book. Jacob pointed at the drawing. "It's you," he said.

"Bertha wrote a book?" Baruch asked.

Rebekah put her arm around Sadie's shoulder. "Read it out loud," she said.

Sadie flipped to the first page and read.

"The weather was frightful. The wind blew angrily like a giant passing gas after eating a bad piece of fish. The rain poured in torrents like the tears of a Jewish mother who discovered that no one liked her matzo ball soup. A sudden flash of lightning brought a brief moment of bright illumination to the inside of the apartment on the fourth floor of 97 Orchard Street. Sadie Rosen woke up from a restless sleep to see a dark figure looming over her. Another bolt of lightning revealed the figure to be that of an ugly man with an eye-patch. He had a wooden peg where his left leg used to be. He wore a pirate's hat. Sadie screamed loudly at the top of her lungs. Her handsome brother Jacob dashed into the room to rescue his beloved little sister, but the pirate had vanished."

Sadie put the book down. The family burst out laughing.

"Thank you, Bertha," Sadie said. "I can't remember the last

time I laughed."

"That was truly terrible," Baruch said.

"As I recall, Bertha was a sweet girl," Rebekah said, "but not very bright."

"She was sweet all right," Nathan said. "Sweet on Jacob." Nathan nudged Jacob.

Jacob grinned. "She was a cutie."

The family sat quietly, each in their own thoughts. Meir wondered how many times they had lapsed into extended silences.

"If you like, you can keep reading the books I brought you," Meir said. "But sooner or later, we need to talk."

Sadie put her hand on Baruch's arm. "We can read later, Papa."

Baruch patted his daughter's hand then faced Meir. "Let's talk now."

CHAPTER THIRTY-ONE

Meir asked the Rosenfelds to sit at the dining table in the same position as they had on the night of the seder. The family stared at the table.

"Why?" Baruch asked.

"I think it may have something to do with the time bubble," Meir said.

"But you're not sure."

"No, I'm not sure. I figure it's as good a place to start as any to find out how to escape."

Baruch looked at the family and shrugged.

"I think Mama sat next to Papa," Sadie said. "But I can't remember where I sat."

"Mama didn't sit next to Papa," Nathan said. "I did."

"Did I sit at the table or in the kitchen?" Rebekah asked.

"It was a hundred years ago," Baruch said. "How can you expect us to remember where we were sitting?"

"Why do we have to sit in exactly the same place?" Jacob asked.

Meir's head pounded. He had to keep in mind that although their bodies were frozen in time, their minds weren't. They had more than enough time to forget where they had sat on that fateful night.

"Forget it," Meir said. "Sit wherever you want."

Baruch sat at the head of the table with Rebekah to his left and Nathan to his right. Jacob sat next to Nathan and Sadie sat next to

Rebekah. They didn't realize it, but they were seated exactly where they had been for the seder.

There was an extra chair. Meir placed his hands on it. "Who sat here?"

The family stared at the chair as if it had walked in uninvited and placed itself at the table.

"I think I sat there," Jacob said.

"You sat in two chairs?" Meir asked.

"Maybe. We recline on Passover. Maybe I needed the extra chair to lean onto."

"Then why don't we all have two chairs?" Nathan asked.

Jacob shrugged. "Not enough chairs?"

"You're the last person to get two chairs. Papa would get two chairs before you would."

Nathan and Jacob glared at each other.

Baruch stood. "It's time for afternoon prayers."

The family left the table. Meir couldn't believe they would put off finding out what happened to them the night of the seder. He tried to argue but they had already begun their afternoon prayers. Reluctantly, Meir joined them.

Days passed and a routine developed. In between morning, afternoon, and evening prayers, Meir looked for clues on how to burst the time bubble. He kept coming back to the seder, certain that the answer was there but he couldn't see it. Not yet. Every day, he had the family sit at the table and try to remember what took place at the seder. While they were unable to recall the events of that night, the family recalled things about their life before they were trapped and shared their memories with Meir. Baruch's stories were mainly about his growing dress business, while Rebekah, Nathan, Jacob, and Sadie's stories were about their friendships with other tenants.

Meir didn't try to steer them away from telling their stories. He enjoyed listening to them. He liked hearing what life was like for Jewish immigrants in the early twentieth century. Also, he hoped that one of their stories would trigger a crucial memory.

Sadie explained how she established when it was day or night by watching Rebekah. She proudly showed Meir how she marked down the days beginning with the slashes on the wall. Her discovery led to the family going to sleep at the same time every night, with Baruch and Rebekah retiring to the apartment's single bedroom behind the kitchen, the kitchen becoming Sadie's bedroom, and Nathan and Jacob arranging the chairs in the front room to act as their beds.

The first night Meir slept in the apartment with the family was the hardest. The lights were on all the time, and he was used to sleeping in a dark room. He stayed in the front room with Nathan and Jacob and made a bed using the only stuffed chair and a dining table chair.

In the morning, his back ached. He did his best to hide his irritation, and he didn't dare confess that he felt the walls were closing in on him. Whatever suffering he endured was nothing compared to what the family had already experienced.

Though the Rosenfelds' memories were cloudy, Meir hadn't forgotten that he was there to end their lives. He still hadn't explained that part to them. The longer he stayed, the harder it was going to be to tell them.

And then one day during morning prayers, Meir realized that

he'd lost the nerve to look them in the eye and tell them he was essentially their executioner. He would keep it a secret. Meir told himself that he was being merciful because what good would it do for them to know, but deep down he knew the real reason. He was a coward.

CHAPTER THIRTY-TWO

Esther Luna located an empty bench in Washington Square Park and unpacked her lunch. She had ninety minutes before her next class. As she ate the chicken empanadas Gus had made her, she watched children scream with delight as they got drenched in the fountain. The water sparkled on their bare arms and in their hair.

One of the students in Esther's Modern Jewish History class walked by.

"Hey, Professor Luna," he said as he waved.

Esther waved back. "Hey, Rashad."

She enjoyed teaching at NYU. The students were engaged, and she liked the faculty. But the pay for an adjunct professor was dismal and she missed working at the Tenement Museum.

She couldn't think about the Tenement Museum without thinking of Rabbi Poppers. Even though he'd been in the time bubble for weeks, she hadn't given up hope.

Esther stopped eating when she saw a Worms coming from the Washington Square Arch. He was younger than the one who had followed Meir. Esther considered leaving before he had a chance to see her but decided to hell with him. She wasn't going to let a Worms scare her.

He walked directly to her bench and gave her a slight nod.

"Esther Luna," he said.

She clutched her amulet. "I have protection."

"You are correct. If I had any intention of harming you, your amulet would prevent me from doing so."

Esther looked at the amulet and then glared at the Worms. "How did you find me?"

The Worms shrugged. "Magic. Of course."

"What do you want?"

"May I ask you a few questions?"

Esther took a bite of her empanada, and the Worms waited.

"No," Esther said. "Go away."

"My name is Beryl Stein. I knew Meir before I joined the Worms."

"Were you friends?"

"Best friends."

"Are you still friends?"

Beryl sighed. "A friend would not have treated him the way I did recently."

Esther wrapped up the rest of her lunch. "Sounds like you're feeling some regret."

"I am."

Esther pointed at the bench. "We could share, but I know an Orthodox man can't sit next to a woman he's not married to."

"I can." Beryl sat on the bench and tried not to look uncomfortable.

"You sure you won't be distracted by sexual desire?" Esther said. "I wouldn't want you to forget why you came here."

Beryl shook his head. "Though you are quite attractive, your beauty won't distract me."

"Good to know." She pulled a strand of hair behind her ear.

"What did you want to ask me?"

"Why did you hire Rabbi Poppers?"

Esther gazed at the fountain. "I saw a girl in the window of an apartment that had been sealed shut for decades. I was freaked out at first, but then I had to find out who she was, and what she was. I tried to hire the Worms, but your people wouldn't have anything to do with me."

Beryl winced. "So, you hired Meir instead?" he asked.

"That's right."

"How do you know the girl's name is Sadie?"

"There are ways to find out things other than using magic. I looked her up in the census records."

"And you're absolutely sure you saw her?"

"Yes."

Beryl rubbed his forehead. "I was led to believe that only Baruch and Rebekah Rosenfeld were in the time bubble."

"Whoever told you that lied. My friend, Stan, saw the whole family."

"Family?"

"Along with Baruch and Rebekah are their three children, Nathan, Jacob, and Sadie."

Beryl paled. "Three children? In the bubble?"

Esther narrowed her eyes at Beryl. "You really didn't know?"

Beryl stood. "I have to go. Thank you for answering my questions."

"Are you going to help Meir?"

Beryl didn't reply. He had already hurried away.

CHAPTER THIRTY-THREE

One day after morning prayers, Meir asked Sadie how long he'd been there. She counted the slashes in her calendar.

"Thirty days."

The number was like a kick to Meir's stomach. He'd been here a month and had accomplished nothing.

That wasn't entirely true. When he first entered the time bubble, the Rosenfelds were a family unit in his mind. Each member a part of a whole. He'd been in the tenement apartment long enough to get to know them as individuals.

Baruch was the proud leader. His leadership had been earned through his diligence to the daily routine of prayer, and through his wisdom. When an argument broke out between family members, they brought their grievance to him, and instead of making a strict judgement, he gave them advice so that they could work it out themselves.

Rebekah was the doting mother, always checking to make sure everyone was comfortable. She hugged everyone at least once a day. Somewhere around Meir's third week in the bubble, she'd started treating Meir as if he were another child of hers.

Nathan was a contradiction. He was serious and the joker. He acted stern but was the first one to invent a new game, or a silly challenge to pass the time. He'd already talked Meir into seeing who could stand on their head the longest. Nathan won.

At first, Meir thought Jacob was the frightened rabbit hiding in corners. But over time, he realized that Jacob was the thinker, observing the others. The phrase that fit him best: *still waters run deep*.

Then there was Sadie. She was everyone's favorite, including Meir's. She was the curious one who asked questions and whose smile got the others to smile. She was the one who still dreamed.

These were good Jews. Meir shook his head. He put aside their shared religion. The Rosenfelds were people robbed of their hopes and dreams. What right did Meir have to end their lives?

Meir sobbed in pity for the Rosenfelds and in pity for himself. No one tried to console him. The family must have been used to someone crying. They let him sob until he was able to stop. He used his handkerchief to dry his eyes and blow his nose.

"Feel better?" Sadie asked.

"Yes," Meir said. "Thank you."

"Don't worry. A month is nothing."

CHAPTER THIRTY-FOUR

Beryl Stein stood on the sidewalk in front of the Tenement Museum gift shop on the corner of Orchard Street and Delancey Street. Shlomo Feintuch joined him.

"Reb Feintuch," Beryl said. "How are you?"

Feintuch leaned against the building. "Terrible. I may be over the Black Fly potion, but my tired feet still need time to heal."

"Then why are you here and not soaking your feet in a nice hot potion?"

"Why do you think?" Feintuch said. "I'm spying on you."

"Rabbi Chaim sent you?"

"What do you expect? You've been missing for a month."

Beryl gazed toward 97 Orchard Street. "I had to find out for myself."

"You've been standing here for a month?"

"Of course not. I take food and bathroom breaks. I got a hotel room where I sleep at night. I just wish I'd brought a change of clothes." Beryl held up his arm and sniffed. "These are starting to smell."

"Rabbi Chaim is very upset," Feintuch said. "You lied to him. You told him you were going to study and instead here you are."

Beryl scowled. "He lied to me. He told me only Baruch and Rebekah Rosenfeld were in the time bubble."

"Who else?" Feintuch asked.

"Their three children."

"Are you sure? Did you see them with your own eyes?" Feintuch pointed at his own eyes.

"Most of the time, I saw no one. Then one day, I saw Meir. A week later, I saw Meir again, but this time a girl stood next to him. She had a bow in her hair. I haven't seen the rest of the family, but I believe they're in there."

Feintuch looked at 97 Orchard Street. "What are you going to do?"

That was what Beryl had been trying to figure out. "Rabbi Chaim is our rebbe," Beryl said. "Our spiritual leader."

Feintuch nodded. "You're right. We can't jump to conclusions."

"He may not have known."

"And even if he did know, he can still make this right."

Beryl stood up straight. "I will go see Rabbi Chaim and give him a chance to explain."

Feintuch put his hand on Beryl's shoulder.

"I will go with you," Feintuch said. "You won't have to face him alone. Of course, first you must change your clothes."

Beryl smiled. "Thank you, Reb Feintuch. I could use the company."

CHAPTER THIRTY-FIVE

Meir dreamed he was kissing Camilla. He could feel her soft lips pressing against his. Delicious sensations spread through his body. He would have been content to continue the dream, but the pressure on his lips felt too real. He opened his eyes and saw someone really was kissing him, but it wasn't Camilla.

Sadie pulled away when she realized he was awake. "I tried not to wake you," she whispered.

Meir pulled himself into a seated position. "You kissed me," he said.

Sadie's eyes grew wide as she touched her lips. "I'm sorry," she squeaked before hurrying into the kitchen.

Meir stared after her, confused. Should he go to her? Should he go back to sleep and pretend it never happened? Nathan came over and sat on the floor next to Meir.

"I didn't mean to watch," Nathan said. "But your voices woke me."

"Why did she do that?" Meir asked.

"Who else can she kiss? She can't kiss me or Jacob."

Turning toward the kitchen, Meir saw Sadie huddled in her bed with a blanket over her head.

"What should I do?" he asked.

"Go back to sleep," Nathan said. "Forget it ever happened."

"I suppose you're right."

"Of course, I'm right."

"Besides, it's not like she's ever going to kiss anybody else."

Meir paled. The words had slipped out before he could stop them.

"That's not true," Nathan said angrily. "She'll have plenty of opportunities once we've escaped."

"You're right. I don't know what I was thinking."

Nathan stood over Meir, grabbed his shirt, and pulled him to his feet. With his face inches from Meir, Nathan said, "You're lying. Tell me the truth, rabbi. Why won't Sadie kiss anyone else?"

Icy dread spread through Meir. The moment he'd hope to avoid had come. He had no choice. He had to tell the truth.

"When the time bubble bursts, she'll die," Meir said. "You all will."

Nathan let go of Meir's shirt. Meir braced for a punch in the face, but it didn't come. Nathan went over to Jacob and shook him.

"Get up, Jacob," Nathan said. He stormed into the kitchen. "You too, Sadie. Get up. Wake Mama and Papa. Rabbi Poppers has something to tell us that won't wait for morning."

Meir winced. He would have preferred getting punched. By the time he'd gotten to his feet, the family had gathered in the front room.

"What is so important that you woke us in the middle of the night?" Baruch asked.

Nathan pointed at Meir. "Rabbi Poppers hasn't been completely honest with us. Tell them what you just told me, kishef macher."

Facing the family in the small room, Meir froze. He was too afraid to speak. Rebekah stood next to him and stared at the others.

"You're scaring him," she said. "Can't you see? He's just a boy."

She turned to Meir. "I can tell you're a good person. I'm sure whatever you did is not that terrible. Tell us what you told Nathan."

"I should have told you when I first arrived, but I chickened out." Meir took a deep breath. "You're never going to leave the apartment."

The family gawked at Meir.

"I thought you were here to get us out," Rebekah said.

"The bubble has kept a hundred years from entering the apartment," Meir said. "When it pops…"

Baruch looked around the apartment. "All that time will come rushing in."

"Exactly."

The family showed no emotion, except for Rebekah. She cried quietly. Meir suspected that her tears were not for her but for her children.

"How long will it take us to age a hundred years?" Sadie asked.

"I'm guessing ten to fifteen minutes at the most," Meir said. "The pressure from aging that rapidly will be intense. Your bodies won't survive."

Nathan stepped forward. Meir expected another angry outburst, but he spoke calmly. "Good. I'm tired of waiting for death."

Jacob shook his head. "Not me. I don't want to die."

Rebekah went to his side and put her arms around him. She stroked his curly hair. "You know there's no other choice."

He pushed his mother away. "How do we know that?" Jacob demanded. He pointed at Meir. "He's a kishef macher. A stranger. Maybe he came here to kill us."

Meir was afraid that all the Rosenfelds would react like Jacob, but he was the only one who rebelled against the inevitable.

"Forgive my son," Baruch said. "When we heard your knock on our door, he thought it was the Angel of Death. At that moment, he may have believed he was ready to go to Heaven, but when faced with the certainty of death, life becomes precious. Even this life."

"I think I understand," Meir said.

Jacob began to cry. Rebekah held him and this time he didn't push her away. He buried his face in his mother's chest. The family sat silently as Rebekah comforted her son. A minute later, Jacob stopped crying and dried his eyes with his sleeve.

Meir went to his satchel, took out a liter bottle and a half pint bottle, and placed them on the dining table.

"I brought two potions," He held up the liter bottle. "This one contains an anti-aging potion. You'll be aging too quickly for it to save you, but it will make your death less painful."

Rebekah gasped. "It's going to hurt?"

Meir sighed. "I'm afraid so."

Baruch nodded at the half pint bottle. "What is in there?"

Meir almost didn't make this potion despite Rabbi Katzerman's recommendation. "A potion that will kill you instantly. Painlessly."

Baruch crossed his arms. "When were you going to tell us about these potions you brought into our home?"

Meir cringed. "I was hoping to find a way out first."

"How is that going?"

Meir glanced at the clouds covering the windows. "Still working on it."

Nathan picked up the half pint bottle and gazed at the dark liquid inside. Meir was about to warn him to handle it carefully, but the potion didn't have any effect inside the bubble.

"Nu?" Nathan said. "Until you find a way out, you're trapped in here too."

"That's right," Meir said.

"You could be here a hundred years. Like us."

"I knew that when I decided to come here."

Nathan handed Meir the bottle. "You might have to choose which one of those potions you want to take."

CHAPTER THIRTY-SIX

Meir's two potion bottles were placed on the mantle next to the clock frozen at 10:45. The anti-aging potion had the light pink of a *rosé* wine. The instant death potion was as black as a black licorice liqueur.

Nathan put them there without asking Meir's permission. Meir thought he did it so that they would be seen as a constant reminder that Meir had not been completely honest with the family.

That assumption proved to be wrong. The family didn't blame Meir for their fate. He had made a mistake, and now that they knew the truth, they forgave him. Meir assumed they had forgiven each other for a multitude of transgressions over the past century. As for Sadie's kiss, though she acted as if it had never happened, the kiss had happened and somehow that small act of intimacy had made them closer.

Two days later, Meir and Sadie sat at the dining table together. While the rest of the family re-read the books Meir had brought with him, Sadie told Meir about how she used to help Rebekah in the kitchen.

"Did you do part of the cooking?" Meir asked.

"Mama let me do a few things here and there. She wanted me to learn. A good wife needs to know how to cook."

"Did you do any of the cooking for the seder meal?"

Sadie shook her head. "Oh no. The seder meal was special. I wasn't ready for that."

"How was the seder meal the night this happened?" Meir asked. He gestured at the clouds covering the windows.

Sadie smiled. "Everything Mama cooked was wonderful but that night she outdid herself. She made roast chicken, matzo ball soup, carrot pudding, and I can't remember what else. But it was all delicious."

"It sounds delicious."

Sadie giggled. "One time, Jacob told me that he missed being hungry."

She glanced at Jacob. He had his nose buried in a book.

"When I get out of here," Meir said, "I'm going to be starving."

"What kind of eater are you?" Sadie asked.

"What do you mean?"

"Good table manners? Or do you attack your food like an animal?"

Meir grinned. "I have good table manners. What about you?"

Sadie frowned at him. "What do you think? I also have good table manners!"

"What about the rest of your family?"

Sadie's eyes widened. "The beggar ate like a beast."

"Beggar?"

Sadie pointed at a chair. "He sat there. Papa brought him home to celebrate the seder with us."

"Where is he now?"

"He left without saying goodbye."

A tingle ran down Meir's spine. He called the family to join him and Sadie. They reluctantly put down their books and took their seats at the table. "Tell me everything you remember about the beggar,"

Meir asked.

The Rosenfelds glanced at each other.

Nathan slapped the table. "The beggar. Of course. How could we have forgotten him?"

"The beggar was ungrateful," Rebekah said. "Baruch brought him into our home, and nothing was good enough for him."

"He complained about everything," Jacob said.

"He made disgusting slurping noises when he ate soup," Sadie said.

Meir felt immense relief. They were finally starting to get somewhere.

"If Papa hadn't brought the beggar home, none of this would have happened," Nathan said. "This is all his fault."

"Nathan!" Sadie shouted. "You said Papa was a good man. You said it wasn't his fault."

Nathan jumped to his feet, scraping the chair on the wood floor. "I changed my mind."

"How can it be my fault?" Baruch said as he picked up a Haggada. "It says in here, 'Anyone who is hungry should come and eat.' I did as HaShem commanded me. There is no sin in what I did."

Meir leaned forward and put his elbows on the table. "Gentlemen. Arguing isn't helping. You're finally starting to remember. Stay focused on what happened at the seder."

Sadie placed her palms on the table. "I remember everything," she said. "It's all come back to me."

Meir motioned for Nathan to sit back down. Nathan complied. Meir turned to Sadie. "Okay, Sadie. Tell us."

She sat up straight. "He said his name was Eli. He had red hair and a red beard. He stank. His clothes were rags, and he had a dirty blanket that he wore over his shoulders like a tallit. He squeezed my arm so hard that he left bruises."

Sadie rolled up her sleeve so that Meir could see the five bruises on her arm left by the beggar's fingers.

"Please continue," Meir said.

Sadie rolled the sleeve back down and buttoned her cuff. "He congratulated Mama for having three children."

"That's right," Rebekah said. "He kept arguing with Baruch. It got so bad that he offered to leave, but I insisted he stay. I should have let him leave." She covered her face with her hands. "This is all my fault. My beautiful children would be grandparents by now if it hadn't been for me."

Meir's heart broke for poor Rebekah, but he couldn't let her feelings of guilt sidetrack the progress they were making. "None of you are to blame for what happened," Meir said. "Sadie. Please continue."

"He complained about everything," Sadie said. "He said my brothers should be studying Torah instead of making dresses. He said the Manischewitz's Matzos was chometz. He reached inside his shirt and took out a piece of handmade matzo wrapped in a filthy cloth. He wanted Papa to replace our matzo with his."

Sadie wrinkled her nose in disgust.

"Sounds like he was a terrible guest," Meir said.

"So terrible. He said I shouldn't be allowed to recite the four questions because I'm a girl."

"Anything else?"

Sadie looked around the room. "After the seder meal, he walked around the apartment talking to himself."

"Did you hear what he said?"

Sadie shook her head. "He was speaking too softly. I couldn't even tell you what language he was speaking."

Meir scratched his beard. "Okay. He came into your home, acted all judgmental, tried to get you to eat stinky matzo, and then wandered around the apartment mumbling to himself. Anybody want to add anything?"

The family members either stared at the ceiling or the table.

"Eli left while we were looking for the afikomen," Jacob said.

"I felt something right before he disappeared," Nathan said. "Like when you're walking by the shore and the wind shifts. You feel like the sea is calling you."

Meir pointed at Nathan. "Repeat what you just said."

"Like walking by the shore and the wind shifts. You feel like the sea is calling you."

"That's the moment the time bubble began." Meir had most of the pieces of the puzzle, but he wasn't quite sure how to put them together.

CHAPTER THIRTY-SEVEN

Beryl and Feintuch stormed into Rabbi Chaim's office.

"We must speak with you, rebbe," Feintuch said. "Now."

Chaim pointed at the door. "Leave my office, Feintuch. Close the door on your way out."

"No!" Feintuch stomped his foot and winced from the pain. "We stand together. We demand answers."

Chaim glowered at Feintuch. "I wish to speak with Beryl. Alone. Get out. Don't make me tell you again."

Feintuch paled. "Yes, Rabbi."

He hurried out of the office and closed the door. So much for standing up to Chaim. With Feintuch gone, Chaim focused his anger on Beryl.

"Did I not forbid you to go to the museum?" Chaim asked.

"You did," Beryl said calmly.

"And yet, you went anyway."

"I had to know the truth."

"You think you know the truth?"

"Not all of it. I want to give you a chance to explain."

Chaim sprang to his feet. "I should explain to you! How dare you."

Beryl stood straight with his hands clasped behind his back. "Sooner or later, I will find out about the Rosenfelds. And why you've kept it a secret."

Chaim stroked his red beard. He gestured at the visitor's chair. "Sit. Sit."

He and Beryl sat and faced each other.

"Rabbi Poppers must be stopped," Chaim said. "He must not free the Rosenfelds."

"For the sake of all Jews?" Beryl asked.

"For the sake of the Worms, the kishef dynasty you have dedicated your life to." Chaim looked around the room as if expecting to find a spy lurking about. "What I'm about to tell you must not leave this room. You must promise me you'll never say a word to anybody."

Beryl shook his head. "I can't make that promise."

Chaim fiddled with items on his desk. "You were a good student. Tell me the history of the Worms."

Beryl crossed his legs. "The Worms started in Worms, Germany in 1694. In 1887, Rabbi Ezekiel of Worms, your zayde, moved the sect to America and established our community here in New York. Your father inherited his position as leader of the Worms, and you became leader after your father died." Beryl didn't mention that some Worms weren't happy when Chaim took over from his father because they felt Chaim was too young. "What does our history have to do with the Rosenfelds?"

Chaim held up his hand. "Hold your horses. I'm getting to it." He tapped his fingers on his desk. "Before moving to America, Rabbi Ezekiel had a special Passover tradition. He would go to a nearby village that didn't know him, disguise himself as a beggar, and wait for a good Jewish family to invite him to their seder."

"I've heard of famous rabbis doing that," Beryl said. "They wanted to celebrate as just another Jew. Then at some point during the service, the great rabbi would reveal his identity, much to the delight of the family."

Chaim smiled. "That's exactly what Rabbi Ezekiel did."

"Have you ever done it?"

"I wish I could, but I'm too well known. The price of fame in the modern world."

Beryl tugged at his shirt cuff. He was glad he took Feintuch's advice and changed into clean clothes before he came to see Chaim.

"Did Rabbi Ezekiel ever do his special Passover tradition here in New York?"

Chaim wagged his finger at Beryl. "You're a smart boy. I've always said you were smart. That's why I found an intelligent girl for you to marry. Let's arrange a meeting. I'll call her parents." He picked up his phone.

"Please, Rabbi," Beryl said. "Stop stalling."

Chaim reluctantly put his phone down. "Rabbi Ezekiel did indeed do it here in New York. But only once and never again."

"The Rosenfelds?" Beryl asked.

"The Rosenfelds."

"Is that the problem? The fact that they know that Rabbi Ezekiel of Worms trapped them in a time bubble?"

Chaim grimaced. "No! Barukh HaShem, he didn't tell them. He said his name was Eli."

"Why didn't he tell them?"

"It was his intention to wait until the right moment, then tell them. But he got too upset. They had machine-made matzo. They let a girl recite the four questions. The Rosenfelds were shedding Jewish traditions like a snake sheds its skin. He created the time bubble in the hope that it would lead them back to the proper ways of our faith."

Beryl narrowed his eyes at Chaim. "How would the time bubble do that?"

Chaim looked at Beryl like maybe he wasn't so smart after all.

"Simple. The Rosenfelds would be trapped in the bubble until they did the seder according to Orthodox tradition."

"That's all they had to do?" Beryl asked.

Chaim held out his hands. "They didn't even have to start over at the beginning. Rabbi Ezekiel left after the meal. The Rosenfelds just had to pick up from there. Each part of the service they observed correctly was a step closer to getting out. I don't see how zayde could have been more generous to them."

Beryl took a moment to digest this information. "If that was all they had to do, then why are they still inside the bubble?"

Chaim shrugged. "I don't know."

"I don't see why they didn't do what Rabbi Ezekiel told them to do. I can't believe they don't know how to do the service according to tradition."

Chaim shook his head. "Oh no. He didn't tell them what they had to do. If he had, they wouldn't have learned anything. They had to figure it out on their own."

Beryl gawked at Chaim. "He didn't tell them?"

"It's their own fault. If they had been observant Jews, they would have understood the clues he left them and gotten out the same night he created the time bubble."

"The fact remains that he enslaved Jews during a Passover Seder, the holiday that celebrates God freeing the Jews from bondage."

Chaim pointed at Beryl. "How dare you accuse the great Rabbi Ezekiel of Worms of enslavement! I'll tell you what happened. Having come to America, the Rosenfelds became too assimilated to remember how to do a seder properly. It's their own fault that they forgot how to be Jews."

Beryl rubbed his forehead. Chaim's twisted logic was giving him a headache.

"I can't believe Rabbi Ezekiel never went back to check on the Rosenfelds," Beryl said.

"Who says he didn't?" Chaim asked.

"He did?"

"Of course, he did. He went back a month later and saw they were still in the bubble. He couldn't believe it. They were completely ignoring the seder table. The answer was right in front of them. In his infinite generosity, he decided to give them another month."

Beryl waited for Chaim to go on, but he didn't.

"Nu?" Beryl asked. "Did he check on them a month later?"

Chaim fussed with items on his desk again. "No. He didn't."

"Why not?"

"He forgot."

Beryl sprang to his feet. "He forgot?"

Chaim motioned for Beryl to return to his chair. "Sit, sit," he said. Once Beryl was seated, he continued. "He was busy."

"Busy? That was his excuse? He was busy?"

"It took a lot of time and effort to establish a kishef macher sect in a new country. America may not have had pogroms, but there was plenty of anti-Semitism. Not to mention, he worked tirelessly to get our fellow kishef machers out of Europe during the Holocaust."

"If he forgot the Rosenfelds, then how come you know about

them?"

"When he was on his death bed, he remembered them, but he was too frail to see if they were still in the bubble. He asked my father, the great Rabbi Yaakov of Worms, to check on them."

"And they were still there."

"Can you believe it? They'd had decades to figure it out."

Beryl gripped his chair's armrests. "Why didn't Rabbi Yaakov free them then?"

Chaim sighed. "Rabbi Ezekiel was a legend among kishef machers and the Worms were one of the most powerful kishef macher dynasties in the world. Yaakov realized that if someone found out the Rosenfelds had been in there for that many years, it could potentially hurt Ezekiel's reputation. Any damage to his exalted legend would hurt the Worms. Yaakov had no choice. He had to keep it a secret."

Beryl imagined the scene. Rabbi Yaakov peering at the poor Rosenfelds in their tiny apartment and worrying more about what others would think of the Worms than their suffering.

"It would have been criminal to sully Rabbi Ezekiel's good name for one mistake," Chaim said. "So, Yaakov kept the Rosenfelds a secret. He told me on his death bed, and I agreed with him that no one must ever find out."

"For the sake of the Worms, you kept it a secret," Beryl said.

"As Rabbi Yaakov once said, '*Es shtait doch geshribben: chochmoh shtikoh.*' It is written: silence is golden. That's why you must stop Rabbi Poppers. He's not as smart as you, but he's still plenty smart. He might figure out that Eli the beggar was actually Rabbi Ezekiel."

Beryl glared at Chaim. "Why don't you stop Meir yourself? Why do you want me to do it?"

"I'm the leader of the Worms. It's not proper for me to do it myself. That's why I had Feintuch give the Black Fly Potion to that woman's husband. I give the orders and my people follow them."

Beryl shook his head. "I'm not going to stop Meir."

Chaim's cheeks turned as red as his beard. "Have you not listened to a word I said?"

"I listened but I'm not sure you heard yourself. Rabbi Ezekiel made a terrible mistake. We must tell the kishef macher community what he did. It may hurt his reputation, but I don't think it will destroy the Worms. If it does, then we don't deserve to exist."

Beryl stood and walked to the door.

"Where do you think you're going?" Chaim asked.

Beryl opened the door. "I'm going to tell Meir how to free the Rosenfelds."

"Wait!" Chaim shouted.

Beryl paused. "I'm listening."

"Take a couple of days to think it over."

"There's nothing to think about."

"You have the reputation of one of the greatest kishef machers of all time in your hands. Second only to the Maharal of Prague and Moses. And you say you have nothing to think about?"

Beryl looked down at his shoes. "I don't want to hurt Rabbi Ezekiel's reputation, but I have no choice."

"You're making a rash decision. Two days won't make a difference for either the Rosenfelds or Rabbi Poppers."

"No," Beryl said.

"Two days. You can't wait two days?"

Beryl groaned. "Okay. Okay. I will wait two days."

Chaim smiled. "Since you're going to be around, you have time to meet that smart girl I found for you."

Beryl held up his hand. "Until this is resolved, I won't be meeting any potential mates."

"So, make the poor girl wait. Break her heart. If you see Feintuch, tell him to come see me. He's a good man and I should apologize to him."

Beryl left and a minute later, Feintuch entered.

"Forgive me, Rabbi," Feintuch said. "I don't know what came over me."

Chaim rose from his desk and draped his arm over the old man's shoulder.

"Tell me, Shlomo," Chaim said. "How are you feeling? Have you recovered from the Black Fly Potion?"

Feintuch nodded. "Yes, rebbe. I'm much better now. Thank you for asking."

"That was a dirty trick Rabbi Poppers pulled on you. I understand he sprayed the potion into your face."

"That's right."

"Did it get into your eyes?"

"I managed to close them in time."

"Good. Good." Chaim led Feintuch to a chair and had him sit. "I know I shouldn't ask you to do something for me so soon after your recovery."

Feintuch shook his head. "Oh no, rebbe. I'm fit as a fiddle. Ask me. I am a loyal Worms."

"You sure? Your feet are too sore from all the walking around you did while you followed Poppers around the city?"

Feintuch lifted his feet off the floor. "My feet are fine."

Chaim looked around the office before focusing on Feintuch. "What I'm about to ask you to do is for the sake of the Worms, the kishef dynasty you have dedicated your life to. Our very existence is in your hands."

Feintuch blinked in astonishment. "For the sake of the Worms? Ask. Ask. I'll do whatever you need me to do."

"Go to 97 Orchard Street and stop Rabbi Poppers from saving the Rosenfelds."

"How?"

"Use your imagination. You'll think of something."

"Rabbi. You know I have no imagination."

Chaim growled. "Are you not a kishef macher? Curse him. Spray a potion in his face like he did you. Not only will you save the Worms, you'll get your revenge on that young pisher."

Chaim went back to his desk. Feintuch stared at the floor.

"But Rabbi," Feintuch said. "What about the Rosenfelds? Is it true this family has been trapped in their apartment for a century?"

"Are you willing to sacrifice the Worms for a family you've never met?" Chaim asked.

"Do I really have to choose?" Feintuch asked.

"No. I made the choice for you. That's what leaders do. Now, go. You must act quickly."

"I must prepare first. I have to decide how best to stop Rabbi Poppers."

"You have two days. Do you understand me, Feintuch? You only have two days."

CHAPTER THIRTY-EIGHT

Two days passed. During that time, Meir didn't participate in the daily prayers. Instead, he studied the objects on the table and read a Haggada from start to finish. The family stole glances at him, but they let him be. Finally, Sadie sat next to him at the table.

"What are you doing?" she asked.

"Waiting," Meir said.

"For what?"

"For HaShem to speak to me."

"We've been waiting too." Sadie crossed her arms. "For a very long time."

"I'm sorry. I'm doing the best I can."

The answer finally came to Meir during the family's evening prayers. He had been watching them pray and noticed the way Baruch cradled the prayer book in his hand. He obviously loved the book and the message contained in its pages. Meir waited until Baruch closed the prayer book before asking the family to sit at the dining table.

"Only on rare occasions does God speak directly to us," Meir said. "Most of the time He sends us clues and it's up to us to catch them." He held up the book he'd found in Esther's apartment. "This is a book of Jewish folk tales. I love this book. It has one of my favorite stories."

"What's the story?" Sadie asked.

"I thought you'd never ask. Four men are traveling together. They come upon the ruins of what had once been the stone castle of a great kingdom. An old man appears out of the woods. He tells the four men that one of the kingdom's stones is out of place. Whoever puts the stone back in its proper place shall restore the kingdom and be made its king. There is a path that leads directly to the crumbled castle. The first three men follow the direct path again and again, but nothing looks out of place. The fourth man is a Jew. He approaches the castle from many different paths. He sees which stone is out of place, moves it back, the castle and the kingdom are restored, and he becomes the king."

The family stared at Meir.

"Not bad for a folk tale," Sadie said. "What's the moral of the story?"

"You have to look at life from different perspectives to truly understand God's plan," Meir said.

"Is that the clue God gave you?"

Meir shook his head. "The part about the stone is the clue. The Jewish man moved the stone to its rightful place and the kingdom returned. We move the matzo box and the clouds part."

Everyone stared at the matzo box.

"You are the victims of a powerful curse," he said. "To break the curse, you must complete a series of tasks. Moving the matzo box is only one of the tasks."

"In other words, we have to move many stones back into their proper place," Baruch said.

Meir nodded. "I believe that's what we have to do."

"That is impossible!" Nathan shouted. "There could be a million things in this apartment that are out of place. We'd have to move them all."

Meir jumped at Nathan's sudden outburst, but the other members of the Rosenfeld family didn't flinch.

"I don't think the tasks are random," Meir said. "I believe that they're all part of the same lesson."

"That doesn't tell us anything." Nathan glared at Meir. He wasn't the joker now.

Meir understood his anger, but it didn't solve anything.

"How can we be victims of a curse?" Baruch asked. "Who would curse us? We're just a humble family. We never hurt anyone."

"It's obvious who cursed you," Meir said.

Baruch glared at Meir. "It's not obvious to me."

"It was Eli. He was a kishef macher. When Sadie saw him walking around speaking what was most likely Aramaic, that was Eli creating the time bubble and the curse that went with it."

Baruch stood. "It's not possible. He couldn't have done it."

"What makes you so sure he didn't?"

Baruch banged his fist on the table. "He was a Jew!" he shouted.

Meir felt a flutter in his stomach. Baruch had moved a stone into its proper place and Meir saw why the family had never figured out how to escape the time bubble. It had been inconceivable to them that a Jew would imprison another Jew.

"Before I came here," Meir said. "I asked one of my teachers for advice on how to break the curse. He asked me if I knew why one Jew punishes another Jew."

"He didn't just answer the question?" Baruch asked.

"He still sees himself as my teacher. He wanted me to figure it out on my own."

"What was your answer?" Sadie asked.

"For not being a proper Jew."

Sadie wrinkled her nose. "What is a proper Jew?"

"Depends on which Jew you're asking. My teacher said when I found out why the kishef macher trapped you, it would help me figure out how to free you."

The family stared at the table. The answer was close, but they still had to move more stones.

Rebekah threw her hands in the air. "The answer is right in front of us," she said. "Eli didn't think we were proper Jews. He trapped us here until we learned how."

Meir was impressed. Rebekah had just moved the biggest stone of all. He studied the matzo box.

"Who found the afikomen?" Meir asked.

"The afikomen?" Nathan said.

"From what you've told me, time stopped while you were looking for it."

Nathan sniffed. "I didn't look for it. Jacob and Sadie did."

Meir looked at Sadie.

"We never found it," she said.

Meir turned to Baruch. "I'm assuming you're the one who hid it," Meir said.

"I put it in a pot on the kitchen shelf," Baruch said. "But when we looked inside, it wasn't there."

"Show me the pot."

Baruch and Meir went into the kitchen. Baruch lifted the lid on the iron pot.

"As you can see, it's empty," Baruch said.

There was nothing inside the pot, not even dust.

"Put the lid back on the pot," Meir said.

Baruch replaced the lid. Meir stood in the doorway between the kitchen and the front room.

"Lift the matzo box," Meir said.

Jacob lifted the box. The clouds parted. Meir turned to Baruch.

"Remove the lid," Meir said. "If there's something inside, take it out right away."

Baruch lifted the lid. His eyes grew wide. "It can't be! It was empty!"

"Quick. Take it out," Meir said.

Baruch reached into the pot and removed a soiled white cloth. Wrapped inside was an oval sheet of handmade matzo.

"I don't understand," Baruch said.

"Moving the matzo box is the first task," Meir said. "Taking the handmade matzo out of the pot is the next task."

Sadie pointed at the matzo. "That's the missing afikomen."

CHAPTER THIRTY-NINE

Baruch sat in the stuffed chair and sobbed. Cradled in his hands was the handmade matzo.

"It was here all along. All these years, the missing afikomen was here."

Rebekah knelt at his feet and rested her head on his knee. Sadie sat on the armrest and the boys stood on either side of their father. Meir stood outside the family circle.

"Is that the afikomen you hid in the pot?" he asked.

Baruch wiped his tears with his sleeve and studied the matzo. "No. This is Eli's."

"That he kept in his shirt?"

Baruch held the oval at arm's length. "Oy! It is. Where's the matzo I hid?"

"Eli took it," Meir said.

"But he hated the Manischewitz's Matzos."

Sadie held out her hand. "I think I understand. Papa. Give me the matzo."

Baruch looked at Meir, who nodded.

Excitement grew inside of Meir. He was finally starting to understand the curse.

Baruch handed Sadie the matzo. She went to the table, removed the box of machine-made matzo, and put Eli's handmade matzo in its place. The clouds cleared away from the window. Sadie put the box on the mantle next to the two bottles of potion and the clock stuck at 10:45.

"Meir said the curse requires that we complete a series of tasks," Sadie said. "Replacing our matzo with Eli's must be one of the first tasks."

The family looked at Meir for confirmation.

"Let's wait five minutes and see," Meir said. Five minutes later, Meir nodded at the window. "The clouds haven't returned. And the box hasn't gone back to the table."

The family gathered at the window. A crowd had gathered in front of the tenement building. They could hear their chatter over the constant rumble of traffic.

"Not only have the clouds not returned," Baruch said. "We can hear the world."

"So many strange sounds," Jacob said. "I love them all."

"Look," Sadie said. "It's Roland."

She pointed at a tall man with blond hair. He was speaking to the crowd.

"Roland?" Meir asked.

Rebekah draped her arm over Sadie's shoulder. "Every day we watch the same people below us," Rebekah said. "We had to call them something, so we made up names for them."

Meir nodded. "Just like you gave Esther the name Alma. Roland's real name is Stan Jolly. He works for the museum."

"A museum?" Jacob said. "That's the kind of entertainment we are? I never would have guessed."

Meir explained how 97 Orchard Street had become the Tenement Museum.

"People pay to see this?" Baruch said. He gestured at the apartment.

"Exactly," Meir said. "There are apartments below that have been restored to look like your home."

Nathan banged on the window, but no one on the street responded. Stan led the group into the building.

"They still can't hear us," Nathan said.

"We've only done enough tasks for sound to get in," Meir said. "We need to complete more tasks before our sound can get out of the bubble."

"There's a man with the same Fisherman's hat that Eli wore," Sadie said.

She pointed at a Worms pacing back and forth on the sidewalk. Meir was surprised to see that it wasn't Beryl, but Feintuch. Though Meir wasn't happy to see him, he was relieved to see that Feintuch had survived the Black Fly Potion.

"Are you sure it was the same kind of hat?" Meir asked.

"Yes," Sadie said. "I even asked Eli if he was a fisherman."

Meir crossed his arms. "You just confirmed my suspicions. Eli was a member of the Worms, a powerful kishef macher sect based here in New York. They wear fisherman's caps. And they're militant about being observant."

"They're here in the city?" Baruch asked. "Is it possible they knew we were here. All this time?"

Meir nodded. "I believe they did."

Baruch sat in the stuffed chair. "I should be furious. I should be tearing out my beard in anger and shouting my own curses. But I only want this to be over. Let's observe the seder according to proper Jewish tradition or at least proper in the eyes of Eli the beggar."

"That means I can't participate in any of the readings," Sadie said.

"And we must lean when we drink the wine," Nathan said.

Rebekah stared at the empty cups on the table. "Four or two cups of wine? We had just finished the meal when Eli imprisoned us. Do we pick up where we left off or start from the beginning?"

"Eli gave us the keys to free ourselves," Jacob said, "but didn't explain the rules."

"That would have been too easy," Meir said. He went to the kitchen. "The kitchen is clean and there's nothing cooking on the stove. If Eli meant for you to start over, the seder meal would be waiting to be eaten again."

Baruch clapped his hands. "We just need to complete the service to end the curse!"

CHAPTER FORTY

Since Jacob and Sadie were going to grow into adults, Meir had them change their clothes. Jacob put on his father's second suit and Sadie put on the red and white dress that was on the wooden mannequin.

Meir bit the inside of his cheek to keep from smiling. Though Jacob and Sadie looked comical in oversized clothes, it didn't seem appropriate to laugh. But then, Baruch laughed, and his laughter was contagious. Everyone joined him. Jacob let his sleeves drape over his hands and he shook the loose fabric about, which led to more laughter.

Once the laughter subsided, everyone took their seat at the table. Baruch gazed out the window and then held up his hand. "We have to wait for sunset."

Rebekah left the table and stood by the window. The late afternoon sun bathed her in a golden light.

"Since our lives are coming to an end, there is something I want to tell you. Perhaps I should keep these thoughts to myself. They may make our demise more painful. But they are from my heart."

"Speak, Rebekah," Baruch said. "No matter how painful. I want to hear what you have to say."

"Me too, Mama," Sadie said.

"Yes, Mama," Jacob said. "Tell us."

Rebekah didn't seem to know what to do with her hands. She wiped them on her dress and ran her fingers through her hair. Finally, she dropped her hands to her side.

"Often, I imagined how our lives would have been if, well, if. Baruch would have opened his clothing store. Rosenfeld and Sons would have been a great success because my husband is an honest man, and he works hard. We would have moved out of this apartment into a house with a kitchen I could turn around in without bumping into something. Everyone would have had their own bedroom with real beds. The house would have had a yard. Not necessarily a large yard, but big enough for me to plant a vegetable garden."

"After all these years, you still surprise me," Baruch said. "I never knew you wanted to grow vegetables."

Rebekah put her hands on her hips. "I told you I wanted to grow vegetables. You just don't remember."

Baruch shrugged helplessly. "I'm sorry. Continue."

"Nathan would have married Edna Oxenhandler," Rebekah said. "Edna would have been a good wife. She would have given him many beautiful children."

"And I would have had to give Nathan many raises to afford those children," Baruch said.

"Actually, Papa," Nathan said. "I had other plans. I was going to take a job at Frankel's Bakery."

Baruch gaped at Nathan. "Is this true?"

"Oh, Papa," Sadie said. "Everybody in the whole building knew but you."

Baruch shook his head. "Nobody tells me nothing."

"I imagined Nathan someday owning his own bakery," Rebekah said. "Every week, he would bring us a freshly baked challah for the Sabbath meal. The sweet smell would fill our home and bring us great joy."

"I would need something sweet after working my fingers to the bone alone all week at the clothing store," Baruch said.

"You wouldn't be alone. You still have another son. Jacob would be by your side. He would have grown up to be the most handsome man in New York. Rosenfeld and Son would be filled with women eager to have him wait on them."

The family laughed, even Jacob.

"What about me, Mama?" Sadie asked. "Did I marry and give you lots of grandchildren?"

Rebekah gazed at her daughter. "You, Sadie. You studied hard and went to college. Then, as you traveled the world, you wrote me long letters of your adventures in London, Paris, Rome, and Jerusalem. Eventually, you settled in one place long enough to compile your stories into popular books."

Sadie stood and hugged Rebekah.

Meir swallowed the lump in his throat. He silently prayed to HaShem to give him strength for what was about to transpire. When the sun was safely below the horizon, Baruch took Eli's handmade matzo and broke it into pieces. He handed a piece to everyone at the table.

"Now we will eat the afikomen," Baruch said.

Nathan studied his piece of matzo.

"We haven't been able to eat for decades. How will we eat this?"

"You can eat it because eating the homemade matzo is part of the seder service," Meir said, "which makes it one of the tasks you must complete."

"Wait," Jacob said, "you have to give a reward to whoever found the afikomen."

"You're right," Baruch said. "It's a tradition, so it must be one of the tasks as well."

He reached into his pocket, took out a Buffalo nickel, and handed it to Meir. The date on the coin was 1916, but it was shiny and new.

"You found the afikomen. You get the reward."

"But you were the one who removed it from its hiding place," Meir said.

"I was only able to do so because you figured out how to make it appear. Take the nickel. You earned it."

"I will cherish it." Meir put the coin in his pocket.

Jacob left the table and went to the window. "Let's see if the task worked." He banged on the windowpane. "Hey! You down there. Can you hear me?"

He came back to the table.

"Nu?" Nathan asked. "Could they hear you?"

"A man looked at me and did this with his hand," Jacob said. He raised his middle finger.

Baruch, Nathan, and Meir laughed, Jacob and Sadie looked confused, and Rebekah scowled.

"He definitely heard you," Nathan said.

There was a moment of hesitation before everyone ate their piece of matzo. Meir wasn't sure if it was because they were embarking on the final journey of their lives or if it was because of the rank smell coming from the matzo.

"This tastes terrible," Jacob said. "But not as terrible as I thought it would."

"Time for the third cup of wine," Baruch said.

He picked up the bottle of wine and filled his wineglass to the brim. He passed the bottle to Rebekah. She did the same. The bottle traveled around the table. Once everyone's glass was filled to the brim, Baruch recited the *Bircas HaMazon*.

They continued the service. When it was time to drink the third cup of wine. They recited the *Borei pri Hagafen* and drank while reclining to the left.

The bottle was passed around again, and everyone filled their glasses to the brim for the fourth and final cup of wine. Baruch filled an extra cup of wine and set it in the middle of the table.

"Elijah's Cup," Baruch said. "Jacob. Open the door so that the spirit of the prophet may enter our home and sip from this glass."

Jacob rose from his chair and opened the apartment door. He gasped. "There's a man standing in the hallway," he said.

Everyone at the table peered at the open door, but the clouds made the hallway too dark to see who was out there.

"Invite him in," Baruch said.

"No!" Jacob said. He slammed the door shut and returned to his seat.

Baruch started to rise, but Meir held up his hand.

"I think I know who it is," Meir said. "Let me talk to him."

"Don't go," Jacob pleaded.

"It's okay. He's not here for me."

CHAPTER FORTY-ONE

Meir stepped out the apartment and closed the door. Except for a semi-circle just outside the door, the hallway was shrouded in clouds. Meir could feel temperature for the first time since entering the bubble. It was freezing cold. His breath came out as puffs of air. But it wasn't wintertime. The cold was caused by the tall man standing in the hallway.

He wore a rumpled black raincoat, a wrinkled black suit, scuffed black shoes, and a black slouch hat. A rose pinned to the suit's lapel was so old and dried up petals flaked off and drifted to the ground. He had lines so deep in his face that streams could run down them. His eyes were a pale blue. Meir knew an angel could appear in any form they wanted and was relieved that this one chose to have only two eyes. In his true form, the Angel of Death was full of eyes so that he could see all creatures.

Meir took a deep breath to calm his nerves. "Shall I address you as *Malach Adonai?*" he asked. "Or as *Mavet?*"

The angel gave a weary shrug. "Call me Marvin. Marvin Edelbaum. I collected a Marvin Edelbaum recently and I like the name."

His baritone voice reminded Meir of the distant rumble of a train that he heard occasionally late at night when he was about to go to sleep.

"Marvin," Meir said.

"Marvin Edelbaum. It sounds best if you say the entire name. It rolls off the tongue as if you were announcing a destination. Where are you off to today? I'm going to Marvin Edelbaum if it doesn't rain."

"I'm sorry. Marvin Edelbaum."

"I'm kidding. You can call me Marvin."

Meir rubbed his arms to generate some warmth. "I knew you would be coming but didn't think you would appear to us."

Marvin examined his nails. He had long slender fingers. "This is a unique situation. I've waited a long time for this family."

"They've been waiting a long time too."

"Jacob Rosenfeld prayed many years for me to take him yet when I come to his door, he slams it in my face."

"You must have heard what his father said. Now that the time has come, he clings to life."

Marvin took a pack of cigarettes from his suit, shook one out, and lit it. He sucked on the cigarette and exhaled. The smoke joined the clouds. "Even if Jacob had listened to Baruch and invited me in, I wouldn't have accepted. I will wait until the bubble breaks." He waved his cigarette at the doorframe. "In keeping with the original purpose of the lamb's blood."

"But you won't be passing over them tonight," Meir said.

As Marvin drew on his cigarette, he made a sucking sound and Meir thought he could hear the echo of death rattles and women wailing.

"I will not," Marvin said as he exhaled. "Go inside. Finish the service. Tell Jacob I will see him soon and that I wasn't insulted when he slammed the door shut. I'm used to such behavior."

Meir stopped feeling cold the second he re-entered the apartment. He joined the family at the dining table.

"Was that…him?" Jacob asked.

"It was," Meir said. "He said he didn't mind that you shut the door in his face."

Jacob hung his head. "I didn't mean to be rude."

Meir looked at the two bottles of potion on the mantle. "We're getting close to the end of the service. Does anyone want a potion?"

"Not me," Nathan said.

The others shook their heads.

"We haven't felt hunger or cold, or pain, or desire for a hundred years," Baruch said. "This is our last chance to feel anything."

"Okay," Meir said. "Let's pick up where we left off."

"Wait," Rebekah said. She took the anti-aging potion from the mantle. "What if only one of us drank the potion?"

Meir sucked in his breath. "Just one of you?"

Rebekah placed her hand on her chest. "I have no intention of drinking it. Before we became trapped, I lived a good life. I have a wonderful husband and three excellent children. I'm ready to die. But what if one of the younger children drank the potion? Would that save them?"

Meir had suggested this to Rabbi Katzerman, but she said it wasn't his decision to make. She was right. It was the Rosenfelds.

"There's no way to know for certain," Meir said, "but it's possible that a person would age slower and live a little longer. Maybe for a day at most. More likely, just a few hours. What's more, they can't start drinking it until the moment the bubble bursts."

Rebekah looked at Baruch. He nodded. She faced her family. "Either Jacob or Sadie will drink the potion. They are the youngest."

"Sadie should drink the potion," Jacob said.

"No, Jacob should drink the potion," Sadie said.

Rebekah handed the bottle to Meir. "Give it to Sadie," she said. "She has the best chance to live long enough to leave the apartment."

"Mama's right," Nathan said. "Give it to Sadie."

The family faced Sadie. Her eyes welled up with tears.

"I don't want to leave you. I don't want to die alone."

"You won't die alone," Rebekah said. "Meir will be with you. Won't you, Meir?"

Meir felt a small ray of hope. Here was an opportunity to get at least one member of the family out of the apartment alive. "Absolutely," he said.

Sadie glanced at Meir and then held out her hands toward her family. "It's not the same. He's not my family."

"Please, Sadie," Nathan said. "If you can escape, even for a moment, then you must do it."

"He's right," Jacob said. "When you leave, our hearts will go with you."

Sadie gathered up her skirt and shuffled over to the pile of books that she used as her daily calendar. She opened the book on the top of the shelf and took out a postcard. She shuffled back and handed it to Meir.

"If I'm going to leave my family then this is where I want to go," she said.

Meir studied the postcard. "Coney Island?"

Baruch chuckled through the tears that had started to fall down his face. "I had promised to take the family there the Sunday after Passover. Sadie was looking forward to it more than anyone else."

"This card shows the entrance to Luna Park," Meir said. "The original Luna Park burned down a long time ago, but Coney Island is still an amusement park."

"I don't care about the rides," Sadie said. "I just want to see it. And I want to see the beach. I've never been to one. Before I die, I want to feel sand on my toes."

Meir nodded. "Okay. I'll take you to Coney Island." He tried to give the postcard back to Sadie, but she waved her hand.

"You hang onto it," she said. "That way we won't lose it."

Meir put the card in his jacket pocket. "Do you mind if Esther joins us? She would love to meet you."

Sadie smiled. "That would be lovely. If she hadn't seen me at the window, then you wouldn't be here."

"Come," Baruch said, gesturing at the table. "Let us finish the seder."

"Wait," Jacob said.

He retrieved his blanket from the corner of the room and handed it to Sadie. "Take this with you."

Sadie held the blanket to her chest. "Are you sure?"

"We shared my secret. It belongs to you as much as it does to me."

Sadie turned to Meir. "Will you carry this for me as well?" she asked.

"What is it?"

"Jacob's blanket. That's all I can tell you."

Meir glanced at the others. Baruch shrugged. Meir stuffed the blanket into his satchel.

"Are we ready now?" Baruch asked.

"We're ready," Rebekah said.

Everyone returned to their places at the table. Rebekah drank the wine in Elijah's Cup in one long gulp and wiped her mouth with her napkin. She filled the cup with pink anti-aging potion and placed the cup and the bottle in front of Sadie.

They continued the service with the *Hallal*. When they reached the time to drink the fourth and final cup of wine, they said the prayer for wine and then leaned to the left as they drank.

Then it was time for the *Nirtzah* and one final prayer.

"L'shanah haba'ah b'Yerushalayim!" they said in unison.

Next year in Jerusalem. Meir was sure none of the Rosenfelds missed the irony.

The seder and the curse were officially over.

CHAPTER FORTY-TWO

"Sadie!" Meir said. "Drink the potion."

Her eyelids fluttered as her facial features shifted.

"Hurts," she mumbled. "Hurts."

Meir took the cup and held Sadie's mouth open as he poured the potion down her throat. Some of the precious liquid spilled down her chin and onto her dress.

The clock on the mantle began ticking again. The hands spun faster and faster until they flew off the face and cracked the glass cover. Dust gathered on every object. Coal soot covered Sadie's slashes on the wall as the wallpaper faded and then peeled off in chunks. The foul stench of mildew, decay, rotting food, and aging bodies brought tears to Meir's eyes. The curse was broken, and an ocean of time was rushing into the Rosenfelds' apartment.

The lights flickered and then went out as the lamps burned through the rapidly dwindling supply of gas. The apartment was dimly illuminated by light coming from the streetlamps outside the windows. Meir felt a month's worth of hunger and exhaustion, but the adrenaline coursing through his system pushed them aside.

The Rosenfelds hunched over and moaned. Hair poured from their heads, cascading over their shoulders and down their backs. Their fingernails grew into long twisted strands. Jacob and Sadie sped past puberty toward adulthood. Their bodies grew, and their faces matured. Crackling noises signaled that their bones were expanding.

Meir managed to get Sadie to drink another cup of potion.

"It still hurts," she said, "but not as much." Her voice had matured from a child to a teenager.

Meir poured a third cup. Sadie had gained enough strength from the potion to drink it on her own.

"We have to go," Meir said.

Sadie stood, wobbled, and slumped back into her chair. "I can't control my legs. They're still growing."

"I'll carry you," Meir said. He slung his satchel over his shoulder and reached for Sadie.

She pushed him away. "Wait."

"Time is not on our side," Meir said.

"I have to say goodbye."

The family was buried in age, their skin mottled and wrinkled. Their clothes had dissolved into strips of fabric and hung on skeletal bodies that hadn't eaten anything in decades besides the matzo and wine they consumed at the end of tonight's seder. Even seated, Meir could see that Jacob had grown taller than his father. Despite their intense pain, the family had managed to grasp each other's hands.

"Goodbye, Mama, goodbye, Papa," Sadie said. "Goodbye my sweet brothers. I love you all."

"Saaaaadie," Baruch whispered. And then he died.

His face shriveled, and his mouth hung open as death ravished him. Meir was equally horrified and fascinated. He was reminded of nature films in which time-lapse photography showed how a dead animal decomposed, with the flesh rotting away to expose the skeleton underneath.

Baruch was quickly followed in death by Rebekah. Her body

slumped against her husband. Death rattles announced the demise of Nathan and Jacob.

Meir reached for Sadie—he needed to get her out of the apartment. She didn't resist him this time as he lifted her out of the chair. She wasn't heavy, but he could feel her body shifting underneath her dress. Her hair flowed to her waist. She put her arm around his shoulder and rested her head against his chest.

The clouds in the hallway were gone. Meir stopped at the top of the stairs and looked over his shoulder in time to see Marvin Edlebaum entering the apartment. A wave of guilt washed over Meir. Whether he had done it for mercy or necessity, the bald fact was that he had delivered death to this family. He rushed down the stairs with Sadie in his arms.

They set off an alarm when they exited the building. The clanging echoed off the surrounding buildings. Though it was still dark, Meir could detect the damp scent of dawn approaching. Sadie took a deep breath of outside air.

"The city smells wonderful," she said.

To Meir's surprise, Feintuch hobbled toward them.

"Is this the little girl?" Feintuch asked. "She's not so little."

Meir put Sadie on the sidewalk and took the anti-aging potion from his satchel. Though her face was too thin, she had grown into a beautiful woman. "She's aging," Meir said. "Here, Sadie. Drink some more." He held the bottle for her as she swallowed more potion.

"I was supposed to stop you," Feintuch said. "That's what Rabbi Chaim told me to do. Instead, I defied him and did nothing. I'm not doing anything for anybody ever again."

"Will you hail me a cab?" Meir asked.

"Certainly."

Feintuch hailed a cab. That was one of the good things about New York. There were cabs on the street twenty-four hours a day. The driver wore a turban on his head and had deep bags under his eyes. If he noticed the alarm from the Tenement Museum, he didn't show it. Meir picked up Sadie and placed her inside the cab. He slid in next to her.

"Where to?" the cab driver asked.

"Coney Island," Meir said. "But first, stop by the closest open bodega."

Feintuch waved goodbye to Meir and Sadie as the cab drove away from 97 Orchard Street.

"Goodbye, my home," Sadie said. "My prison."

Once the car turned onto Delancey Street, Sadie pointed out to Meir the details of the modern world that fascinated her most. This included the video screen on the back of the seat, the feel of the cab's vinyl seats, the jerk of the cab coming to a stop, the other cars on the street, the traffic lights, the colorful billboards, the smorgasbord of stores that lined the streets, and the few night owls and early risers on the sidewalks.

The cab stopped at a bodega that was an oasis of light on a dark corner.

"I'll be right back," Meir said.

He ran inside and bought an armload of sports drinks. The cashier was a bored young man who rang them up and put them in a plastic bag. Once Meir was back in the car, he opened one of the bottles and handed it to Sadie.

"What is this?" she asked.

Meir realized she wouldn't be familiar with a plastic container or a sports drink.

"The liquid in this bottle will work with the slow growth potion to restore some of your electrolytes," he said.

"My electric lights?"

"Something like that. There's electricity in our bodies."

Sadie peered at the bright green liquid inside the bottle. "It looks like pickle juice," she said.

"I guess it does," Meir said. He took the bottle back from her. "Here. Let me open it for you."

Her eyes grew wide as he twisted the cap off. Meir handed her the bottle, and she sipped the green liquid. "It's not terrible."

Meir opened a bottle of red liquid and drank. He needed the electrolytes as well. Taking out his cellphone, Meir saw he had a signal again. He dialed Esther's number. It rang so many times, he was sure it would go to voicemail, but then Gus answered.

"What the hell?" he said in a sleepy voice. "Do you know what time it is?"

"Actually, I don't."

"It's 4:00 a.m. Who the hell is this?"

"Rabbi Meir Poppers."

Gus's attitude changed immediately. "Meir? You're out? Hold on. Esther. Esther. Wake up. It's Meir."

He heard fumbling and then Esther was on the phone. She sounded wide awake. "Are you still at the apartment?"

"The time bubble has been popped," Meir said. "Sadie and I are on our way to Coney Island."

Esther gasped. "Sadie? She's with you?"

"She doesn't have much time. Can you meet us at Coney Island?"

"Where? Coney Island is a big place."

"On the beach by Luna Park."

"We're on our way."

Esther hung up. Meir put his phone away. Sadie was watching him. There was pain in her eyes.

"You were right. There's just too much time to catch up with. I can feel my body aging. Will I live long enough to see the beach?"

"Don't worry," Meir said. "I know a shortcut."

He recited the kefitzat ha-derekh. The cab driver yelped in shock. They were on Surf Avenue at the entrance to Luna Park. Meir paid the startled driver, got his satchel and bag of sports drinks, and scooped Sadie out of the car.

"Let me stand for a moment," Sadie said.

He placed her on the sidewalk in front of the ticket office. She linked her arm with Meir's as if they were on a date. She pointed at the electric sign above the entrance, four circular star bursts with the word Luna wrapped around the bottom of the circles.

"They always made me think of flowers," Sadie said.

Meir recited a spell that sent a jolt of electricity into the sign. A multitude of tiny lights came to life and created the illusion of flowers blooming in various colors. As bright and colorful as the lights were, they were nowhere near as bright as the smile on Sadie's face.

"Wonderful," she said. "Now take me to the beach."

Meir lifted Sadie into his arms and carried her toward the boardwalk. Along the way she waved at the rides and read the names written on them as if she were reciting the words to a magic spell.

"Cyclone. Thunderbolt. Steeplechase. Oooh, The Tickler."

"Can you smell it?" Meir asked. "Salty and wet?"

She breathed in. "The ocean?"

"We're almost there."

They came to the boardwalk. Meir clomped across the wooden slates, down a short flight of stairs, and onto the beach. With lights from the boardwalk behind them, their shadows trekked ahead of them as Meir marched passed benches and volleyball nets until he reached the ocean.

He set her down so that the water washed over her bare feet and soaked the bottom of her dress.

"It's cold!" Sadie said.

"I'm sorry," Meir said.

"I love it. I haven't felt hot or cold for so long."

He waited for a few more waves to lap up her feet before he carried Sadie away from the ocean and placed her on the beach. Meir's sneakers and socks were soaked. Sand caked the legs of his pants. Sadie wiggled her toes. She picked up seashells and rubbed her fingers over their bumpy surface. She smiled shyly at Meir.

"That night I kissed you," she said.

"I remember," Meir said.

"I was pretending you were my boyfriend, Hershel."

"You had a boyfriend?"

Sadie shook her head. "Not a real boyfriend. Only in my mind. When you appeared at our door, my first thought was that you looked exactly how I imagined Herschel would look." Sadie winced and Meir felt her bones shift. "I used to imagine that he brought me to Coney Island."

"And here we are," Meir said.

"Would you mind terribly if I called you Herschel?"

Sadie had aged from a young woman to a mature woman, though she was too emaciated to fill her dress.

"I don't mind at all," Meir said.

They drank sports drinks as they watched seagulls float over the ocean. It was dark where they sat, but they were surrounded by the electric lights in the apartment buildings and the streetlamps on the boardwalk.

"I feel a chill, Herschel," Sadie said. "Would you put your arm around me?"

Meir answered by wrapping his arms around her. Her bony hands clutched his forearms, and she had a sour smell.

"Let me know if I'm holding you too tightly," Meir said.

"I dreamed of this moment," Sadie said. "So many times. I can't believe it finally came true."

They sat silently and listened to the waves and the gulls calling each other. The sun broke the horizon creating streaks of pink and orange. The ocean sparkled.

Sadie closed her eyes. Meir heard someone shouting his name. He turned. Esther and Gus were running toward them. When they reached Meir and Sadie, Esther saw Sadie's eyes were closed and dropped to her knees.

"I'm too late," Esther said.

Sadie's eyes flickered open. "Too late for what?"

Esther's lower lip quivered as she reached out and touched Sadie's arm. "Hello, Sadie," Esther said. "No matter what age you are, I know it's you."

Sadie squinted at Esther. "Alma? I'm sorry. That's not your name. Meir told me, but I forgot."

"My name is Esther."

"Do you mind if I call you Alma? It's easier to remember."

Esther looked at Meir.

"I'll explain later," he said.

She turned back to Sadie. "I don't mind at all. I can't believe I'm really here with the girl with the yellow ribbon who waved at me from the window."

"And you waved back."

Sadie patted Meir's arm. "Give her Jacob's blanket," she said.

Meir took the folded blanket from his satchel and handed it to Esther.

"I couldn't take this," Esther said.

"Please. I trust you to take good care of it."

Esther hugged the blanket. Gus put his arms around his wife.

"Who is that handsome man?" Sadie asked.

"This is my husband, Gus."

"Pleased to meet you," Gus said.

Sadie looked up at Meir and whispered, "Does he know about Roland?"

It took him a moment to remember that Roland was the name the Rosenfelds had given Stan Jolly.

"It's okay. Alma and Roland are just good friends."

Gus nodded at Meir. "I see you're growing your hair out."

Meir touched his hair and beard. Time had caught up with him as well. He had over a month's worth of untended growth.

"How does it look?" Meir asked.

"I liked it better shorter," Esther said.

Ocean waves pounded the shore. Early morning joggers hurried past them. Meir could feel Sadie's body shifting again. She closed her eyes and arched her back. She groaned and dug her fingers into Meir's arm. Esther and Gus watched in amazement as Sadie's hair turn gray and crow's feet formed around her eyes. Age spots appeared on her hands. Her body shrank.

"Did she drink the anti-aging potion?" Esther asked.

"She did," Meir said. "It's working better than I thought it would."

Sadie opened her eyes. She had aged into an old woman. Esther moved closer to Sadie and held her wrinkled hand.

"I wish I could have done more for you," Esther said.

"Meir told me you studied Jewish history," Sadie said.

Esther smiled. "That's right. I did."

"Then you must know the song we sing at Passover," Sadie said. "*Dayenu*."

"Dayenu means it would have been enough."

Sadie squeezed Esther's hand as she gazed at the ocean. "If you had only seen me in the window and acknowledged my existence, dayenu. If you had only found Rabbi Poppers and asked him to find me, dayenu. If I had only taken one step out of the apartment, dayenu."

Meir could feel Sadie's body shifting again. Her hair turned white and clumps of it fell out. The wind carried the strands across the sand. Her dress hung on her shriveled frame.

"And I came to Coney Island. Just like Papa promised me I would. I got to feel the sand on my toes. I spent the day with Herschel and Alma. Dayenu."

Sadie closed her eyes for the last time and let go of Esther's hand.

Gus held Esther in his arms as she sobbed. Meir was crushed. He knew Sadie's death was coming, but he was still consumed with grief. He felt like he'd lost a family member. He gently rocked her withered body as he listened to the waves crashing against the shore.

When the restaurants and souvenir shops along the boardwalk began to open, they stood and wiped the sand off their clothes. Meir felt sticky and worn out. Esther and Gus had driven to Coney Island in the El Plato de Oro van. Gus went to a shop and bought beach towels. They carefully wrapped Sadie in the towels and placed her in the back of the van. Esther hugged Meir.

"I'll call Rabbi Fruman and arrange for Sadie to have a Jewish burial at Falk Yeshiva's graveyard," Meir said.

"We'll drive you there," Esther said. "Right, Gus?"

"Of course," Gus said.

"I don't know what to do about the rest of the family," Meir said. "I suppose I could find a way to get into the museum and collect their remains."

Esther put her hand on Meir's arm. "The museum will figure out what to do with them. Bury Sadie. Dayenu."

CHAPTER FORTY-THREE

They had just passed Secaucus when the sports drinks and adrenaline that had kept Meir going since leaving the Rosenfelds' apartment wore off and he struggled to keep from passing out. Also, everyone noticed how bad Meir smelled from not bathing for over a month.

"I'm going to use the shortening of the way before I pass out," Meir said.

"Camilla told me about this," Esther said. "I've been wondering what it's like."

He recited the kefitzat ha-derekh.

"Wow!" Gus said. "That was fast."

"If I could do this, I would never sit in traffic," Esther said.

They had gone from driving on a highway through an industrial landscape in New Jersey to a forest back road in rolling tree-covered hills in upstate New York. They came to an iron gate. The gate swung open.

"They're expecting us," Meir said.

Once beyond the gate, they drove over a hill and got their first clear view of Falk Yeshiva. It looked like any mid-size college in America with wide sidewalks connecting a series of Neo-Georgian structures. Students studied or played frisbee on lush green lawns.

"That's your school?" Esther asked.

"Yes," Meir said. "That's it."

"I can't believe it."

"Why? What were you expecting?"

"I don't know. A castle?"

The road ended in front of a white building with a domed roof and a large Star of David over the entrance. A group of people waited for them in front of the structure. Meir's heart sank when he saw the gurney for Sadie. Another sign that she was gone.

Gus parked the van. He and Esther got out. Rabbi Zelig Fruman stepped forward. He wore his Met's logo ballcap and had rubber bands in his beard.

"Welcome to Falk Yeshiva," Zelig said. "May I see the body?"

Gus opened the back of the van. Zelig peeled back the beach towel covering the body. "Nu? This is Sadie Rosenfeld? A lovely woman."

"She must be handled carefully," Meir said.

"She will be."

Sadie's body was loaded onto the gurney and wheeled away to the mortuary.

"The funeral will be held tomorrow," Zelig said. "Gus. Esther. I hope you can stay and join us. We have guest rooms that are quite comfortable."

Esther and Gus nodded.

"We wouldn't miss it for the world," Esther said.

"Excellent," Zelig said. "My students will show you to your room."

A boy wearing a wool cap and girl wearing a bucket hat stepped forward. Meir wondered if he had looked as young as they did, when he was a student here.

"Dinner is at seven," Zelig said. "I hope you're not vegetarians.

We serve the best brisket you'll ever taste."

"It's true," Meir said. "The brisket is the most magical thing they create at Falk Yeshiva."

"As long as it's not chicken," Gus said. "I'm still not ready to eat chicken again."

He and Esther followed the two students toward the dormitories.

Zelig turned to Meir. "Come," Zelig said. "We have a room ready for you in the infirmary. After you clean up and rest, our medical staff wants to look you over."

As they walked, Meir couldn't believe he was back at Falk Yeshiva. He had come here right after his bar mitzvah. For years, the school had been his entire world.

"I'd never done anything as difficult as entering a time bubble," Meir said. "If I'd had more experience, I would have done a better job."

Zelig put his hand on Meir's shoulder. "There's a first time for everything."

"I know. But why do I feel guilty?"

"We never feel like we've done enough. You did a good job because you're alive and the time bubble is no more. The fact that a member of the family lived for more than a few minutes outside the bubble shows that you succeeded beyond expectations. Your training at Falk Yeshiva served you well."

"Thank you, Rabbi."

"Besides, we were standing by in case something went wrong."

Meir stopped walking. "You were watching me?"

Zelig nodded. "Sure. If you hadn't gotten out of the time bubble, I would have gone in and rescued you."

"How long would you have waited before you came in to help me?"

Zelig squinted at the sky. "I suppose I would have waited a year. That should have given you plenty of time to figure it out on your own."

"Why didn't you tell me this before I went into the bubble?"

"I didn't want you to think we didn't believe in you."

Meir felt dizzy and had to hold onto Zelig to keep from falling.

"I didn't mean to upset you," Zelig said.

"It's not that," Meir said. "Time is catching up with me."

"Let's get you to the infirmary."

Meir stayed still. "One more thing, Rabbi. From what the Rosenfelds told me, I am certain that it was a Worms who trapped them in the time bubble."

Zelig stroked his beard. "We came to the same conclusion. Why else would the Worms have tried so hard to keep you from helping the family?"

"They said his name was Eli. Have you ever heard of him?"

Zelig snorted. "I'm sure that's not his name."

"What should we do?"

"You have done enough. Let us deal with it kishef macher sect to kishef macher sect."

They continued to the infirmary.

Once the doctor on staff saw that Meir wasn't at death's door, she took him to his room. The room wasn't as nice as the New York Hilton Midtown, but compared to the Rosenfelds' three-room apartment, it was luxurious and spacious.

Meir took off his shoes. There was sand from Coney Island in them. He poured the sand into a wastebasket. As Meir removed his clothes, he found the Buffalo nickel that Baruch had given him in his pants pocket, and Sadie's Coney Island postcard in his jacket. He put them in his satchel.

After a long hot shower, he put on the clean T-shirt and sweatpants that had been provided for him. He was about to go to bed when there was a knock on his door.

"Come in," Meir said.

Rabbi Rhea Katzerman entered.

"You made it," she said.

"I did," Meir replied.

She sat in a chair and Meir sat on the bed.

"Did you give them the anti-aging potion?" Rhea asked.

"Only Sadie," Meir said. "It was the family's idea."

"I'm not accusing you of talking them into it."

Meir rubbed his forehead. "I'm sorry, Rabbi. I'm not thinking clearly."

Rhea stood. "Of course. We should talk after you've had a chance to rest." She narrowed her eyes at him. "Before I go, I have to ask. Did you also make the instant death potion?"

"I did," Meir said.

"Did anybody take it?"

Meir shook his head. "None of them wanted it."

"What did you do with the potion?"

"It's in my satchel."

Rhea's eyes widened. "I'll be right back."

She left the room and came back shortly wearing a pair of rubber gloves. She carefully took the half pint bottle of instant death potion out of Meir's satchel.

"I will make sure this is properly neutralized," she said. "Now get some rest."

Meir got under the clean sheets and turned out the lights. He began to go over everything that had happened that day, but sleep claimed him immediately.

CHAPTER FORTY-FOUR

Meir gazed at his reflection in the mirror. Rabbi Fruman had lent him a suit to wear to Sadie's funeral. The pants didn't cover his ankles, and he could have hidden a basketball inside the jacket, but he appreciated his former teacher's generosity. At least Meir still had his trusty Trilby hat.

There was a knock at the door. Was it time for the service already? He thought he still had more time. Opening the door, he was surprised to see the student with the bucket hat. Standing behind her was Esther Luna. She carried a large shopping bag.

"I brought Esther to see you," the student said.

"We need to talk," Esther said.

Meir gestured. "Come on in."

Esther glanced at the student with the bucket hat. "Thank you, Hanna. I never would have found him without you."

"No problem," Hanna said. She waved and walked away.

Esther entered Meir's room.

"Nice dress," Meir said.

Esther wore a floral dress.

"Rabbi Katzerman lent it to me," Esther said. "She has good taste."

"What did you want to see me about?"

Esther took the blanket that Sadie had given her out of the shopping bag. "What do you know about this?"

Meir remembered what Jacob said to Sadie as he handed it to her.

"We shared my secret. It belongs to you as much as it does to me."

"Not much," Meir said.

Esther unfolded the blanket on Meir's bed. Meir gawked at Jacob's portrait of the Rosenfeld family. He appreciated the skill and dedication that went into creating the artwork, but since he had spent time with the Rosenfelds, he could see how perfectly Jacob had captured Baruch's crooked smile, Rebekah's kind eyes, Nathan's dour expression, Sadie's curiosity, and his own impish grin by stitching together hundreds of small strips of fabric. He even managed to include the ribbon in Sadie's hair with a bit of yellow silk.

"When me and Gus unfolded it last night, we freaked out," Esther said. "Look. He even stitched his name in the corner. Jacob Rosenfeld."

"Truly a work of art," Meir said. "I had no idea he'd done it. I remember my first impression of him was still waters run deep."

"Why did Sadie give it to me? She should have given it to you."

Meir went to his satchel and took out the Coney Island post card. He handed it to Esther.

"She gave me this," he said.

"A postcard?"

"Sadie pretended it was from her secret boyfriend. She trusted me with her secret and Jacob's secret with you. It makes sense. You were the one who found her and her family. She knew she could trust you."

"I'll do my best."

Esther carefully folded the blanket and put it back into the shopping bag.

"Is it okay to mention that you look terrible in that suit?" she asked.

"You're only saying it because it's true," Meir said.

There was another knock on the door. Rabbi Zelig Fruman entered before Meir could let him in. He grinned at Meir.

"You look good in that suit," Zelig said. "Almost as good as I do."

Esther giggled.

"Thank you, Rabbi," Meir said.

"Come on," Zelig said. "It's time to bury your friend Sadie."

CHAPTER FORTY-FIVE

A week had passed since Sadie Rosenfeld's funeral, and Esther Luna was still thinking about her. She had Jacob Rosenfeld's blanket framed in a glass case and decided to hang it in her apartment.

"I don't know, Esther," Gus said. "It feels like it belongs in a museum."

"I agree," Esther said. "But no museum is going to take artwork from an unknown artist."

Gus studied the blanket. "What about one of those outsider museums? They're always looking for self-taught artists who created masterpieces out of old underwear and chewing gum."

Esther crossed her arms. "It's not a bad idea, but for now, I want it here. Hold it up against the wall so I can see how it looks."

Gus held the framed art against the living room wall while Esther scrutinized the position from the other side of the room. Flan the cat slept on the couch and ignored them.

"A little higher," Esther said.

Gus inched it a little higher.

"A little to the left."

Gus inched it a little to the left.

"Make up your mind," Gus said. "My arms are getting tired."

"Hold it right there," Esther said. She came over and marked the top of the frame with a pencil.

Esther sat on the couch while Gus hammered in nails and hung Jacob's blanket. Despite the noise, Flan stayed asleep. When Gus was done, he joined Esther on the couch.

"I've been thinking," Esther said.

"Don't hurt yourself," Gus said.

Esther rolled her eyes at the old joke they shared.

"I feel like there's something else I can do for the Rosenfelds."

"What are you talking about? You did enough. Like Sadie said, 'Dag nab you.'"

Esther snorted. "The word is dayenu. It's not that I should do more. I'm not ready to let go of them."

"I can tell from that look in your eye, you have an idea."

Esther grinned. "I want to write a book about them. I've already done the research."

Gus gawked at Esther. "You can't write about what happened. People will think you're crazy."

"Camilla won't."

"Okay. Everyone in our respective families won't think so, but the rest of the world will."

Esther laughed. "Don't worry. I won't write about the time bubble. I'll write about how they disappeared, and how nobody knows what became of them." She gestured at the artwork. "I'll write about Jacob's blanket."

"How are you going to explain where you got the blanket?"

Esther shrugged. "I haven't figured out that part yet. But I already know what the title is going to be. *The Orchard Street Mystery*."

"Isn't that the title of Bertha Rose's book?"

"You can't copyright a title."

Gus rubbed his mustache. "You know. I think it's a great idea. People love a real-life mystery."

Esther draped her arm over Gus's shoulder. "Thank you. I can't do this without you."

Gus kissed his wife. "I got your back."

"I never mentioned this before, but Meir told me what you said to him when we first met him in Atlanta."

Gus's face turned red. "That mamabicho!"

"He said you threatened to beat his ass if he told me."

"I might have to do that."

"If you did, he might turn you into a frog."

"He can't do that." Gus's eyes widened. "Wait. Maybe he can."

"The point is you were wrong. Sadie had nothing to do with Sophie. I was sad when Sophie died, but women often lose the baby the first time they get pregnant."

Gus gazed into Esther's eyes. "Do you think you might ever want to try again?"

Esther kissed her husband. "I always thought we would."

"Any idea when?"

"Now is as good a time as any."

Gus grinned. "Now. As in right now?"

Esther pointed at Jacob's blanket. "In front of the Rosenfelds? No way."

CHAPTER FORTY-SIX

Two weeks had passed since Sadie Rosenfeld's funeral and Meir was almost ready to go home to Atlanta. The medical staff at Falk Yeshiva told him he shouldn't suffer any long-term effects from his month and a half inside the time bubble, but he should take it easy for a few weeks. Meir had said his goodbyes and was now back in New York City to take care of a few last details.

First, he got a proper haircut and his beard trimmed by a professional. Then he went to Yonah Schimmel's. He loved their potato knishes. He had meant to go before he entered the time bubble but hadn't gotten around to it.

The dining area was a cramped space with barely enough room for the tables and chairs. There were stacks of cardboard boxes in the back. Yellowing photos and framed newspaper articles cluttered the walls. The welcoming warm scent from generations of baked dough had seeped into every nook and cranny of the aging building.

With his satchel and rolling suitcase beside him, Meir ate his knish and flipped through a copy of *The New York Times*. He looked for any stories about the Tenement Museum. He found none. He had checked local and national news every day since the curse on the Rosenfelds' had ended. So far, the only report that he'd seen had been in *The New York Post* on the day after.

The paper reported a break-in at the Tenement Museum. The intruder set off the alarm. Museum officials said nothing was stolen or damaged. There was no mention of the sudden appearance of four ancient corpses and rotting, turn-of-the-century furniture in a fourth story apartment.

How the Tenement Museum and the police department had managed to keep this bizarre discovery from leaking to the public had been a mystery to Meir until he spoke to Stan Jolly. He informed Meir that the Tenement Museum's officials believed someone had placed the Rosenfelds' bodies and their furniture in the apartment as an elaborate prank. Nobody considered it the least bit humorous. They kept it a secret because they didn't want to give the pranksters any publicity. Meanwhile, the NYPD was carefully examining everything in the apartment.

Meir wished he could have explained everything to the museum and insist they give the Rosenfelds a proper funeral. But few people accepted the existence of kishef machers like they did in the old days. Meir knew there was no way he could convince the museum officials that he had rescued a family trapped for a hundred years.

Other than Meir and the owner, Yonah Schimmel's was empty. The owner sat on a stool behind the counter and read the paper. Meir took out his phone and called Sylvia Solomon. He had been looking forward to calling her. His heart needed the hope of making a romantic connection after what he'd been through.

"Hello, Sylvia?"

"Who is this?"

"Rabbi Meir Poppers."

"I seem to recall someone by that name. But that was a long time ago. I thought sure he had died. Otherwise, why would he have ignored all my calls?"

Meir took a sip of his coffee. "I'm sorry, Sylvia. I tried to explain that I wouldn't be reachable for an unknown amount of time. But my mission is completed, and I was hoping I could get the number of the woman you wanted me to meet."

"You're joking, right?" Sylvia said. "Did you really expect her to wait for you? She never even had a chance to meet you. This is a good woman. I introduced her to other men, men who don't turn their back on an opportunity to meet a good woman."

Meir scratched his beard. "I assume she met someone."

"Of course, she did! A nice podiatrist in Sandy Springs. She's already met his mother. I'm expecting an invitation to their wedding any day now."

"Mazel Tov for them. Do you have someone else I could meet? I'm returning to Atlanta later today."

"Even if I could find someone on such short notice, why should I bother? I can't help you if you don't meet me halfway. It's hopeless, Rabbi Poppers. Hopeless."

Meir got a lump in his throat. "You're right, Sylvia. I shouldn't have wasted your time. I can't even keep my cat from being lonely. How could I possibly imagine that I could maintain a relationship? Maybe kishef machers aren't meant to find love. Our lives are too unpredictable. I'm sorry. I'm carrying on and you have better things to do than listen to me. I'll let you go."

"No wait, Rabbi," Sylvia said. Her voice softened. "When you hired me, I did some research on kishef machers. You are a strange bunch, that's for sure."

Meir chuckled. "That's putting it mildly."

"I understand that to be a kishef macher, you have to study, but you also have to have inherited Jewish magic. Do I have that right?"

"We call it Moses mishpocha because our bloodline started with Moses."

"Not sure I buy it, but here's the thing, Rabbi Poppers. To inherit this Moses mishpocha means that there was a kishef macher in your family tree."

"My great great grandfather, Lev Poppers, was a kishef macher."

"And I assume you had a great great grandmother?"

Meir smiled. "I did. Sulah Poppers."

"Was Sulah a kishef macher?"

"No, she wasn't."

"There you go! If you alter zayde Lev could find a wife, why not you?"

Meir sighed. "Yes. Why not me?"

"I misspoke. You aren't hopeless. You're a challenge and there's nothing I like more than a challenge. I'm going to find your bashert."

Meir felt a weight lifted from his heart. "Thank you, Sylvia."

"I'll call you later. Have a good trip back to Atlanta."

Meir put his phone away and forked the last bite of his knish into his mouth. As he chewed, Beryl Stein entered the bakery. He ordered at the counter before joining Meir. Beryl's face was drawn, and his clothes looked like he'd slept in them. He looked barely strong enough to bear the satchel on his shoulder.

"Are you okay?" Meir asked. "You look terrible."

Beryl brushed away Meir's concern with a wave of his hand. "I'm fine."

The owner brought a mushroom knish and a cup of black coffee, both steaming hot, and placed them in front of Beryl who tore into the knish as if he hadn't eaten in days. Meir read the paper while Beryl ate his breakfast. When he was done, Beryl wiped his beard with a napkin and drained his coffee cup.

"I'm sorry about Gustavo Ramos. We should never have given him the Black Fly Potion."

"It caught me by surprise," Meir said. "I never thought of the Falks and the Worms as enemies."

"We aren't enemies. At least, we shouldn't be. I didn't join the Worms because I hated the Falks. I felt spiritually unfulfilled by their unOrthodox approach to Jewish magic. I needed the Worms' dedication to tradition and strict observance of Judaism."

"Do the Worms recognize the Falks as Jews?"

Beryl tapped his fingers on the table. "Some don't. But this one does."

Meir sipped his coffee. Beryl held up his cup to let the owner know that he wanted a refill. The owner came to their table, filled Beryl's cup and then Meir's without Meir asking him to, then he went back to the front counter.

"I get the impression that when I was in the time bubble, you were as busy as I was," Meir said.

Beryl nodded. "You could say that. I asked Rabbi Chaim about Sadie Rosenfeld. He said you made her up. Said she didn't exist. Meir, I have known you to be stubborn, impetuous, and not near as smart as you think you are, but I have never known you to be a liar. That's why I decided to find out for myself."

"Is that when you went to see Esther Luna?"

"Yes. I had no reason to doubt what she told me, but I had to be completely sure. Too much was at stake if I got it wrong. So, I waited on the street and watched the apartment."

Meir nodded. "I saw you."

"And I saw you. And Sadie Rosenfeld." Beryl's face darkened. "That's when I confronted Rabbi Chaim and demanded he tell the truth."

Meir chuckled. "Wish I could have heard that conversation."

Beryl shook his head. "Be glad you weren't there. He told me how the great Rabbi Ezekiel of Worms trapped the Rosenfelds and then forgot about them."

Meir felt a flush of anger. "He what?"

"Rabbi Chaim said he was too busy to remember them."

"I don't believe it. They suffered all those years for nothing. This isn't right, Beryl. The kishef macher community needs to know what he did. We can't let Rabbi Chaim keep this a secret."

Beryl held up his hand. "Calm down. Why do you think I looked like I've been run over by a truck?"

"I'm sorry. I should have asked. Why do you look worn out?"

A couple entered the restaurant, took an eternity to place their order, and then sat at a table in the back. Beryl glanced at them, then leaned forward.

"When Rabbi Chaim told me what Rabbi Ezekiel did, I was going to come to the time bubble and get you and the Rosenfelds out. Then, I was going to reveal the truth about Rabbi Ezekiel."

Meir narrowed his eyes at Beryl. "But you didn't do any of those things."

"Rabbi Chaim begged me to think it over for a couple of days before I did anything. I agreed out of respect to the Worms. Then before I could act, you burst the bubble. And Rabbi Shlomo Feintuch beat me to the punch."

"Wait. Feintuch was at 97 Orchard Street. He saw me with Sadie."

Beryl nodded. "I know. After he left you, he came back home and told the Worms what he'd seen. He said Rabbi Chaim had lied. Then, I added the rest about Rabbi Ezekiel."

"How did Rabbi Chaim react?" Meir asked.

"He denied it. He was furious we would even suggest he lied and locked himself in his office. Some of the Worms believed him. They stood outside his door and begged his forgiveness."

Now Meir understood why Beryl was so disheveled. The Worms were in the midst of a crisis.

"For weeks, the Worms were divided. They sent someone to the Rosenfelds' apartment to investigate. They found their bones, but Rabbi Chaim said that didn't prove anything. Yesterday, he finally caved and admitted everything."

"He did?" Meir said.

"Rabbi Chaim stepped down as leader of the Worms," Beryl said.

"Who took his place? Or have you decided that yet?"

Beryl scowled. "Don't laugh."

"Why would I laugh? This is serious business."

"They appointed Feintuch as our new leader. He is now officially Rabbi Shlomo of Worms."

Meir guffawed. "I'm sorry, Beryl. I know I shouldn't laugh. This is actually wonderful news. I'm sure he'll be a fine leader."

"All I know for sure is I'm still hungry. I'm going to order another knish."

"Me too."

Meir and Beryl ordered more knishes and coffee. As they waited for their food, Beryl took from his satchel a plastic bag with a Midtown Comics logo on it and handed the bag to Meir.

"You were in such a hurry to save Gus Ramos, you left these behind," Beryl said.

Inside the bag were the issues of *The Phantom Stranger*, *Moon Knight*, and *Doctor Fate* Meir had picked out at the comic book store.

"Wow. This is amazing," Meir said. "What do I owe you?"

Beryl grinned. "Nothing. It's a going away gift. Tell me you really are going this time."

"Yes. I am going home today." Meir gazed at the comic books. "You know what this means, don't you?"

"I'm almost afraid to ask. What does it mean, Meir?"

"You wouldn't have kept the comics for me if you didn't believe I'd find a way out of the time bubble."

"Is it so hard to believe that I have faith in Rabbi Meir Poppers?"

Their knishes and coffee arrived. They put aside their burdens for a moment and chatted about comic books. When they were done, Meir put his hand on Beryl's arm.

"You could leave this mishegoss and rejoin the Falks. We'd love to have you back."

Beryl patted Meir's hand. "I appreciate the offer, but the Worms is my home now. Would you leave the Falks if Rabbi Fruman lied to them?"

Meir shook his head. "No. I would do everything I could to save our sect."

Beryl brushed crumbs off his suit. "Nu? What time is your flight to Atlanta?"

"Late afternoon."

"Are there any other Jews in Atlanta or are you the only one?"

Meir laughed. "There are plenty of Jews."

Beryl glanced around the room. "But are there any other kishef machers?"

Meir sighed. "I'm the only one."

"I suppose that means less competition."

Meir nodded. "It does."

"But it must also be lonely."

"It is."

There was nothing more to be said. It was time for them to go home. They shared an awkward hug before going their separate ways. Meir was about to hail a cab but changed his mind. The Tenement Museum was just a few blocks away.

He walked to the museum, stood on the sidewalk, and looked up at the fourth-floor apartment where Esther had seen Sadie with her yellow ribbon in her hair. A white sheet covered the window.

Thinking back on the events that took place in that cramped three-room apartment, Meir remembered something that Rabbi Fruman had said when Meir was a student at Falk Yeshiva. He said that a kishef macher wasn't an athlete or a superhero. When he or she performed Jewish magic, his or her goal wasn't to win or lose. A kishef macher's only goal was to relieve someone's suffering. The same goal of all Jews. The same goal of all humanity.

Acknowledgements

Thank you to Walter Biggins, Frank Reiss, and Andy Rogers for their excellent advice. Thanks to my writing group Jef Blocker, Robert Gawltney, and Marissa McNamara for their insight and encouragement.

Special thanks to Esther Luna for allowing me to name one of the key characters after her. A visit to the Tenement Museum proved inspirational. I appreciate and admire the museum for keeping the stories of immigrants alive. Much gratitude goes to my mother, Dorothy Dubrow, for instilling in me a sense of wonder about the world, and to my father, Dr. Reuben Dubrow, for teaching me how to land a punchline.

To Jessica Handler for just about everything.

There really was a Meir Poppers. Meir ben Judah Leib Poppers was a Bohemian rabbi and kabbalist. He was born in Prague in 1624 and died in Jerusalem in 1662. As for the Meir Poppers in my novel, I was inspired by occult detectives in comic books like the Phantom Stranger and Doctor Spektor, and in paperback novels like Manly Wade Wellman's John the Balladeer and Jory Sherman's Dr. Russell V. Chillders in the Chill series.

There is a rich history of Jewish myth and magic. A lot of the magic my characters perform come from two of the best resources for Jewish magic: *Jewish Magic and Superstition A Study in Folk Religion* by Joshua Trachtenberg and *The Encyclopedia of Jewish Myth, Magic and Mysticism* by Rabbi Geoffrey W. Dennis.

About the author

Photo By: Royce Soble

Mickey Dubrow is the author of *Bulletproof, Always Agnes* and *American Judas*. For over thirty years, he wrote television promos, marketing presentations, and scripts for various clients including Cartoon Network, TNT Latin America, and HGTV. His short stories and essays have appeared in *Prime Number Magazine, The Good Men Project, The Signal Mountain Review,* and *Full Grown People*. His first novel, *American Judas*, won the 2024 American Legacy Book Award in the category of Science Fiction: Parallel Universe/Alternative History. He lives in Atlanta, Georgia with his wife, author Jessica Handler.